LEE BROOK

The Miss Murderer

Don't walk 'round Morley in the dark!

Lee

MIDDLETON PARK PRESS

L Brook

First published by Middleton Park Press 2022

Copyright © 2022 by Lee Brook

All rights reserved. No part of this publication may be reproduced, stored or transmitted in any form or by any means, electronic, mechanical, photocopying, recording, scanning, or otherwise without written permission from the publisher. It is illegal to copy this book, post it to a website, or distribute it by any other means without permission.

This novel is entirely a work of fiction. The names, characters and incidents portrayed in it are the work of the author's imagination. Any resemblance to actual persons, living or dead, events or localities is entirely coincidental.

Lee Brook asserts the moral right to be identified as the author of this work.

Lee Brook has no responsibility for the persistence or accuracy of URLs for external or third-party Internet Websites referred to in this publication and does not guarantee that any content on such Websites is, or will remain, accurate or appropriate.

Designations used by companies to distinguish their products are often claimed as trademarks. All brand names and product names used in this book and on its cover are trade names, service marks, trademarks and registered trademarks of their respective owners. The publishers and the book are not associated with any product or vendor mentioned in this book. None of the companies referenced within the book have endorsed the book.

First edition

*This book was professionally typeset on Reedsy.
Find out more at reedsy.com*

For you, Mum—
Thank you for encouraging my love of reading.
Without you, this book wouldn't exist.

Contents

Chapter One	1
Chapter Two	5
Chapter Three	12
Chapter Four	17
Chapter Five	25
Chapter Six	33
Chapter Seven	39
Chapter Eight	46
Chapter Nine	54
Chapter Ten	63
Chapter Eleven	69
Chapter Twelve	74
Chapter Thirteen	80
Chapter Fourteen	89
Chapter Fifteen	95
Chapter Sixteen	101
Chapter Seventeen	108
Chapter Eighteen	114
Chapter Nineteen	121
Chapter Twenty	128
Chapter Twenty-one	135
Chapter Twenty-two	146
Chapter Twenty-three	155
Chapter Twenty-four	159

Chapter Twenty-five	166
Chapter Twenty-six	175
Chapter Twenty-seven	182
Chapter Twenty-eight	189
Chapter Twenty-nine	194
Chapter Thirty	200
Chapter Thirty-one	208
Chapter Thirty-two	213
Chapter Thirty-three	219
Chapter Thirty-four	225
Chapter Thirty-five	233
Chapter Thirty-six	241
Chapter Thirty-seven	247
Chapter Thirty-eight	254
Chapter Thirty-nine	257
Chapter Forty	267
Chapter Forty-one	274
Chapter Forty-two	283
Chapter Forty-three	289
Epilogue	296
Afterword	300
About the Author	301
Also by Lee Brook	302

Chapter One

The man's heart hammered in his chest as the woman he had been waiting for exited the door of the secondary school. It was a little after seven o'clock in the evening, and as she hefted her tote bag over her shoulder, she used her other hand to push a stray blonde hair from her face. Every Thursday, she left reception just after seven. Alone. He was thrilled that she was right on schedule.

She heard the patter of rain against the windows of the school and the angry rush of wind across the deserted car park. She glanced up at the dark, sinister sky.

He watched in ecstasy as her eyebrows met and her forehead wrinkled. Her blue eyes flickered in his general direction, but he would have been invisible, a black blur against a dark wall. She paid him no notice and looked down at her mobile. Her hands rapidly fired off a text. Stood there in the alcove of the entrance, protected against the wind, he thought she had never looked more beautiful.

But for her, the ominous clouds above her threatened to burst and shower her with those cold, northern rains that she was still not used to. And the April light was fading, too. Whilst it was getting lighter every night, the sun had already set. What little light was left had hastily followed night into day.

She hesitated. The man had an inkling of what she was thinking.

Do I take the long way by the main road or the short route through the woods?

The man smiled to himself as she turned left out of the main gate, opting for a speedy route through the woods over the security of the main road.

Perfect.

He kept his eyes on her as she trudged up the lane. Cottages about a hundred years old lined the field to her left. To her right, a new housing development comprising mammoth-sized houses stared back, their orange bricks reflecting the glowing light from the streetlights, casting long, hazardous shadows across the surrounding lawns.

Her pace quickened once she passed by the cottages and the houses, her red coat pulled tight around her slender frame. He could hear her shoes crunching on the gravel path as she made her way through the gap between the brick fence posts that separated Gipsy Lane from the South Leeds Golf Club.

As the man had done his research, he knew what route she would take. So, he kept a wide berth, climbing over the remnants of the brick wall to her left, far enough away that she wouldn't see or hear him. She'd follow the lane into the woods for just under a kilometre, after which she'd get to the aforementioned Golf club, or its remnants anyway. Just before a deadly virus hit at the end of 2019, the business had failed, and the building was left to rot. Next, she would cross through its empty car park, follow the path for another hundred metres, and turn left, continuing through the woods for another hundred metres, where she would meet the road that ran through the woods. Her house was on the outskirts of the woods, on Town Street, one of the old houses they had built for the managers of the mines.

As she left the lane—and the cover of the trees—out into the car park, the heavens opened, and the rain began crashing down. The man bent down, keeping under the trees, as she struggled to get the heavy tote bag from her shoulder to search for her umbrella.

She frantically rummaged in the large bag. "Where the heck did I put you?" Once she found what she was looking for, she pressed the button and launched the nylon canopy against the cold, wet barrage. The man was getting frustrated and becoming impatient with her ridiculous actions, especially considering she was going to be entering the woods a minute or two after opening her umbrella.

Then she trudged off through the car park and into the woods, and he almost lost sight of her.

The mud path between the trees was secluded along this stretch, which was why he'd chosen it. He could have easily pounced before she reached the car park and pulled her into the foliage, but the cottages and houses there formed a risk. Here, there was the impenetrable canopy above, an impassable tangle of trees and thick vegetation on the ground to protect him from any onlookers. There was nobody around—not even keen dog walkers who would be closer to home—thanks to the time of night and the weather. Except for her, of course.

Soon the man had no choice but to narrow the distance between them, careful to keep to her left, where the trees would hide him, but still had enough space between their trunks so that he could manoeuvre through freely. The winter they'd just suffered through had broken records for being one of the coldest ever in Leeds, but the leaves had done an excellent job of growing back.

She hated this part of the woods, especially in the fading light, as the gnarled branches stretched out like skeletal fingers reaching for her.

The moment that the man had been waiting for was approaching. There, in the darkness below the canopy, she wouldn't see him coming. He wore his black tech shoes to mask his footsteps and, where he could, walked on tufts of grass and fallen leaves, attempting to be as soundless as possible. She was almost there, at the point where the mud path met the concrete road, where the trees by the border were more expansive and the undergrowth thicker. The point of failure, he called it—the point where the opportunity would be lost.

The man thought about the anniversary and how the conditions tonight had been perfect as if it were inevitable. He had been given the ideal opportunity, and he would not waste it.

His heart rate sped up, as did his pace. He slid between two wide trunks and crouched into a low walk through the undergrowth. She was right there, and he was sure he could smell her fruity perfume, and the occasion nearly got the better of him as he almost ran the last few metres. Instead, he forced himself to keep a slow and steady pace so she wouldn't hear him. But he needn't have bothered. She was deaf to any sound other than her shoes on the gravel and the rain lashing down on the canopy.

He was fifteen metres behind her.

Ten.

Five.

Chapter Two

This was his chance, the perfect moment he had been waiting for. His moment of revenge. He turned full circle and took one last look around him, checking the woods were deserted.

They were.

It was time.

He sprinted towards his victim from behind, forcing his left hand over her mouth and his right arm around her neck. He longed for the feeling of her hot breath against his palm and shivered as she tried to scream, but he had worn gloves to avoid leaving evidence. The man gripped her mouth tighter. She dropped her tote bag and umbrella as she struggled against him, grabbing at his arms with her hands, her sharp nails digging into the black, merino wool fleece he was wearing. But as he was so much stronger than her, it was hardly a fair fight. Within seconds, he'd lifted her from the ground, pulled her into the undergrowth—it was wild and abundant and swallowed them up almost immediately—through a thicket and into a grove he had discovered months before.

Her black skirt caught against a sharp branch just as a jogger passed by, taking the man by surprise. Luckily, the motion had caused her to stagger down to her knees, and the momentum carried him with her. Upon landing on the wet ground, he was hit in the face by a wet branch. Despite her attempts to scream, he clamped down harder over her mouth, and the jogger didn't hear her muffled moan. Instead, the jogger glanced briefly at the abandoned tote bag as he ran past, unaware that the owner was being attacked only metres away.

He knew it had been a close call.

Her wriggling continued, so he tightened the hold around her neck until he felt her strength ebbing away. All he needed was to hold her neck like that for a few more seconds, and she would be unconscious.

She would be his to do whatever he wanted.

There.

Breathing hard, he laid her gently on the wet ground and took in the beautiful features of her face. Her eyes were shut, but he knew they were a marvellous shade of cornflower blue. Her ample bosom rose and fell in an even rhythm as if she was asleep. The light was fading by the second, yet despite this, he saw her flawless, pale skin glisten from the rain, her damp blonde hair a contrast against the dark leaves. She looked so serene, and if it weren't for her chest that rose and fell, he would have been sure that she was dead already.

"Soon, my sweet, soon." Once he was finished with her, he'd end her.

But first, he would make her pay for what she had done.

* * *

Erika's lungs filled with damp, cold air as she awoke. The memory of the attack flashed through her mind as she looked around. Where was she? Everywhere she looked was the same.

CHAPTER TWO

A tangle of foliage and trees. And Darkness.

"Finally awake?" a voice asked. She couldn't pinpoint where the voice came from. It sounded familiar but gruff as if his voice was caught in his throat. It wasn't what she was expecting.

She blinked against the darkness, her eyes darting around the grove. Erika couldn't see a face to match the voice, just two eyes staring down at her. Then the light changed, and a monster appeared before her, its beady eyes hovering just above a red nose and razor-sharp teeth that protruded from ruby lips. The image shocked and terrified her, and for a fleeting moment, she thought she had been attacked by some kind of demonic clown. But when she blinked again, her eyes adjusted, and she realised her attacker's hood was up. He was wearing a face mask, a remnant from the pandemic, one of those popular ones that were all the rage with her students.

The man stepped closer, and Erika's heart pounded. Terror rose and threatened to choke her. She opened her mouth to scream, but she couldn't. Black duct tape had been used to seal her mouth. Erika tried to move, but her hands had also been taped together at the wrists behind her back. The tape wouldn't budge. She rolled over and tried to continue the movement, but her wrists kept digging into the soft ground, and after three revolutions, she came to a dizzy stop. The man came closer, and she kicked out with her legs, noticing with alarm that he had a knife in his hands. A fixed blade hunting knife, its blade glinting in the failing light. He laughed and said, "There's no escape, Miss Allen, so you may as well calm the fuck down and do as I say."

He unzipped and unbuttoned his jeans.

"Please, God, no," she tried to cry out through the tape, but only a muffled noise came through, and all he saw was her writhing on the damp ground.

Her writhing turned him on even more.

Erika began heaving against the tape as bile rose into her throat. She tilted her head to the side and took deep breaths through her nose to counter it.

"Calm down, Miss Allen. And don't move. I'm sure you wouldn't want this knife to penetrate you in any way." He rolled her over so that she was facing him, wrapped the duct tape around her ankles, pulled her black skirt up, rolled her tights down to her knees, and used the knife to slice the waistband of the tights in two. Then he sat down, pinning her to the ground just above her knees, and spent agonising seconds cutting the straps off her white, lace panties. The drops of rain felt wet and cold on her bare thighs.

"Please. Please, don't do this," she tried to say. But the tape wouldn't allow her to speak.

The man wasn't done yet. He pocketed the remains of her panties and pulled at her white blouse. She noticed her coat and cardigan had already been removed, probably, she thought, before her hands had been bound. Buttons flew in all directions with satisfying pings, exposing a lacy white bra. He did the same to the bra as he did the panties, slicing each strap delicately as if he were creating a piece of art.

With a gloved hand, Erika's attacker gripped a nipple that had been exposed to the cold. Erika squirmed away at the sharp pain, but it did nothing but harden the already erect penis she could feel against her leg.

She saw him pull down his pants, exposing himself, saw a pink wrapper being torn, and heard the crinkling sound. The man dropped his knife to the floor to free his hands, its sharp

CHAPTER TWO

blade embedding into the wet earth, and more bile threatened to rise up Erika's throat. Rough hands forced her onto her front, her face planted in the mud. She couldn't break the fall with her hands behind her back. Those rough hands found their way between her thighs and pushed them apart. He was too strong, but she tried to resist anyway. He punched her in the back of the head, her nose hitting the ground, and she went dizzy from the shock. A tiny bead of blood snaked down her pale face and dripped down. Despite the shock, she fought as he tried to manoeuvre himself between her legs.

"Keep still, Miss Allen," he said, panting, "or I swear to God that I'll fucking hurt you!"

Erika flailed once more with her legs, ignoring her attacker. He caught the blow with his hand and then threw her feet back down towards the earth. He rolled her onto her back, so she was facing him. "OK, Miss Allen. We'll do it your way." He rifled through her coat and found her iPhone. "How about I send an image of you to Ian? I'm sure he'd get a kick out of seeing you this way. Or how about to your family and friends through Snapchat? Or Instagram? I know the passcode. I've been watching you, you see. Or how about I film it, and once I've finished, I'll send it everywhere? Think of your students. Or you can behave, and I'll toss your phone to one side?"

She nodded and lay there, her eyes closed, breathing deeply, her chest rising and falling, rising and falling. "Thank you, Miss." He soon became entranced, watching the blood from her nose trickle slowly down her stomach, watching her breasts with their stiff nipples rise and fall to a steady rhythm.

Then suddenly, she flailed again, bent her knees and kicked out with both feet until they connected with the bare flesh of his thigh. With his pants and jeans wrapped around his ankles, the impact meant that he lost his balance, and he fell down on top of her with a crash. His left elbow caught her in her right breast, and she tried to cry out in agony. He forced the gloved knuckles of his right hand into her face with a crack. "You stupid, crazy bitch! You will not enjoy this. I'll make sure of it." He turned off her mobile and pocketed it.

Blood oozed from her nose and drenched her blouse. Her vision blurred, and it was only a mix of rhythmic breathing and the chilly rain that kept her from passing out. The man rolled her over onto her front once again, pushed her stomach tight onto her raised knees, and spread her thighs.

Miss Erika Allen had no more fight left in her, and she futilely squirmed as he entered her, desperately trying to scream words through the tape.

He thrust, his body shaking with ecstasy. For her, there was only pain.

Trying to block it out, she squeezed her eyes shut once more. She panicked, expecting to suffocate because of the broken nose and the tape over her mouth. All she could think about was letting the monster finish. Then he might let her go home.

She had plans tonight, plans at home, anniversary plans with Ian. Now those plans would never happen. She knew that, deep down. There was no way he would allow her home after this.

Her rapist's thrusts grew more and more frantic, and she knew he was close to finishing. The man placed his strong hands around her neck and thrust harder and faster as he clenched his fingers tightly. She suffocated as he made a low, rasping sound.

He rolled her onto her back just as her oxygen ran out. Tears ran down her face as she noticed the knife in his hand, the blade glistening in the rain.

But as he plunged the knife into her stomach, Erika Allen was already gone.

Chapter Three

Emilia Alexander rolled off George Beaumont and noticed a smile on his face. "You're incredible, Mia, you know that?" he said as he turned his head to kiss her full on the lips.

She nibbled his lip, ran her hand through his thick blond hair and smiled a slow, satisfied smile. Mia kissed him back. "You know I enjoy being in control."

Blonde curls framed an oval face, her chin sharp, her nose just a button, and he swore that when he looked deep into those cornflower blue eyes, it was like she could see within his very soul. Her smile grew wider as he stroked a rosebud nipple, his finger moving over the hardened tip. George took in the view of her body, one that had been partly crafted in the gym, partly from her being a PE teacher. He often found her doing yoga on the living room floor, twisting herself into positions that a contortionist would be proud of. She had done some modelling as an undergrad student but gave that up when she decided to teach. Somehow he had found himself sharing his life with a woman so charming, so caring, so beautiful, and he couldn't believe his luck. He was hooked from the first time he saw her. "I'm all for giving you control," he said. "Fancy putting that underwear back on and going for round two?"

CHAPTER THREE

Mia laughed and tried to find the white lacy bra and matching panties that had been hastily discarded somewhere on the floor at the side of the bed. "Well, I'd only just put them on fresh from the shower. And anyway, why do you want me to wear them? You got little use out of them earlier." She smiled that sexy smile of hers and pulled the quilt tightly around her naked body. The cold April evenings hadn't retreated just yet, but they soon would, and then it would be time to get ready for the day of their wedding. "You better get some use out of what I've bought for the wedding night." She said it with a wink, her Yorkshire accent broad and, to George, incredibly sexy.

"You know, it's evenings like these where I could murder a beer. Sit out on the porch in just a pair of boxers and enjoy it whilst watching the sun go down." Partly to prove to himself that he could, and partly because of the wedding, he'd given Dry January a go. But it had gone a step further when Oliver, a DC from work, challenged him on who would last the longest and he was determined not to give up now. As of yet, neither had faltered, and he also had the wedding to think about. The lack of beer had helped him lose a few pounds. It was extra motivation; in his book, any motivation was excellent motivation. "It was always part of my routine when I was younger when I'd just joined the force. We'd always go out after—"

"Do you have to work this weekend?" she asked, changing the subject. "I want it to be just the two of us on Saturday, and I have no marking or planning. Plus, the mornings are still freezing, and your body would do a great job of warming me right up."

"I could warm you up right now. You never said whether you wanted to go another round or not?" George asked with a grin

13

just as his phone rang. He glanced at the number and held up a hand. "Sorry, babe, it's work."

Mia's smile disappeared, and she gazed out of the window. They'd left the windows open during their hurry to rip each other's clothes off. But that wasn't unusual. She saw only the darkness; the sun had set hours ago.

"DI George Beaumont," he said.

Detective Superintendent Jim Smith's voice boomed out of the speaker. Jim, a Geordie who supported Newcastle United, was his boss, head of the Leeds Homicide and Major Enquiry team based at Elland Road Police Station. He loved it when Leeds lost and hated how close the station was to the stadium. "George, the body of a female has been found in Middleton Woods. From the call, it looks like she's been stabbed and sexually assaulted. The DCS has given me permission to take control of operations out of Elland Road. I want you to lead a team as the SIO."

"Really?" George struggled to keep the surprise out of his voice. He'd been working hard, keeping his head down, but had never been asked to be the senior investigating officer for a homicide.

"Yeah, this is your chance; we're short-staffed, George. The ambulance is already there. Patrol officers have begun preservation of the scene and the Crime Scene Co-ordinator, Stuart Kent, is on his way with a team of SOCOs. This is your lucky break. You'd be a fool not to take it. But if you aren't ready—"

"I'm ready," George said. "Thank you, sir."

DSU Smith grunted. That was all the approval he would get. "Wood is already there. The DS will be your deputy SIO on this." George liked DS Wood. She was a detective sergeant in her late twenties with long brown hair that was usually tied in a ponytail. George had worked with her before, a few days after she'd transferred from Wakefield Central. She was intelligent, thorough, and had a keen initiative, something George appreciated.

George was beaming as he ended the call, but then he saw Mia's expression. She looked through him, rather than at him, as she spoke. He didn't envy those students of hers who let her down or misbehaved. Recently, she had made an issue out of him leaving at all hours of the day and night to go to crime scenes. "This is big, Mia. Huge. This could be what my career needs." He reached over to squeeze her arm, but she got up, taking the duvet with her. "Look, I'm sorry, but I've been put in charge of the investigation."

"Sorry?" she said as she bit her nails. They were long and the colour of sapphires. "Tell your face that, George. I'm not sure I've seen you happier. You forget how well I know you. And how well I know police officers." Her father had been a relatively successful DCI who had unfortunately been killed whilst hunting a serial killer.

"You're right. I am happy that I've finally been recognised for my hard work. It's my job, Mia. My career. It's what I do. I thought that you'd be happy for me."

She turned to face him in the door to his en-suite. Her eyebrows met, and her forehead wrinkled. "You've been at work all day. You didn't get home until after eight. It's only just turned eleven. Isn't there anybody else?"

He ran a hand through his hair and tried to keep his voice kind but firm. "It's my job, Mia. You knew what you were signing up for. I'm finally getting a chance to prove myself. I'm only a DI, but he's making me the SIO on this one. If I want a promotion, I need to go."

Why was it so hard for her to understand?

Something had changed recently, something his detective skills hadn't figured out. He was clear from day one about his job, and she had been clear about the effect her father's job had had on her. But it was only recently that they had begun to argue about it. Yet, when he thought about it, it wasn't them even arguing. It was him apologising whilst she pouted and protested. She never stayed angry for long, but that wasn't the point.

She shrugged. "I guess I'll get in the shower alone. You can sleep in the spare room tonight so that you don't wake me when you get in at ridiculous o'clock. It's Friday tomorrow, so I have to be at work early." He reached for her, but she turned away and began to close the door. "It's your loss, George."

He heaved a sigh and let her go.

The en-suite door slammed shut.

Chapter Four

DS Wood showed George the way to the crime scene. "At least it's stopped raining," she said. "I thought at one point it would never stop. April showers and all that." In the distance, George saw a hive of activity, with blue lights blaring from the park's access road. He had intentionally left his vehicle at the park gates and had walked the path to where the body had been found. He angled his torch down onto the way ahead, wary of holes and debris hidden by shadows.

"The body's just off the path and through there." Wood pointed towards an area that had been cordoned off with police tape. She'd told George that she'd made the trip several times this evening already, looking for evidence of a vehicle. But George knew that this road was gated near the entrance, and only certain people had the keys. There was also a camera stationed at each gate. It would be easy to check if anybody had unlocked them. "Watch your step. It's quite slippery."

"What on earth was she doing walking out here alone? And at night, too?" George questioned. What was thought to be the deceased's bag was covered by a small tent. George shone his beam to the right of the bag, off the road where gigantic trees stretched up towards the heavens, and saw a steep drop illuminated by artificial light. This place was dangerous.

"My thoughts exactly."

"What time was she found?" George asked.

"About ten by a dog walker," Wood explained. "There had been an apparent break in the rain, and he had risked taking the dog out. He lives on the opposite side of the main road in the Bodmins and takes his dog for a walk along this path every day, though usually much earlier. He noticed the bag, and his dog had started to bark as if it were afraid. It was quiet, so he had let the dog off the lead. He followed his dog into the thicket here and saw her body. The killer made no attempt to conceal the body. Poor guy is beside himself. I've made him aware he needs to come in tomorrow to give an official statement so that he can be excluded from the case. We've taken footprints already."

George nodded, closed his eyes, and shivered. At ten, he'd started slowly stripping Mia of her underwear while some poor girl was lying out here in the cold. He remembered the rain battering the windows whilst they had finished their bottle of wine.

"Any ID?"

DS Wood shook her head. "I used a lantern, but whoever this is isn't known to us." A lantern device was a handheld fingerprint reader they used to ID people, but like DNA, it only worked if their prints were on the database.

"OK, thanks Wood."

The pair reached the common approach path, a designated path all the officers used, so they didn't accidentally tread on any evidence. The officer who was on guard at the tape nodded at George after he showed his warrant card and signed in. A police photographer that George recognised, but couldn't name, was taking pictures of the scene. He heard the incessant click as he put on the protective coverall and shoe covers the guard had provided.

They ducked through the thicket to find a blue forensic tent that had been erected to protect the body. The emergency lighting that had been erected gave the tent an eerie glow that opposed the nature that surrounded it.

"I'll wait here if that's OK?" Wood asked with a thin smile. "I've seen enough for one night."

George greeted the uniformed officer and lifted the flap, blinked, blinded by the light from the fluorescent bulbs. After his eyes quickly adjusted, he entered the tent and glimpsed the victim at the far end. A young woman was lying on the wet ground, her hands behind her body. Dizziness overcame him as he walked towards the corpse and bent down to check whether her hands had been bound. They had. Blood covered the ground. That coppery smell, along with the heat of the suit and the cloying atmosphere of the cramped interior of the tent, caused George to pause on the spot. He struggled with nausea rising in his throat and nearly turned around to leave the tent.

A man was bending over her, thoroughly inspecting the body, while the photographer continued her job. The deceased was young, probably mid-twenties. Blonde hair was plastered to her face, but what he could see of it was black and blue. One eye was swollen shut, and her nose was clogged with blood. Her left eye, a cornflower blue now devoid of life, stared up through the canopy above, unblinking, unseeing. A strip of black duct tape, the same tape that bound her wrists, covered her mouth.

Her crimson-stained blouse was open, her breasts exposed, and her stomach was a bloody mess. He exhaled and moved closer. Her dress was up and twisted around her waist. There was no underwear, and it looked as if her tights had been cut and rolled just below her knees.

Shit.

He had seen dead bodies before, of course, and a wave of familiarity hit him. It was the smells and sounds of a murder scene, the tingle of excitement in his bones and adrenaline pushing him forward, protecting him in part from realising that he was about to deal with a dead body, something he'd never entirely come to terms with.

"Sexual assault?" he asked the man.

"I can't guarantee anything until I get her back, but I'd say almost certainly. I'm the Crime Scene Co-ordinator, Stuart Kent."

DI Beaumont nodded his head. "DI Beaumont. You got here faster than I expected."

Kent nodded back. They'd worked together previously, but he hadn't been in such a senior position then, and they hadn't spoken for long. "I can't tell yet whether she was strangled or stabbed to death. The stab marks are obvious, but can you see the bruising around her neck?"

George moved closer, stepping on the tiles they used to preserve the scene.

"You can also see large clots in her nose," Kent said, pointing. "With the tape around her mouth, she probably couldn't breathe anyway. But once we get her back, the pathologist will be able to tell you which injury killed her."

George nodded and moved around the victim in order to get a better look at her face and neck. The discolouration of her neck was substantial. "Any prints?"

"Not yet. It looks as if they were wearing gloves. In terms

of the strangulation, their hands were large, larger than mine anyway." The Crime Scene Co-ordinator demonstrated this by circling her neck with his own hands. "Strong, too. Strong fingers and thumbs, at least. A tight grip. You can see where the culprit's fingers caused the deep patches of bruising."

"What happened to her face?" George said as he inspected her nose.

"Whoever killed her was a bully; really roughed her up. My guess was they punched her to subdue her. She put up one hell of a fight. I can tell by the bruising on her wrists and the cuts and scrapes on her legs where she lashed out."

"Here's hoping that we can get some DNA from the culprit off her."

"Sorry to disappoint you, but I have already checked, and there's nothing under the fingernails. The culprit most likely secured her hands with the tape before she had a chance to defend herself. And with the amount of rain this area has had tonight, any fibres on her skin or clothing may have been washed off. Nothing is ever easy or plain sailing, I'm afraid."

"And you found no DNA internally?" George glanced at her partially naked body once again and shivered. His voice wavered. "When can we cover her up?"

"Any internal DNA will only be found during the post-mortem." Kent glanced up at him. "I won't be long. I'm just finishing up. Then we can get her decent again."

"Tell me about her stomach?" George asked.

"It was a frenzied attack. We've measured the entry wounds, and once I send the report to the Calder Park lab, they will be able to check the profile against known weapons."

"Let me know as soon as you do, Stuart. If it's a unique weapon, we can check shops for CCTV."

Stuart Kent nodded. "With an attack like this, there would have been a lot of blood spattered on the killer's clothes. The rain may have washed it away, but I've advised a SOCO to check the surrounding area. They may have left you a trail."

George knew that as the time between the kill and finding the killer increased, it would be harder for the SOCOs to discover anything as the killer could easily destroy or wash their clothing and other belongings. They needed a lead and fast.

"I'll be honest with you, though, DI Beaumont, this rain will have severely reduced the amount of forensic information that we might have collected."

DI Beaumont nodded as he fought against the claustrophobic atmosphere. He watched the SOCOs take photos and videos of the scene and was confused by his reaction. After surveying every centimetre of the poor woman's defiled body, George could no longer bear it and took a step towards the exit. As he attempted to push the flap to the side, he made eye contact with one of the SOCOs, and opened it, welcoming the rush of cold wind outside.

In spite of his desire to rip the suit from his body, George peeled it off slowly, and the dizziness subsided as soon as it was removed. He didn't need to see the victim or the crime scene any more, especially not with her being in that state. The fresh, bitter air helped him to refocus. "DS Wood, do we know who she was?"

Wood handed him her driving licence. "This was in her purse," she said, nodding her head back towards the main road. "It was in the tote bag."

He glanced at the driving licence. "A Miss Erika Allen."

"She lives close to the woods, close to the entrance where our cars are," noted Wood. "I checked whilst you were inspecting the body. We found this too." She passed George a lanyard with an ID card.

"Beeston Park Academy, Learning for Life," he read. "That's the school back along the path. I can only imagine that she must have been walking home from work when she was attacked."

"She was stupid to have come this way," Wood remarked. "The only CCTV cameras are by the gates, and with the trees, it's pitch black by seven."

"Was there any cash in her wallet?"

Wood nodded. "Yeah, a ten-pound note and some change. This wasn't a burglary."

Was this an opportunistic attack, or was it premeditated? Whoever it was, was a predator. One sick fuck. "Phone the school. Somebody will be in. They may know what time she left." Wood nodded. "It could have been a colleague," George said, thinking aloud. "Or maybe it was someone who knew her and had it in for her. An ex-lover or a disgruntled parent?" It was highly unusual for a teacher to be murdered.

"I'll interview her colleagues tomorrow. See if they know anything," Wood said. George nodded.

As they were walking back to their cars, George asked, "Is there anything else I need to know, DS Wood?"

She nodded toward a closed umbrella in a plastic evidence bag. "We think it's hers. It was found open on the path. The likely scenario is that she would have dropped it when she was attacked. It's on the list to be tested. You never know; she may have hit the culprit with it."

"I certainly hope so."

"We also found no underwear. The killer must have taken it

with them."

They continued walking, and George pictured the series of events. "So, my guess is that she was walking home through the woods when the culprit grabbed her from behind and pulled her into the undergrowth. Because of the weather and how late it is, there was nobody around to witness it. The culprit then pulls her through the bushes and subdues her, most likely by punching her in the face, before taping her wrists and ankles. He cuts her clothes off, then either he rapes and strangles her, or rapes and stabs her to death."

"What a bastard." Wood was shaking her head, her fists clenched. George had never heard or seen her like this before. "To have raped and then killed her…"

George narrowed his eyes. "Not necessarily, DS Wood. I know what I said, but it may have happened differently. Stuart Kent will let us know."

"What do you mean? You think the culprit could have raped her after they'd killed her?"

George gave a curt nod.

"Jesus."

Chapter Five

George took family liaison officer Cathy Hoskins with him to notify the deceased's next of kin. She was the kind of woman you wanted beside you during this situation, a vigorous, kind woman with a compassionate nature and a calming voice. Whilst he hadn't worked with her before, George knew of her reputation, and DSU Smith couldn't have recommended her any higher. She'd spent many years working as a rape counsellor before she joined the West Yorkshire Police.

"Mr Ian Kennedy?" George asked when a partially balding man in his late twenties, or early thirties, opened the door. "I'm DI George Beaumont, and this is DS Cathy Hoskins." George showed him his warrant card. Cathy did the same. "We're from the West Yorkshire Police Homicide and Major Enquiry Team. May we come in?"

The man nodded and opened the door wordlessly. He wore blue and white striped pyjamas, was barefooted, and had a confused expression.

"Thank you," Cathy said, offering a smile. They followed him into a living room lit by a lamp on a small coffee table. A tattered novel sat next to it. The television was on, the sound low, but the shrill laughter permeated the awkward silence.

"Do you mind if we turn that off?" Cathy asked. Another smile.

Ian nodded and reached for the remote. "Of course. I wasn't watching it anyway. Not really. Is this about Erika? I've been worried sick." He turned off the TV and sat down in the chair by the lamp. The two detectives sat on a small brown leather sofa. Ian gazed from one to the other as the detectives craned their necks to face him. "Is it bad news?" As Ian said it, he sobbed.

George nodded. He found this part of his job extremely difficult, but he knew that most people were killed by people known to them, and he reminded himself that in most cases, the victim's partner was the culprit. So being compassionate but also alert for any clues was part and parcel of this investigation section. Any piece of information, no matter how small, might help them solve the case.

"We found a young woman's body tonight in Middleton Woods. We found a driving licence that suggests that it was Erika."

Ian stared at him uncomprehendingly, and George wondered if he'd heard him. "After she didn't return home from work, you reported her missing earlier?"

"Yes. Yes, I did." Ian's eyes filled with more tears, but he coughed and said, "I knew it. I could feel it. She's never late for anything. And she texted me when she set off like usual. I was cooking tea, so I never replied." George had detected the smells of cooking as he entered, and now, as he swept his gaze around, he saw the said meal was left untouched on the table.

Ian wiped the flowing tears away from his eyes and grabbed a tissue for his nose. It always took a few moments for the news to sink in, so George and Cathy waited patiently. They knew that denial or anger would surface next.

"Are you sure that it's her body?" he eventually asked, his voice stretched. Denial. At least it wasn't anger. Poor Ian, he couldn't quite believe that she was dead. Not yet, but that would end soon, usually once a person had identified the body.

"We're sure," said Cathy softly. "We found her purse and tote bag and her lanyard from work in it."

Ian let out a shallow, shaky breath. It was sinking in. "Can you tell me how she died?"

"She was murdered. We don't have the full details from the pathologist yet, but she was strangled and stabbed," said George.

He glanced at Cathy, who said, "There was also evidence of a sexual assault."

The tears flowed once again. "You mean—you mean Erika was raped?"

George nodded. "It looks that way. I'm so sorry."

"Oh, no. Please." He buried his head in his hands as the tears rolled down his cheeks. "My poor Erika."

Cathy stood up and walked over to him. "Can we call anybody, so you're not alone right now?"

Ian shook his head. "No, I have no family. Erika's family was my family, you know? So I suppose it'll be down to me to tell her parents?" More tears fell. "I don't know how I'm going to do that. Her mother will—her mother will be devastated. They both will. They love her so much."

"I can do that for you if you like?" said Cathy.

Ian thought for a moment and then nodded. "Thanks, but I think... Could I be there when you tell them? I think it will be better if I'm there."

She nodded and spoke softly. "Of course. Whatever you think

will be for the best. And I'm always available if you decide you want to talk." She passed him her card. George knew she would be available for Ian whenever he needed her and would be his point of contact when wanting an update.

"Do you know who did it? Have you caught the bastard?" Ian asked. "Is it that arsehole from school? One of the kid's dads?"

"What do you mean?" George asked, twisting in his seat. He took out his notepad and pen.

"She disagreed with a parent about one of her students. So he waited outside for her about five or six months ago. September. It was lucky that I was picking her up, and she got into my car whilst he was shouting abuse at her," Ian explained. "She told me he'd started watching her from the gates when she left at night. It scared her, freaked her out."

"I'm sure it did." Cathy kept her voice neutral. "After the verbal abuse, did either of you report him?"

"Yes," said Ian. "I told her to. So she filed it with the school, and a police sergeant from Morley came and interviewed her. I can't remember his name. But what that guy did was a crime, right?"

"Yes, it certainly was," Cathy confirmed.

"Did Erika say whether she had any trouble with him before?" George asked.

"She said not. The child was new. They'd put him in the bottom set for maths. Dad wasn't happy." Ian closed his eyes. "If I remember correctly, the school took it seriously, and after she reported it, he backed off. So the head moved the child sets, and the dad wasn't allowed to pick him up on school grounds. Then they changed schools. I think Erika said he moved up to one in Morley."

CHAPTER FIVE

"It may not be connected," George said carefully. Cathy looked over and caught his eye. It was a great start to their investigation. He sent a quick message to DS Wood to check tomorrow when she took the statements. "But it's something we'll look into." The suffering man nodded. "Ian, what we want you to do right now is piece together Erika's movements over the last week or two. Then, if the killer was following her, we might have a shot at identifying them, especially if it is the dad from the school."

"You think he's the one who did this to her?"

"It's one line of inquiry," George said vaguely.

"Right, OK. Erika liked to be at school by half seven every morning, and she was usually picked up by her friend, Amanda."

"Do you know Amanda's surname?" George asked.

"Milbury. Amanda Milbury. They're best friends. They spend so much time together. In fact, they were in Leeds last weekend. They went shopping and had a meal. Erika mentioned something about a man following her then, actually. Well, she said she was being paranoid. What if—what if that fucker had been following her? Maybe we could have saved her."

He made a mental note. "Ian," he said, "you can't blame yourself. What about after work? Did she always come home via the park?"

"No, it was weather dependent. And also whether I could pick Erika up. I work in Hunslet and often fly up Dewsbury Road to pick her up. But not always." Ian's voice faltered, and he stared down at his hands. "I knew that I should have picked her up. But unfortunately, she stayed a little later, and when I offered to pick her up, she refused. It was our anniversary of getting together, so I thought I'd get tea on instead. An M&S deal. A treat, you know?" He pitched forward onto the table, sobbing.

There was a brief silence before George said, "This is not your fault, Ian. She had, I assume, safely made her way home through the woods before?"

He could see Ian fighting against the sobs. He nodded at George's question.

"That's right. It was quicker than going down Gipsy Lane and back up the Ring Road. Walking through the woods halved the journey. But I should have collected her." He choked up again, and George felt terrible for making him relive it. "She texted me just before she left and told me she was on her way. I didn't get it until I had finished making tea. I waited. I called her phone. Nothing. It was turned off. That's why I panicked and called the police. I knew deep down that something awful had happened to her."

The culprit must have stolen Erika's phone because CSI hadn't found it. They'd applied to her network for her phone records, but they often took the piss.

"Thanks, Ian. So what usually happens on the weekends? Did she go out without you last weekend?"

"No, she went to Leeds on Saturday morning with Amanda, as I already said. They spent nearly the whole day out. United was on at half-five on Sky. She got home around half-time. I'm sure of it. Bet it's a nightmare at the station when they play. And on Sunday, Erika had coffee with a friend at the White Rose. The shopping centre." He clicked his fingers. "They met at Costa. I think."

"Do you know the friend's name?" George asked.

"Noelle," Ian said. "But I'm afraid I don't know her last

name. They're old colleagues who kept in touch. I've never met her. She was home by 2 pm."

George made another note for Wood to follow up. He'd get her to visit the school in the morning. They'd have Noelle's details. He questioned Ian about their whereabouts the weekend before, but Ian couldn't remember much. He recalled that on Saturday afternoon, Erika had walked to the avenue alone but returned empty-handed as the butcher had shut early. He wasn't sure of the time.

"I'm really sorry, mate. I really am," George said. Ian's shoulders shook as he took in a few deep breaths. "But I have to be honest, there's only one person to blame here, and that's the culprit. Whoever did this? Not you. Unless you did this, Ian?" George paused. "Did you do this? Did you kill Erika?"

There was a short silence before Ian began sobbing.

Eventually, Ian sat back up and rubbed his haunted eyes. "I still can't believe she's dead. And to answer your question, no. No, I did not kill my fiancée. I did not kill the woman I love."

Fiancée? That was news to George. He cast his mind back to the victim's bruised and battered body. He pictured her discoloured wrists tied behind her head. "There was no ring on her finger. When did you get engaged?" he asked.

"Last weekend," Ian said mournfully. "We were going to pick out a ring tomorrow." Ian burst into tears again.

"Did anybody know about the engagement?" George asked.

"Just her colleagues." Ian dabbed at his face. "Am I allowed to see her?"

"Of course," Cathy said.

"We'd like you to identify her formally, but there's no rush. It doesn't have to be tonight. It can wait until tomorrow," George added.

"No, that's OK. I want to see Erika now. If I can? I'd really like to see her now." He got up and started looking around the living room. "I want to make sure—make sure that it's definitely her."

"I understand," said Cathy. "We can arrange that for you if you're certain?"

"I need to. I'll just get my coat and shoes."

He walked out into the hall, and the detectives followed him. He grabbed a brown jacket from a cupboard under the stairs, put on a pair of Adidas trainers, and searched his pockets frantically for the house keys.

"They're in the living room," Cathy explained. She smiled. "The keys. Next to your book."

"Oh, yeah. Of course. Sorry, my mind is a bit of a mess right now."

Whilst Ian returned to collect them, George and Cathy stood there in silence.

"Are you sure that you're OK to do this?" Cathy asked once Ian was back. "Perhaps it would be better to do this later in the morning?"

"It's fine." Ian turned to Cathy. "I'd like to do it now." Ian patted the keys in his pocket. "It's not as if I could sleep anyway. I need to know it's her."

"Sure, I understand," she said. "Let's go."

As they exited the house, George yawned. It was one in the morning.

Chapter Six

Cathy took Ian to the mortuary to identify Erika Allen's body, and George went back to the station. He was surprised to see that despite it being after 1 in the morning, the whole team was there, including DSU Smith.

"Ah, George. Now you're back; I feel it's important that you brief us on the situation," he explained. "Incident Room Four, please, everyone; DS Williams has set up a CCTV unit in Five."

Whenever a murder occurred, an Incident Room was set up at the station, and as a picture of the victim emerged, it would be up to George and his team to update the information stored there.

His team filed in. He knew after the briefing he'd need to spend the rest of the morning organising the roles and duties of his team. The few chairs in the room were filled quickly by the higher-ranking detectives from CID while everyone else stood at the back. He could feel their anticipation. George went to stand beside DSU Smith at the front of the room. Wood whispered in his ear to let him know she had pinned three photographs of Erika Allen up on the whiteboard. The one on the left was from her licence. To the right was one of her dead at the crime scene. He couldn't face looking at the one in the middle. Underneath was a map, her route home from work drawn with red ink.

"This is an important case, and I thank you for coming in so late," DSU Smith said. "DI George Beaumont is in charge of the investigation, so all instructions will come from him. East Ardsley and Robin Hood have offered their support if we need more officers on the streets, and should we need help, the surveillance team from Laburnum Road."

Everybody's eyes were on him, and George became paranoid that they were all thinking the same thing he was. Could he really handle a case this size? Of course, he could. It's what he had trained for, right?

Smith nodded at him. "The floor's yours, George."

Despite his nerves, George had done this before. It was how he met Mia. They had been surveying Leeds for a pickpocket who had been involved in an altercation that had turned fatal. The fight had been caught on various CCTV cameras. They'd also had many witnesses at the scene and DNA evidence to convict. They just had to find the bastard. And George did. Their suspect had stolen Mia's purse, and so George had given chase. Unfortunately, there hadn't been a lot of investigating involved.

For George, this was a whole different kettle of fish.

George pointed at the photograph of the victim behind him, took a deep breath, and composed his thoughts. "The victim is twenty-five-year-old Erika Allen." The before and after pictures were in stark contrast to each other. In the before picture, she was at the beach, and her hair was loose, flyaway in the wind, as the sun shone on her face. She was smiling at the camera, an ecstatic glint in those cornflower blues. She looked full of life. Happy. Content. Suddenly, anger towards the person who had taken that away from her surged through his veins, and his fists balled tight. He needed to calm down. George had a wicked temper, one he tried extremely hard to control. "Erika was walking home from work through Middleton Woods when she was attacked."

When George explained what they knew, especially about the sexual nature of the attack, he observed the collective expressions of outrage and disgust. "The pathologist will clarify later whether the sexual assault was pre- or post-mortem."

George had to hold up a hand as the inaudible murmur in the room increased in both volume and voracity. "I share your disgust, which is why we're going to do whatever it takes to catch this bastard."

There were nods and cheers all around.

"Yolanda, DS Williams, is on CCTV, but I need a few officers who can help her trawl through. I don't know what there is around the woods or the school, but see what you can find. Her route home is mapped up here on the board. Take copies of it. I also need you to make sure you look at previous days and earlier; I want to know if anyone was following her."

Three detective constables volunteered.

"Thank you." He had helped secure convictions based solely on video evidence in many of the cases he worked on, yet George knew that studying CCTV footage was a very tedious job. Despite it being arguably one of the most essential tasks, officers still didn't like it, as they'd invariably be shut away in a darkened Incident Room Five, for hours on end, surveying footage from different cameras.

"DS Wood is going to go to the victim's place of work tomorrow to question her colleagues." Wood nodded. "I want two of you to look into a report the victim filed last year regarding an incident at the school. Apparently, the dad of one of her students waited outside for her after school and verbally abused her. He'd been banned from school, but she felt as if somebody was then following her. Call the school tomorrow and get an ID. Check for any other incidents, and do a background check. This could be our first lead. It could be 'the' lead. Get me something on this guy." From his team, DS Joshua Fry and DS Elaine Brewer nodded.

George pointed at a group of CID detective constables. "I'd like the three of you to look through the records of known criminals that are out in public. Look for other attacks or similar patterns. Bring them in and question them if you have to."

The three shouted, "Sir!" in unison.

George smiled at his team. "I want everything documented on HOLMES. That's it, thanks everyone," George said as the team began filing out of the room, talking among themselves. He knew that they'd do what they could tonight, then all be back first thing in the morning, raring to go.

"Cathy Hoskins and I interviewed Erika's partner. I'll email over the transcript once I've typed it up," George said, turning to Jim Smith. "Guy was in a right state."

"Has he ID'd the body yet?" Jim asked, his deep, raspy voice commanding respect. Jim Smith was nearly as wide as he was tall, with a barrel chest, and George would always describe him as being built like a brick shithouse. The man was in his late fifties, yet it was only the wisps of grey in his hair that gave his age away.

"Cathy took Ian to the mortuary already. The poor guy didn't want to wait."

"I can understand, George. Poor guy, I'd be in denial too,"

CHAPTER SIX

Jim said as he scratched his bristly chin. Jim Smith had been there since 6 am that morning; the hollows beneath his eyes were dark and angry. "I know I don't have to tell you how big this is. Look at this." Jim handed him his phone that showed a message from the popular social media reporter, YappApp. "The media have caught on already, but we've put in a gag order. A popular, young teacher mutilated and raped in a public park." He shook his head. "It's terrible news. And if we don't get to the nationals first, there's going to be a frenzy."

"I agree. When are you giving them a statement?" George asked.

A sly grin appeared on his face. "I won't be giving them one, but you will be," he confirmed. "This is your case. I'll be there if you need me to be, but this is your case. You're the SIO. This is your rodeo."

George nodded, "Thanks, boss." He took a deep breath and smiled. He knew the key was confidence and psyched himself up. There had been no need to deal with the media and put out a press release during the pickpocket murder enquiry, so he hadn't dealt with the media before. He also did not know what went into a press release. He'd seen Jim do it regularly, of course, but it hadn't been on his mind to pay much attention.

As if reading George's thoughts, DSU Smith said, "Juliette Thompson will help you. She's our press liaison officer. You can meet with her in the morning."

"OK, sir." He stifled a yawn. It was going to be a long day. Not only did he need to follow up with his team, but he needed to attend the post-mortem.

"Get yourself home, son," Jim said, "and get some sleep. There's not much else you can do tonight. And even if you did, it'll probably be shite, and you'll have to do it again tomorrow anyway."

George grinned. "Sure, OK. Thanks, sir." He glanced at his watch. It was after three. Mia had given him his orders to sleep in the spare room. He checked his phone and had saw she'd not replied to his messages. She was pissed off with him. He sighed. It was an occupational hazard; he'd told her very early on about his plans to have a long career in the force. In fact, she had practically known the moment they'd first met. As a reward for chasing a thief who had stolen her purse in the city centre, she had promised him one date. With her being a witness, they'd held off for a while. But, she knew that he worked unsociable hours, sometimes for days on end, because her own father had too. Early in their relationship, it had been OK, but recently it hadn't. Why was that? Why did it seem to annoy the hell out of her?

As he walked to his car, his thoughts turned to poor Erika, battered and bruised, lying naked in the bush, having been defiled moments before her death. He couldn't imagine the terror she must have experienced. He made a small promise to himself that he would catch the killer and that any crimes they had committed would not go unpunished.

Chapter Seven

Mia didn't say a single word as she finished her bagel and drained the remnants of her coffee. Friday was her busiest day of the week, where she had classes each period. Tuesday was her shortest, where Mia only taught for three periods and had the rest to plan her lessons. She hated Mondays as she had to stay late for a staff meeting.

"I'm off to work, babe." George opened the door, and outside it was chilly and cloudy. At least it wasn't raining. He pulled on his jacket and lifted his briefcase. Mia allowed him to kiss her on the cheek but stood up as he tried to put his arms around her. "I'll be late again tonight. I love you."

She ignored him.

"Please, Mia, I don't want to go to work like this." He nearly said something about her father he knew he would have regretted and so kept his mouth shut. Mia shrugged and didn't say a word. She simply looked him in the eye, a petulant look on her face. He sighed and walked out the door.

As he drove to work, he thought about ways of somehow involving her, especially as the deceased had been a secondary school teacher like her. George desperately wanted her to know that it was his responsibility to catch the killer, but he didn't know how. He knew exactly why. Her late father. Her lack of empathy towards his career, mixed with her stony expression that morning, meant that he hadn't even tried to discuss what he had written during the early hours that morning.

I know, he thought. *If there's a break in the case today, I'll pick up a Chinese on the way home and surprise her.* The Chinese at the bottom of Middleton Avenue was delicious, and the portion sizes were huge. He'd go the extra mile for her.

* * *

"Sir, I have something," DS Yolanda Williams said, an experienced female police officer whose job it was to trawl through the CCTV footage. She was invaluable during cases with no witnesses. He'd worked with her before and liked her eccentricity. She was constantly changing her hairstyle and was currently sporting a short afro Mohawk. As she blew away a caramel tip that had fallen onto her face, George noticed her cheeks were flushed and that her voice had been rather excited. She'd obviously been waiting for him.

George dumped his jacket on his chair and followed her out of his office and into Incident Room Five, where two large monitors were set up next to one another. Paused CCTV video footage was shown on each.

"What am I looking at?" George asked.

"This is a map of the area of the school and the surrounding houses. I've circled camera one in blue and camera two in red. Camera two has given me this image." She pointed to the monitor on the right, which showed a blurred figure in the background, standing next to a wall, putting a hand to their mouth. They were wearing all black. "It's hard to see because the culprit's chosen a place with little light. But that's definitely someone watching her."

That was quick. His heart hammered deep within his chest. The adrenaline always hits deep.

"What about camera one? It looks as if the angle would be better to see the culprit."

"I agree, sir, but it's in black and white, so whilst the quality of the image and angle is better, it's not as useful as the coloured version."

George grunted. He understood. Footage from both cameras had been provided by the public, but it still frustrated him. "Run the video on, Yolanda, please." He saw Erika Allen bathed in light, standing in the entranceway to the school. She was wearing what they found at the crime scene. The tote bag rested heavily on her shoulder. In the foreground, with the meagre light, he only saw a black shadow. He scrutinised the screen. "It's impossible. The guy's just a shadow. Everything he's wearing is black. They obviously knew what they were doing. That's if this guy is the culprit."

Yolanda nodded. "I'll keep looking. Perhaps I can get footage of the culprit without his hood up."

"Stop. Yolanda, pause the video. Rewind it back slowly. They're doing something. Putting their hand to their mouth. What is that?"

"I know what they're doing, sir—smoking a cigarette. I thought I saw it earlier, but only on camera two. But now that you mention it, I can see it. Let me recheck the footage from camera one. The black and white might help us identify a lit cigarette."

"You're right, Yolanda." On camera one, the black and white footage showed the bright end of the cigarette as the figure touched the other end to their mouth. He called DS Wood and told her to get SOCOs down there to search for cigarette butts. Maybe they'd get lucky with some DNA.

But George was doubtful. He knew that even kids smoked outside school these days, and the culprit may not even be on the system. They also couldn't identify the culprit from these shots. The jacket was all black with no identifiable logos. "You've been extremely helpful, Yolanda. Keep looking and let me know if you find anything else."

Yolanda took her seat, put on her headset, and began clacking away. "You can count on me, sir."

* * *

His team waited patiently for him in the Incident Room. DC Jason Scott's permanent snarl was plastered to his face. George ignored the young constable and studied the murder board before speaking. The pictures of Erika Allen were still there. He still avoided the image in the middle. "Any updates or leads?" he said to the silenced room.

"I'm meeting with Erika's colleagues later at the school," Wood said. "Then I'm off to see her parents."

George nodded. "What have you got for me on the culprit's MO?" George directed his question to Joshua Fry and Elaine Brewer, two experienced detective sergeants.

Joshua was a bright, IT-savvy officer who'd previously worked down south. "Nothing yet, sir. I've been working on the report Erika gave up at Corporation Street, Morley, about the abusive parent. She spoke to the duty officer and gave a full statement."

"Nice, Josh. What information did she provide?"

"To be honest, sir, not a lot. She was fairly vague, noting that the school had dealt with it, but she was worried because she had seen him on Town Street, outside her house. The officer asked for a description, and all she advised was that he was average height and always wore a hoodie and bottoms."

"That could be anybody. But it matches the guy we've got on CCTV watching her last night," George said. "Does it say which date she saw him on Town Street? Did she say anything specific about his facial appearance or any features? Tattoos? Piercings?"

"Nothing that will help to identify him, sir. The school should be able to help. She said the guy outside was always in the shadows."

"But she was sure it was the same guy?"

"According to her statement, she was adamant. It was only once outside her home, but she'd also noticed him on the way home from the supermarket."

"Supermarket? Which one?"

Joshua glanced down at his notes. "Aldi. It's just past the Catholic primary school, close to her house."

"See if you can find the officer she spoke to, and see if he can remember the dates." Joshua nodded and started tapping away. "Let's see if we can dig up the CCTV on that. Elaine, call Aldi. They're bound to have cameras outside the store, particularly in the car park. Jay, I need you to stop looking for the ring this afternoon. Call the primary school, and see if they have CCTV. I also want you and another officer to go house to house and see whether any of them have CCTV."

"On it, sir," both Elaine and Jay said in unison.

The report on her stalker, and the search for CCTV, were a start. He knew they needed to get an ID on this guy. He checked his watch. The post-mortem was scheduled for four. "Are you going down to the school now?" he asked Wood, who was also getting ready to leave. She nodded. "Her friend Noelle used to work there. Get her details."

"Yeah, thanks for your note. I'll get her details from HR and follow up."

* * *

Before returning to his office, George assigned the other officers the rest of the day's duties before dismissing everyone. He'd considered joining Wood at the high school but knew she had it covered. For now, George had to trust his team to make the right calls while he waited for the forensic reports and the post-mortem that afternoon. He wanted to be hands-on but also knew that in his senior position, he needed to delegate.

Information was drip-fed to him through the day: Wood's reports of her interviews with the teaching staff at Beeston Park Academy and her meeting with Erika Allen's parents; a confirmation from DC Scott about the lack of CCTV around Aldi and the Catholic primary school.

Dinner was a sandwich and coffee from the canteen eaten at his desk. He was surprised to see it was already 3 pm, an hour before the post-mortem when his internal phone rang. He had little to show for it, and the day was fading quickly. "DI Beaumont," he said, picking up the receiver.

"Sir, it's Samantha Fields." Sam was the office manager, a harsh woman in her late forties who never had a smile on her face. "I've got a Mrs Edith Jackson on the phone who lives near the school. She tells me she wasn't in when DS Scott and DS Brewer did the original house-to-house calls to collect the CCTV footage. She says she's heard about the death of the teacher via Facebook, and some guy in a dark tracksuit was hovering outside her house last night. The timings fit. She has his discarded cigarette butts in a plastic bag for us. She told me to tell the SIO, 'I wore gloves.'"

He stopped at Wood's desk on his way out of the office, but she wasn't back yet. He called her and asked her to be present for the post-mortem in his place.

"Everything OK?" she asked.

George nodded and explained about the cigarette butts before he left.

Chapter Eight

Mrs Jackson's door opened before George had even knocked. "Come on in, detective," a teenage girl said.

He followed her through the narrow hallway and into a lightly decorated kitchen, where a woman with a face well worn by years of cigarettes and sun was sitting in a wheelchair at a small coffee table. She had a cup of coffee in her hand; it looked like she hadn't slept a wink for weeks. Yet despite this and the apparent frailty of her body, there was a strength to her eyes that George had rarely encountered. She reminded him of his own grandma. "DI George Beaumont, nice to meet you both." He flashed his warrant card.

"Why don't you take a seat, love, and we can discuss why I called you out here."

"Thank you. I appreciate anything you can tell me," George said. "Do you mind if I record this?"

"Will anybody hear my voice?"

"No, this is so I can type up my report later."

"On HOLMES?" George nodded and hid a smile. "Sure," she said. She timidly dunked a rich tea finger into her coffee and nibbled at it, the soft crumbs falling to the table as she did so.

"I heard about the murder of the schoolteacher," Edith

Jackson said. "And, well, I was 'round back on Wednesday night, having a cigarette, love, and I saw..." She looked down sheepishly. "I saw a man in a green car driving up and down the street repeatedly. I wheeled myself out front to be sure of what I was seeing. And he drove up again about five or six times whilst I was out there. Although this time, whenever the car went past me, it slowed. It scared me. It never went into the school. But yet, for an hour, the car kept driving up and down. When we go outside, I'll show you where I was sitting in my chair and where the car kept reversing."

"And what does this have to do with last night?" George interjected.

"I'm getting to that, love, be patient," she said. She was the type of witness he needed to let speak, so he stayed silent. "So Thursday, love. Same time. I saw the same man in the same car. But this time, he was driving even slower up and down the road, as if he was looking for somebody or something."

She took a sip of coffee and paused. "Listen, I know it was stupid, but I wheeled out onto the path. I wasn't sure if he had seen me this time. I hoped he hadn't. What I did love was wheel up to where he had been reversing the day before. And I typed a message to my granddaughter here. Madelaine, dear, do you have the text message?"

Madelaine nodded and passed her phone to George. It was a car registration. He took a photo of the text and emailed it to DS Elaine Brewer with a message for her to look into it.

"," Mrs Jackson said. "As soon as I lit up on the junction, the car disappeared from view. I can't remember the time, but that text will tell you."

About six-thirty, George remembered.

"So I went back home and put a serial killer documentary

on, as I usually do at that time of night. I made a pot of tea and settled into it. They're usually about three-quarters of an hour. But that car was on my mind, love. I'd never seen it before. But two nights in a row, around the same time. Coincidence? Probably. But I watch a lot of crime documentaries, and they always seem to find the culprits through one coincidence or another. So around quarter to seven, I decided I needed another cigarette. I never smoke in the house, dear, never. I went out front to smoke because it's easier to wheel back into the living room rather than the kitchen. On the other side of the low wall, to my surprise, was a figure with their hood up."

Bingo.

"I couldn't tell what their sex was at first. They were just a dark figure with smoke rising into the air. I watched in silence for five or so minutes, not daring to move. They smoked about three cigarettes. I'm a terrible addict, love, but whoever was smoking that night was the biggest chain smoker I'd ever seen, let me tell you. Eventually, they turned around. I think there was a change in the wind; maybe a patter of rain began to fall. I was entranced. But the figure turned and faced me. I didn't like what I saw. His features were hidden in the shadows, but I know they had a cropped beard around their mouth."

"You're sure it was a male?"

"Definitely. He took another drag, the cigarette between gloved fingers, and grinned. The grin made me shiver. It was something about his mouth. I can't quite explain it. I wished him a good night and went back inside. I hadn't had a single cigarette. And I couldn't concentrate on the documentary. I went outside ten minutes later to tell him I was going to phone the police if he didn't move, but he had gone. A few teachers were leaving at that point, too. I can see the entrance to the office from out front."

George looked at her and knew she was telling him the truth. "Could you describe him to me?" George asked her. "What kind of clothes was he wearing? Any logos? Any distinguishing features? Would you recognise him if I got you to look at some e-fits?"

"One question at a time, love; I'm not as young as I used to be." Edith Jackson allowed her eyes to meet with Beaumont's before she took a deep breath and answered the questions. He figured she was concentrating, making sure she remembered everything about their culprit.

"He was wearing casual clothing and was a white man, average height, with brown hair. He had his hood up. I couldn't see over the wall what kind of footwear he had on, but he was wearing black jeans. His coat was made from some kind of woolly texture, which I found off considering it had rained on and off. It wasn't suitable if you understand?"

George nodded but didn't speak, allowing Mrs Jackson to continue. When she didn't, he said, "Tell me about the beard."

"It was dark, so I couldn't see much. I think his beard was brown, like his hair. Probably a darker shade. I wasn't paying too much attention; I was worried more about the littering he was doing. He kept throwing his cigarette butts on the floor by his feet. I was fuming, love, fuming. I made a mental note to sweep them up the next morning. But by then, I'd heard through the grapevine about the teacher that was killed. It might be a coincidence, detective. But a shifty fella waiting by the school hours before a young, beautiful teacher is murdered begs belief. Honestly, I'm so upset. So is poor Madelaine. She didn't go to school today, that's why she's here, love. Miss Allen was her PE teacher. , love, I digress. After finding out this morning about Miss Allen, I got Madelaine out of bed early to push me outside before the school run started. The cigarette butts were still there. I got a plastic bag, put on some gloves, and collected them for you."

Edith looked from George's face to Madelaine's face to make sure that she was clear. Madelaine nodded before Edith opened her eyes wide, waiting for George to understand the significance of what she had just said.

George knew the significance. They could have the culprit's DNA. But only if the guy she saw was the killer. It backed up the CCTV evidence they had, but the problem was that Mrs Jackson could have contaminated the area, and the evidence, too. It probably wouldn't hold up in court. But he fired off another text to Elaine Brewer to get some SOCOs on the scene. They'd take DNA from both Madelaine and Edith, too, to eliminate them. He explained this to them both.

"It's a shame, you know, about that school. When Madelaine's parents went there, it always had such a terrible reputation, but more recently, it's been positive. It's been a long time since there was any scandal there. As I say, a shame."

"Can you explain, Mrs Jackson? I'd like to hear about it, in case it's important for later on in the case."

"Oh, I doubt that, love. I really do." As Mrs Jackson said this, the front door opened and then slammed shut.

"Madelaine. Madelaine? Where the fuck are you? I've just had a call from the school to say you didn't attend today. If this is what happens when you sleep over at your Nanna's, then I'll have to consider—What the hell—"

A woman in her mid-thirties, not too dissimilar looking to both Madelaine and Edith, entered the kitchen. She eyed DI Beaumont warily. "You never said you were having guests today, mother?"

"Janice, this is Detective Inspector George Beaumont. He's leading the case. You know, Miss Allen? The murder? He's here about the cigarette butts."

"Of course he is. Nice to meet you; I'm Janice Mitchell." She closed the distance, and they shook hands. She sat down in the empty chair at the coffee table, and all at once, George became overwhelmed by the odour of nicotine and perfume. He thought he could also detect alcohol but didn't dwell on it.

"So you were telling me about previous scandals, Mrs Jackson."

"Of course, love. Janice would be the best person to tell you, actually."

George turned to his left to find an intense pair of green eyes looking at him. From her demeanour and the way she carried herself, he assumed she was a loud, confident woman. She used a manicured hand to sweep an unruly curl of blonde hair away before she said, "What am I the best person for, mother?"

"You're the best person to tell the story. The one about the teacher who had that affair with one of your classmates, dear."

"Oh. That. Sure. I don't remember much; it was nearly twenty years ago. Madeline, love, could you go upstairs and pack your bag, please? We need to go once I've told the detective my story."

The blonde daughter left the room, and Janice continued her story. "This case is going to cause an uproar, you know? Genuinely. Miss Allen was an excellent teacher. Very popular. She was beautiful. Fit from playing sports. Young. Intelligent. A maths wiz, apparently. , back to my story... My year eleven form tutor was sacked for having sex with a boy from my form."

"What can you tell me about this boy, Janice? Do you remember his name? Where he lived?"

"Bailey? Billy, maybe? Sorry. He was in my form and some of my classes, but he was a nobody, really. We were all shocked when the truth came out. They hadn't told us it was the weird boy she had been sleeping with, but he left the school, and the area, when she had been sacked. We kind of added two and two together. Plus, Jimmy Scanlon from the year below apparently messaged him on MSN. The boy confirmed it was him. He was a weird boy with some kind of facial deformity. I can't remember the details. But the school might know. The current head was just a teacher back then."

"I'm sure his grandad moved him away when rumour got out. I'm sure that's what you told me, dear," Edith explained.

"Do you remember what the boy looked like?"

"Brown hair. Normal height. Normal weight. Normal. But weird, if you get me? I don't remember much other than he got bullied for having a deformity on his face. But what that was, I can't remember."

"OK. And what about the teacher? What form were you in? Do you remember the year? Can you remember her name? What happened to her after the termination?"

"I'm so sorry, but I can't remember. I was in year eleven. That's all I can remember. I'd have been sixteen, so during the middle of 2000. We got a supply teacher in. It was summer, so we had already done our exams. We didn't really see the supply as we left in the June. I'm sorry, it was a long time ago."

"No need. You've been very helpful. You mentioned a man named Jimmy Scanlon. Does he still live in the area?"

"No, detective, I'm afraid he died when we were in our early twenties. We weren't close, so I didn't go to the funeral. I found out through Facebook."

"You've both been extremely helpful, but I have one last question for you, Mrs Jackson if that's OK?"

"Sure thing, Detective Beaumont."

"If I got this killer and put him in an identity parade, would you recognise him? You'd be safe behind a one-way mirror."

"I can't be sure. But I'm happy to try."

"Before you go, Mrs Mitchell—"

"—Ms Mitchell. I got divorced from that piece of shit last year."

"Ms Mitchell, I need to take DNA swabs from you, your mother and your daughter to clear you from the investigation." She nodded, still smiling.

A few minutes later, when DS Elaine Brewer arrived with a team of SOCOs, a smile broke out on George's face. He looked at her, and she was doing the same thing. They had found a break, finally, the first of the case. Not only could they have the culprit's DNA, but they had a number plate they could run, one that they could hunt and stalk, like that bastard had, to that poor girl.

Chapter Nine

On the way back to the office, George called DS Wood.
"Hi, George, are you OK?" she said.

George didn't have any time for small talk. He needed to get back to the office and brief them on what Mrs Jackson and her daughter had told him. "Fine. How did the post-mortem go?"

"The usual stuff, boring, gross stuff. You know, guts and gore. Awful smells. Basically, everything I don't really want to see or smell," said Wood, trying to make light of the ordeal. "But you asked, and I delivered."

"Thanks, Wood. What did Dr Ross find out?"

"The bastard had put her through hell before killing her, as Kent suspected in the woods. The cause of death was asphyxiation. Bruising to the neck and windpipe suggests she was strangled. As Kent mentioned, the pattern of bruises suggests large hands, most likely a male. It would have been brutal for her. The angle suggests she would have been facing away from her attacker. The frenzied stabbing happened afterwards. Dr Ross is also sure that the culprit had sex with her before he killed her. There's no trace of any semen, but there was lubricant from a condom. Ross found some fibres under her nails, and he's sent them off to the lab."

CHAPTER NINE

Battling with the torrid images of Erika laid on the rain-soaked ground, George closed his eyes and tried to repel the thoughts from his mind. The motives behind inflicting such harm on another individual were impossible to comprehend, regardless of their age, but somehow that Erika was a loved and respected teacher made it even more difficult for George to understand. Wood continued on what Ross had advised, that the sequence of events showed the culprit had both organised and planned the killing. They were already attempting to determine whether Erika was the intended target or if the killing was a random act, but George felt as if he already knew that the culprit had intentionally killed Erika Allen.

"I can go through the report with you tonight, George?" said Wood.

"Thanks, but I need to get home at a decent hour tonight. Email it to me."

"Everything?"

"Yes, everything Wood. Thank you," George said, hanging up.

* * *

"Can I have your attention, please?" DI Beaumont barely had to raise his voice, and everyone stopped what they were doing and turned to face him. The air prickled with expectation. They had drawn the squad room blinds to keep the sunlight off the monitor screens, but nobody had complained. Wood had given George the name of the angry student's dad.

George looked at the faces of his team staring back at him and said, "We have a recent development." The faces that stared back were both eager and expectant. He got straight to it and told them what Mrs Jackson and her daughter had told him.

"My train of thought at the moment is that the father who was stalking Erika, Liam Flesher from Beeston, is still to blame. Once he's been located, we'll bring him in and take swabs."

"What about the boy who was sleeping with his teacher?" DC Jay Scott asked. "Any relevance to the case?"

"At the moment, I'm unsure. Unless it's Liam Flesher, then probably not. Edith said she was sure his grandfather had moved him out of the area. I'm going into the school tomorrow to speak to the head. Apparently, she was a teacher during that time period. Once I know more, I'll update HOLMES. Keep checking it and updating it."

"So what's next, boss?" DS Joshua Fry asked.

"We have DNA now. A SOCO has sent the butts off to the lab, and DSU Smith has put in a word with the DCS Mohammed Sadiq to get the results expedited. Hopefully, we get a match on the system for Liam Flesher." The DNA database contained six million profiles, but these were usually previous offenders. Liam may not even be on the system. "DS Wood has also updated me on the post-mortem report. From what Dr Ross has advised, we believe the man responsible had a grudge against Erika Allen. After killing her, he repeatedly stabbed her in the stomach. Dr Ross used the word 'frenzied.' There's no doubt that this attack was personal, but it could also be a message. I need you to look into her past. We're talking ex-boyfriends, old friends, family members who she'd fallen out with, or anyone who might have resented her relationship with Ian Kennedy."

"What about Ian's ex-girlfriends?" Elaine Brewer asked from the back of the room.

CHAPTER NINE

"Excellent, Elaine," said George. Wood had mentioned it to him on the phone, and he was just about to get to it. "We're going to need to talk to Ian Kennedy again."

The DSU entered the room, his presence causing those seated to swivel in their chairs. "We've decided it's best to keep the information about Liam Flesher and the information from both Mrs Jackson and Ms Mitchell from the press for now." He made eye contact with every officer in the room. "If any of these names turn up in the papers tomorrow, I'll know it was one of you lot. To be clear, it isn't worth your career. Understood?"

They all nodded.

George cleared his throat as Wood entered the room. She looked dishevelled, but it only made her look more beautiful, her dark features in contrast to her white blouse. "Ah, DS Wood. I know you've had a busy day, but I'd like you to brief us on what you got from both Erika's workplace and her parents."

"I interviewed her colleagues today at Beeston Park Academy, and they mentioned a stalker, as well as Liam Flesher. Two of the women she works closely with clearly remember her telling them about it in the weeks leading up to the attack. The three of them would regularly talk about it in the staff room, and they widely believed it to be Liam Flesher. They couldn't prove it, however."

"What about her parents? Did they know about this stalker?" asked George.

"Yes. Erika mentioned Liam Flesher to them. Again, they believed he was the person following her. In fact, Erika's mother, Leanne Allen, went out with her for a coffee last week after work in Wakefield. A guy with a hoodie followed them through Trinity and into the car park."

"Right." George looked around for Yolanda and the other three covering the CCTV footage. "I need two of you to call Trinity and get all the footage from them. Speak to the coffee shop too. Liaise with Wood so that you can get the date, too. You're looking for evidence of a guy in a hoodie following them. Thanks. We really need an image with a face, a lead of some sort. There should be quite a few cameras, so we should be in an excellent position."

"I think we may have the killer outside her house earlier in the week, too," Yolanda replied. "I was coming to find you when you started the meeting," she added when she saw the look on his face. "And sir, could I also run something by you, if that's OK?"

"Sure, Yolanda. Give me five minutes; then I'm yours," he said. "Thanks everyone; that's all for now, but if you get anything, let me know."

Smith grabbed George by the shoulder as he headed out of the door and said, "Don't forget the press conference in an hour. I trust you've spoken with Juliette?"

"I just got back, so not yet."

With a tone that didn't warrant arguing with, Smith said, "I'll get Juliette to come down here instead. Meet me in my office in ten minutes."

George glanced at his watch, then marched through to Incident Room Five to find Yolanda. "Let's see what you've got."

Yolanda nodded to the screen on her left. "This is from yesterday morning. The owner of the CCTV camera sent it to us an hour ago. You can see the time stamp shows 7 am as Amanda Milbury's car pulls up. And as she gets in, you can see him watching. You can see him face on. It's a shame the

CHAPTER NINE

camera quality is terrible. He looks as if he's wearing some kind of face mask." George watched as a dark figure in a dark hoodie appeared in the top-left corner of the screen. "As soon as Amanda sets off, he turns back."

"We need to check the CCTV footage further down the street if there is any," George said. "Take young Konrad, add him to your team for a bit. He's new. It's only right he trawls through hours of footage. Take him out house to house tomorrow and search for more cameras."

"Speaking of more CCTV. Brad from Wakefield called. Brad Fox. He's got IT to send over facial recognition software. Once we have a suspect, we can use images, and the computer will search for them: the more images, the better. I'd like to use it if that's OK? I was going to run it by DSU Smith, but you're in charge here."

George nodded. "I'll speak with Josh and see if he can get some images from Facebook. I'm going to arrange a meeting with the head to discuss Flesher and the boy who had the affair with the teacher. It's him, though. It's got to be—that bastard Flesher. Just show us your face," George muttered to Yolanda, who was watching the other screen.

"I've got another video for you to look at, sir. Look, there's Erika." Yolanda pointed to the screen on her left as a petite blonde walked out of the front entrance of Aldi and out of shot. Yolanda pressed a button, and suddenly Erika was back. He remembered the way she was lying on the ground, battered and bruised and covered in blood. Lifeless. She was almost pixie-like in the way she moved. Five foot two, Dr Ross had confirmed in his notes. Yolanda paused the video and put the previous footage back on. The killer entered the shot, having left Aldi a minute after her, according to the timestamp. She let it run on until he, too, was out of shot. The difference in size between the two was stark, and he would have had no trouble subduing her.

Yolanda put a second lot of footage back on, and the pair watched as Erika continued walking home, not noticing that the man was watching her, not noticing that he was following her as she walked down St. Philips Avenue. He stayed at least a hundred metres away from her and kept to the opposite side of the road, head down as if engrossed in a mobile phone. Just a man walking. It wouldn't cross a bystander's mind that the culprit had his face angled downwards so that anybody wouldn't see it.

"Shit! All this footage, and we still can't get an ID on him." George clenched his fists and sighed noisily. He needed to keep calm and not let his emotions get the better of him. *Breathe, George.* "This guy obviously knows what he's doing." He watched until they disappeared off the screen. "Where's the next camera?" he asked Yolanda.

She sighed. "The next cameras are on the park gates, but one only covers the gate itself, and the other is facing east."

"What about Town Street west?"

"Nothing on there until you get to the two we've already seen. This was last week. The owner said he deletes them after four or five days to save space. We can't get in contact with the other owner. It looks as if they're on holiday."

George masked his disappointment. "OK, Yolanda, thanks." She looked downhearted and tired, too, so he added, "You're doing good work here, Yolanda. We're getting closer. And soon, when you get a picture of the bastard, we will have him. And most of that work will have been down to you."

She smiled and nodded her head at him. For George, it was

CHAPTER NINE

necessary to keep morale high. He'd order in tomorrow to show his team how valuable they are. As a DS, he'd been part of murder squads before where the SIO had lost team morale, and it ended up curtailing the entire investigation. He didn't want that for his team.

* * *

Smith was waiting in his office. "Any footage of the killer on the CCTV?" Smith asked before George could say hello.

"No, nothing confirmed as yet." He didn't elaborate. Once they had something concrete, he would inform the DSU.

"Now, I know that this is your first press conference, so Juliette, our liaison, is going to guide you through it. We can say certain things and not others. Integrity and impartiality are paramount. Ah, here she is."

A woman arrived, her auburn hair falling in ringlets framing her round face. Everything about her screamed marketability and efficiency, especially the meticulously applied make-up.

George smiled at Juliette and held out his hand. "Detective Inspector George Beaumont," he said.

"Juliette Thompson, press liaison."

As Juliette outlined the crucial aspects of a press conference, he tried to stay focused. He wasn't used to dealing with the media, even though it was an important part of his job. George knew that the higher his rank, the more he had to do it, but at the moment, his thoughts were preoccupied with catching a killer.

The rest of the hour was spent going over it, and contrary to what he'd expected, he left feeling much more confident about addressing the media.

"I'll take you downstairs," Juliette said. "The press is waiting for you outside."

He shot a look at his DSU.

"Don't worry, son, I'll be there too," Smith said, a Cheshire Cat grin on his face. "I'll need to be to make sure you don't fuck up."

Chapter Ten

"Good afternoon, ladies and gentlemen. My name is Detective Inspector George Beaumont, and I'm the senior investigating officer on this case. The body of a local woman was discovered in Middleton Woods shortly after ten last night. I can now confirm that her name was Erika Allen, aged twenty-five, from Middleton. It is believed she was walking home from the school where she worked when she was attacked and subsequently murdered."

"Was she a victim of sexual assault?" A female reporter shouted from the middle row. George wondered whether they had a mole or whether it was the first question people asked when a woman was murdered. He certainly wasn't expecting to be asked that question straight away.

He glanced at Smith, who furrowed his brow and gave a barely noticeable nod.

"Yes, she was raped, strangled, and stabbed."

The energy changed from one that was calm and solemn to a ripple that became frenetic. The outside of the station buzzed. Every reporter and journalist began firing questions at George all at once.

"Do you know the identity of the rapist?"

"Do you have any leads?"

"Are there any suspects in custody?"

"Is this an isolated incident, or should we be warning teachers?"

"Is there a serial killer on the loose?"

Despite feeling like he was a deer in headlights, George maintained his composure. He emulated DSU Smith and lifted his hand, drawing silence from the press. He barely needed to raise his voice but did so , letting his confidence and competence be shown. "Anyone with information is asked to contact me, or DS Wood, at the Leeds District Homicide and Major Enquiry team quoting reference 13102426766 or online via live chat. We are currently pursuing all lines of inquiry. That's it for now. Thank you."

As they trooped back upstairs, DSU Smith said, "Fuck me, did you hear the question about it being a serial killer? I don't do serial killers, Beaumont, so you fucking find that bastard and quick. It's all we bloody need."

"Serial killer? I'm not so sure. I think it's personal," George said. "A one-off."

Juliette nodded in agreement. "It'll be a jealous ex-boyfriend. Or a colleague. It usually is."

"I hope to God you're right, Beaumont," Smith said as he headed straight to his office. "Keep me updated."

"That was a good job, by the way." Juliette paused outside the staff room. "Not too shabby for your first press conference."

On his way back, George received a call from DS Elaine Brewer. "Sir, it's about Liam Flesher."

"Oh, please tell me you have something on him."

"He's dead, sir. He died about a month ago. Overdose."

CHAPTER TEN

* * *

George left work at seven that night and drove to Erika Allen's house. He wanted to talk to her fiancé, Ian Kennedy, again. The wrought-iron gates were open, and Ian's car was on the drive, so George parked up outside, blocking the exit. A shiver ran down his spine as he stared up at the house. George imagined that Erika's killer had probably been standing here himself and watched as she came and went. It was probably how he got to know her routine, especially as he wasn't Liam Flesher.

DS Wood had called ahead, so Ian was expecting him. George knocked.

"I'm sorry to bother you again," George began when Ian opened the door, "but there's been progress made in the case, and I have a certain line of inquiry I'd like to follow. I wanted to ask you a few more questions. On the record? Is that fine with you?"

"You want to record it?" George nodded. Ian returned his nod with a blank stare and eventually stood back to let him in. George followed him into the living room, which he noticed Ian hadn't tidied since his last visit. Even the meal he'd cooked the previous night was still sitting there on the table. Ian sank down into the armchair next to the small coffee table. The light radiating from the lamp rested on it was the only light in the room. The TV was off. He gestured for George to take a seat.

George eased himself into the nook of the leather sofa and questioned whether he was sitting in a dead woman's seat. "This might seem like a strange question, but do you know of anyone who may have wanted to hurt Erika?"

Ian's eyes widened, but he didn't hesitate. "Other than the

dad from the school? No, of course not. Everybody loved Erika. She was the nicest, most beautiful person I've ever known. Why?"

"What about ex-partners?" George asked, ignoring Ian. "Has anyone she may have dated in the past been in touch recently?"

"We've been together for nearly three years," Ian said. "We started seeing each other just as she started teaching at Beeston Park Academy. I met her at a training course. But to answer your question, as far as I know, she hasn't. I didn't exactly check her phone or social media, but she would have been acting differently, right?"

George's heart sank. "Sure, I understand. You had a very open, honest, and trusting relationship. That's what you're suggesting. Correct?" He was grasping at straws, trying to tease answers from him. He needed something. Anything.

"I'm not suggesting anything. We were very strong. Faithful. I think. I don't know." Ian hung his head. The yellow pallor of his skin and the mess in the living room suggested he wasn't eating or sleeping right. He looked awful. Dark shadows were imprinted under his eyes. George wondered what he'd feel like if Mia ever— He didn't finish the question in his mind.

"OK, not to worry. Thank you." He had Joshua working on her social media accounts, looking for any evidence of harassment or aggressive behaviour. Sometimes stalkers would send threatening messages. But they'd found nothing yet. "So, we've discussed Erika, but what about you? Any ex-partners who might be upset about your engagement with Erika?"

"What? No. Nothing like that." He frowned. "As I said, we'd been together for nearly three years. Before that, I had dated nobody. Not even at Uni. I hate to admit it, but I was a virgin before I met Erika."

George sighed, worried that they might be headed down another dead end. *So much for the jealous-ex theory.* "OK, thanks for your honesty, Ian." George braced himself. "And you weren't having an affair?"

"What?" He held up his hand, stood up, and then sat back down. "How could you ask such a question?"

"I appreciate that Ian, but I have to ask. We will have to look at Erika's past. Is there anything we're going to find? Was she ever accused of misconduct at work? Had she perhaps had, or was currently having, an affair with a parent or student?"

It took a few seconds for Ian Kennedy to understand the questions and what George was suggesting. "Off. Turn that fucking thing off right now!" Ian shook his head. "How can you even suggest that? My poor fiancée has only just lost her life." He threw himself back down, his eyes fixed on a photograph of Erika in a gold frame beside a vase of dead flowers.

He switched off his Dictaphone and got up from the low sofa, a low groan erupting from his stomach. "Thanks for talking to me, Ian."

George was about to let himself out when he turned and asked, "Do you have anyone who can come and stay with you for a bit, mate? Or someone you can visit? I don't think it's a good idea for you to be alone right now."

"I was going to head back up to Glasgow and stay with some extended family," he said. "But I knew how that looked. I'm innocent, and I want to prove that to you."

"Look, mate, you aren't a suspect. Go to Scotland. But before you do, call the station and ask for DS Wood or me. Give us the address where you'll be staying. If we need to ask you any more questions, we will call you. It'll do you some good to get out of here."

Ian's shoulders sank, and George could see the relief on his face. "Thank you, Detective Beaumont. Really. I'm finding it hard living here. She's everywhere. Wherever I go, I can smell her perfume and see her belongings. Her face stares back at me from that picture. I miss her. I just want her to be alive so badly that everything I do reminds me of her, you know?"

George didn't, thankfully. He couldn't even imagine what Ian was going through, but he knew that the man needed support. He made a mental note to call Cathy and ask her to check in on him and then nodded at Ian and said, "I know, mate, I know."

George thanked him and left. He left his car blocking the drive and walked up and down Town Street, searching the houses and streetlights for cameras. There was a camera they'd missed positioned on a streetlight high above, opposite Ian and Erika's home. It was pointing downwards so it would pick up whoever was walking on both paths. If they were lucky, it might even have picked up a decent facial shot. The camera would be council owned, one that the NPT would have requested. They were having issues with the youths in the area.

He fired off a text to DS Wood, who he knew was still back at the office, asking her to ring the council first thing in the morning and request any camera footage they had. There was still a chance they could identify the killer from that.

Chapter Eleven

When George got home, Mia was out. This didn't surprise him. He was glad he'd forgotten to get the Chinese takeaway. It was Friday night. Mia liked to relax at the end of the school week; it wasn't unusual for her to go out with her work colleagues. There were a few of them, Mia included, who enjoyed going out to clubs. It used to be that she would invite him, but he would decline; clubbing just wasn't his thing. Dancing all night without talking didn't appeal to him because he couldn't really dance—hated it, in fact—and he found conversations impossible in noisy environments. It was pubs that George liked; they appealed to him more than clubs.

He had a shower and warmed up a bowl of soup, then made a coffee and sat down in his favourite armchair to eat and think. When Mia got home two hours later, George was still sitting there. It took her a long time to get the key into the lock, so he knew she was drunk before she stepped into the house. A few minutes later, she'd stumbled past the lounge, noticed the light was on and poked her head around the door.

"Oh, George, now this is a surprise," she said with a scornful laugh. "You're actually home before me."

They hadn't gone to a club then. George knew if they had, it would have been closer to 4 am when she would have stumbled in. Getting up from his chair, he smiled and walked over to her.

"I'm going to be honest with you, George Beaumont." She only used his full name when she was mad. Her words were slurred. "I saw you on TV tonight. Everyone did." There was a glazed appearance in her eyes and a slur in her words. "You never told me about that teacher."

"I tried to, but you haven't given me a chance." He desperately wanted to pull her into his arms, but he hesitated. She had crossed the line, not him. "I tried to tell you this morning, but you weren't interested. Think about how I feel. I've barely seen you since it happened."

"As if you give a shit, Detective Beaumont. I knew her, you know? Everybody at work did. They were all asking me about it tonight, and I couldn't tell them a single thing because you didn't tell me." As she stepped back away from him, she stumbled on her heels. "The first I heard about any of it was on the TV. And you know what's worse. That teacher looks exactly like me. Exactly like Michelle, too. In fact, I could list about ten young, slim, blonde female teachers with blue eyes from schools around the area where Erika Allen was murdered. What if the fucker is a serial killer? What if Michelle is next? Or me? Don't you think it would be prudent to tell me? Or don't you give a shit?"

"Mia, I tried to tell you this morning." He gave in and reached for her. "You didn't want to hear from me."

She stepped away into the corridor, just out of his reach. "You tried to tell me this morning?" She laughed. "I could see it in your eyes this morning, Detective. You were desperate to leave the house. Why was that? Somebody at work that you're

CHAPTER ELEVEN

keen on? A conversation about a killer takes time, and that means spending time with them to talk to them. So don't give me that shit about how you were going to tell me this morning. You still could have told me, even if I was being frosty with you."

"I know. I'm sorry. I mean it, Mia. Please, listen; this case is enormous for me. Once it's over, we'll spend some quality time together. We'll book a holiday for May half term. I promise."

She raised a waxed eyebrow but didn't reply.

The silence dragged out its intended purpose of making him feel like shit. It was working. It was working overtime.

She turned to go upstairs and, with a little sigh, said, "I'm tired, George. I need to go to bed."

George followed her to the foot of the stairs and tried to take her arm to help her up. She smacked his hand away. "I can walk up the stairs. I'm not that drunk, OK?" She slurred her words, but George kept his mouth shut. He watched her stagger upstairs, making sure that he was there if she fell.

Next, he locked up and turned off all the lights. By the time he got upstairs, she'd collapsed on top of the duvet and was fast asleep on her stomach, wearing one of his T-shirts. She didn't stir as he placed a blanket over her, nor did she when he climbed in next to her. George pushed a loose strand of hair out of her face and desperately wanted to pull her into him and make love to her. He needed a distraction from the case, from the imprinted image of Erika covered in blood. George knew he needed Mia now more than he had probably ever, yet she was being so selfish.

He gazed at her lovingly, despite her snoring, marvelling at just how beautiful she was and how extremely lucky he was to have her. She was a beautiful woman, both in and out, when she was in a good mood. Most days, she made his world seem so much brighter, his life so much more fulfilled. But recently, that had all stopped, and that was even before this big case had landed on his lap. He turned over, switched off the bedside lamp, and watched Mia sleep.

* * *

At four in the morning, George awoke to Mia's hand grasping his already erect penis and her lips on his mouth. He thought it was a dream at first, but then, as his mind woke up, his body responded. "I only act the way I do because I miss you when you're not here," she whispered in his ear. She panted as he removed the T-shirt she was wearing, the material gliding over stiff nipples. She kicked her panties off, and he slid inside of her. They made love urgently but softly, and when they came together, Mia lay panting in his arms.

"I'm sorry. I know this is hard for you, too. But, I meant what I said. We'll go on holiday in May once I've caught this bastard."

"The guy's a murderer and a rapist?"

"Yeah."

"How bad was it?" she asked hesitantly. "Did you have to look at her body?"

"Yeah," he said, gently stroking her hair. "They had left her there on the ground, wet from the rain. I won't go into the details, but it was bad."

"She was nice. A popular teacher, I'm told. A popular colleague, too. Very good at her job." She shuddered and rolled over, pushed herself into his nook, pulling his arm with her. "Erika was going to interview for our school, you know? There was a vacancy. The last time I spoke with her was last year when we all went on a course, but she spoke with Michelle about the position. And William, too."

"Do you think they'd talk to me about what they discussed with Erika?" he asked. But she never replied, and he could soon tell by her breathing that she'd gone back to sleep.

George lay there for another hour, thinking about the case, thinking about what Mia had said last night. Was the killer after blonde teachers? There was no way of knowing, not unless he struck again. He gripped her tightly, wanting to protect her. After another twenty minutes of tossing and turning in the dark, he got up, showered, and went to work. It was early that Saturday, so the roads would be quiet, and Mia would probably want to sleep off her hangover .

Chapter Twelve

After returning to the headquarters, George found his team at their desks. The motivation was high, and there was a buzz of determination in the air. They were clacking away at their keyboards or on phones, chasing lines of enquiry. It felt good.

He called a briefing in Incident Room Four, knocked on the door of Incident Room Five and passed a message to Yolanda. DSU Smith didn't work weekends. George was on his own for this.

"I'm sure you've all rather heard about Liam Flesher' death or read about it on HOLMES. It means that we're back at square one, but I know we've had some results from the CCTV, if not an actual ID yet. We also have DNA, but that's still with the lab."

At the mention of Liam's death, the atmosphere in the room changed. Where it was positively charged before, it was now as if all the energy had been drained. "I want progress, everybody," George commanded. "I'm going to be checking through your updates, but I want them from you in person first. Somebody, give me some good news."

Yolanda raised her hand, and George nodded at her. "Sir, we have footage from Trinity Walk, Wakefield. We have a clear shot of the culprit, but he looks to be wearing a clown face mask," Yolanda informed them.

George grinned, and he heard a few cheers from the back. "That's amazing news, Yolanda. The CCTV team is doing a great job. You got anything else?"

"Not yet, sir. We've received the requested footage, but we lack the officers to look through it."

George knew they didn't have enough people working on it. "Have you got the footage from the entrance and exit of the car park yet?"

"Yes, sir," she said.

"Good, I want all ANPR data for vehicles leaving that area up to three hours before and after the timestamp. I want every car, van and lorry traced. Document everything to HOLMES." Yolanda looked deflated. "I need at least four more people on CCTV. And for people to work overtime this weekend."

George looked around when no one immediately raised their hands. "You, you and you two." He pointed at two male constables sitting together and two female constables standing together at the back. "You're on CCTV duty. Liaise with Yolanda. She's in charge."

They all nodded. Even with Smith at home, they still followed his instructions.

Good.

"DS Fry, I want you to work with the four constables I've just nominated for CCTV duty. I know I pulled you from that job, but I need you to run the number plate we got from Mrs Jackson and cross reference that with the ANPR."

"Yes, sir," he said.

"DS Brewer, how are you getting on with the social media side?"

"Good, sir," she said. "But we have found nothing."

"Explain."

"She had around fifty Facebook friends, most of them family members who don't live in Leeds. Erika was a very private woman. Her settings were on high, so only her friends could see her profile. They all check out. She didn't even have her picture as the profile picture. Erika had had no new friend requests since before the new year, and we've swept all her messages, too. There's nothing. Not even a flirty, suggestive message from a colleague at work. She had Instagram but had only posted one picture. There's nothing else."

George grimaced and gave an abrupt nod. He couldn't disregard the rumours that Edith Jackson had mentioned on just her social media accounts, however.

"Where are we on the CCTV at Nando's?" George asked Yolanda.

She shook her head, bouncing a loose caramel tip. She blew it away and said, "The inside of the centre has five cameras, but there's only one camera in the street that showed Erika and Amanda both arriving and leaving. We've checked all six, but there was no one matching our culprit's description either before or after her. I checked an hour each way."

"This guy isn't invisible. We have him in Wakefield, wearing a mask. We need him without it. I think we should invest more time in the Wakefield footage." He looked at DC Blake, one of the female detectives he had nominated for CCTV duty. "Ruby, I need you to call Wakefield Council and see what cameras they have in the area. The footage should be of high quality. Use facial recognition software too. We've got to find this guy."

DS Wood, who was sitting directly on George's right, held up her hand. "The press is outside. I've just had a text. We're the

CHAPTER TWELVE

only team working on a murder investigation, so if you leave, they'll likely bombard you with questions about the case."

"Remember what DSU Smith told you. It's not worth your job going to the press. Not that I believe any of you will. You're all doing a great job. Do we have anything else?"

George looked around the brightly lit room. "OK, off you go. It's going to be a late one. Thanks everyone."

* * *

After a frenzied start, the day continued as it had begun. George ordered Chinese food on the department's budget because the press was lurking outside, and the coffee machine was working overtime. They gobbled it up like vultures.

With almost half the squad working the CCTV angle, he'd given the other half the task of calling and speaking to everybody who worked at Beeston Park Academy. Now that Liam Flesher had been cleared from the investigation, they needed to change the questioning. There was a reason why she'd been attacked, and George insisted that they find it.

After grabbing a reluctant DS Wood, they went downstairs and, much to the media's excitement, issued a public appeal for information. Juliette had advised them to give the press a description and to hand out the image they had captured on the CCTV. George gave them the only description he could: a man of average weight and height wearing a dark hoodie and dark jeans with a face covered by a clown face mask. It wasn't much to go on, but with the CCTV image capture, someone may have seen something. It would go out on the six o'clock news.

Next, fearing the reaction to the photograph would lead to

more work than his team could handle, he spoke to DSU Smith, asking if Wakefield could handle the calls for them. Smith got back to him and advised they had agreed, advising that at the moment, they would also take a step back and let George and his team continue to lead the investigation from Elland Road.

The time bomb had stopped ticking for now.

At six, George turned on the news and watched the public appeal with his team. It felt weird seeing himself on TV. What he saw he didn't recognise. The person on the TV was a more efficient, professional version of himself. His hair was perfectly groomed, his jacket buttoned up. Juliette had fussed over him for ten minutes. But it was his confidence and composure that impressed him. He even sounded calm but displayed the correct sense of urgency. A picture of Erika's murderer flashed up on the screen after he had finished talking, and the newsreader read out the emergency number. He wondered for a moment if Mia had seen it. His phone buzzed in his pocket, and thinking it must have been Mia; he said, "Hi honey, did you see me on the TV? I'm sorry I didn't tell you sooner."

A laugh greeted him, one that was deep and stemmed from deep within. One that was male and certainly not Mia's. "George, it's Finchy," he said, his Scottish accent flowing out from the speaker. "Mate, I've just seen you on the telly. SIO on a murder case, are we?"

George closed his eyes and smiled. Mark Finch was his oldest friend and, as luck would have it, an experienced and well-respected criminal profiler. He was going up in the world, Professor of Criminology, and had recently secured tenure at the University of Leeds. They'd known each other since they were little boys, or wee lads, as his mum would say. As a child, his parents ferried George up to Scotland to see his grandparents during every school holiday, and Mark would always be there, hanging by their door, waiting for him. George had many precious memories, most of them beginning with him leaving his suitcase with his grandpa whilst he explored the surrounding woods with Mark. It had gutted him when they left Scotland. Just before George had turned five, his family had moved to Leeds to be closer to his father's parents, and leaving Mark had been difficult for him. "That I am. Sorry about that, Finchy; I thought it would be Mia calling. Listen though, mate, I could do with your help on the case. I need to pick your brains. Are you free later tonight?"

"Erika Allen's killer, huh?"

"Aye."

"As luck would have it, it's Saturday, and I have nothing on. I'll meet you at the Drysalters at eight. United lost; it'll be quiet."

The pub was just around the corner. "Perfect. See you soon."

"That you will, George."

Chapter Thirteen

"My hypothesis on serial offenders, George," Mark Finch said once they'd bought drinks, "is that they don't emerge fully formed but are a long time in the making." Mark had already given him verbal consent for the recording of the conversation, and so he placed his Dictaphone down on the table.

George looked his friend up and down. Mark looked well; he'd grown a beard and looked as if he had joined a gym. In their twenties, Mark had always been heavier than he should have been, not that it bothered him, but something had obviously changed. George suspected that the change was his fiancée, Florence. Like his fiancée, Mia, Florence was a secondary school teacher who worked at an academy in Roundhay. They booked their wedding for next year, and Florence had a bun in the oven. A brief bout of envy hit George for Mark's happy life, wondering whether he should broach the subject of having children one more time. She had made it quite clear early in their relationship that she didn't want children, telling him she'd felt it necessary George knew upfront. But that discussion had been before he'd proposed. It had been non-negotiable, but maybe she would have changed her mind?

CHAPTER THIRTEEN

"So," George said, "are you saying we need to figure out whether this bastard has killed before?"

Mark nodded. "Well, yes, and the challenge for me as a criminologist is to discover when they started to kill and to see whether I can connect them to other unsolved murders. You see, in my experience, people who commit atrocious acts like these never stop. It's common for there to be gaps between murders."

George grimaced and closed his eyes for a second. He didn't like where the conversation was already headed, and neither would Jim Smith. "I also look at the how and the why people commit crimes."

"What do you mean by the how and the why?" George asked.

"Well, to put it simply, to profile your killer, I'd need to know how he killed his victim and why. Murder is rarely accidental. So I'd need to know a wee bit more about what happened so that we could discuss the killer's behaviours towards his victim and why those behaviours were shown. Once I know that I could give an informed guess as to the kind of person you should be looking for."

"An informed guess?"

"Yes, George," he said with a laugh. "But it's a very efficient guess. All killers show patterns, and they can be categorised because of this. There are some, however, that do not fit the mould, but I'll know more once you share the details."

George wondered just how much he was allowed to share with Mark and considered calling DSU Smith for permission. But something stopped him. Yes, this was his first actual murder investigation, and yes, he was relatively inexperienced. He'd shown that on multiple occasions. But he was also a professional with many years of experience. It was time he showed that.

George took a swig of his non-alcoholic beer. He couldn't taste the difference between a bottle of that and his regular, but what he knew was that it tasted incredible, especially compared with the shit instant coffee he'd been chugging all day. "The victim, Erika Allen, was twenty-five, and she worked at Beeston Park Academy. He attacked her on her way home and pulled her into the bushes where the culprit tied her up. Then, he strangled her whilst he raped her. Once she was dead, he got a knife and stabbed her in the stomach. Repeatedly."

Mark didn't react. He took out a yellow pad and a pen from his briefcase. "Do you mind if I take notes? I won't share them with anybody." George nodded. "Was she tied up in a specific way? You said the culprit strangled her as he raped her. Did he strangle her with his hands? How was she raped? Did the killer take anything from the scene?"

George had been expecting questions, but they came quickly, and George needed a moment to catch up. "He had taped together her hands at the wrists behind her back with black duct tape. The culprit had also used the same type of tape over her mouth. He'd tied her ankles together, too." George thought back to the woods and where she lay. "She'd struggled against her bindings, her body bruised and battered. Stuart Kent, the Crime Scene Co-ordinator, said she must have put up a fight. She was covered in mud, too, from where she had fought."

"Those actions would have made it difficult for the killer," Mark said. "Yet he tied her up. How?"

George grinned. "You know, you're good at this. Why don't you become a detective?"

"I'm good, thanks," Mark said with a laugh. "What I'm doing pays much better."

George thought back to what Kent had said and what he remembered from the scene inside the tent. "Kent said the culprit strangled her with his hands, but it wasn't that initial strangulation that killed her. She also had a bloody nose. Either could have subdued her."

Mark nodded. "Makes sense."

George didn't enjoy remembering this part, and a frown appeared as he explained, "Then, he raped her from behind, and as he did, he strangled her. Her knees were bruised, grazed, and covered with dirt. She was definitely on her front as he raped her. The pathologist confirmed death by asphyxiation."

Mark nodded, continued with his notes, and asked, "Anything else?"

George reached for his drink, but it was empty. "Yeah, a few things, really. The killer stabbed her in the stomach after she'd died. Repeatedly. And this is what gets me. She'd noticed somebody following her in the weeks leading up to her death but never reported it. It's a man wearing all black, hood up, wearing a face mask."

"The guy from your appeal." It wasn't a question.

"Yeah. Does the attack mean something? What's the reason for him targeting her? Was it personal or something?"

Mark studied him. "What makes you think it's personal?"

"Well, the sexual assault, the stabbing of the stomach after death, the fact that she was a teacher. Who in the right mind kills a teacher?"

Mark stared at him, cogs whirring. A full minute passed without either of them saying anything.

Finally, Mark broke the silence. "You're right, George."

"What am I right about?"

"About her being a teacher. Why has he killed a teacher?"

"What?"

Mark leaned forward. "A serial murderer selects his victims. It isn't always random. In fact, I'd argue that the victim had triggered your culprit in some way. There's always a trigger in relation to offending. And, George, the killer must have both access to the victim and the opportunity to kill. Then they kill using their MO. Your culprit seems to have a rather long, drawn-out MO. It takes time, and the killer obviously doesn't want to be caught. So, location is key."

"She gave him an easy opportunity to kill her as she walked home alone, and through the woods, of all places."

"Yes, I've heard about Middleton Woods before, and I know students use the same path home the teacher did. A young student would have been easier to kill, no?"

George nodded.

Mark sat back in his chair and picked up his drink. "This is where the selection is key, George. He selected her because she triggered him, and we need to know why. He stalked her, you said?" George nodded. "He selected her specifically, then. Why? Was there anything unique about her?"

George shook his head. "She was just a teacher at the school. My DS spoke with her parents, friends, and colleagues. She found nothing. Neither had any jilted ex-partners or family members. Mia knew of her and said she was very well thought of at work. I spoke with her fiancé but got little from him other than she thought she was being followed. We've confirmed it with CCTV footage. He was outside the school the night he murdered her, nonchalantly smoking cigarettes. He even left us with his cigarette butts. We have sent them off for DNA analysis."

"I don't think your culprit will be on the database, George. So keep looking. Have you spoken with the parents from the school? Any rumours or anything."

George thought back to Edith Jackson. "Actually, now that you mention it, the lady who told us about the cigarette butts, her daughter, told us that there were rumours of Erika sleeping with a parent at the school. Could that be it?" He doubted it, especially after his most recent conversation with Ian, Erika's partner.

"Could be exactly that. Maybe Erika had stopped the affair, and the parent had stalked her? Did you get anywhere with her colleagues?"

George made a mental note to see them himself and specifically ask about any affairs. "I asked her fiancé directly. He wasn't happy that I asked, but I don't think he was lying when he said neither was cheating. We inquired into a jilted parent, but it got us nowhere. It's something, though, thanks, Mark."

"Sure. But I think there's more to this. You asked me to profile the guy. From what you told me, he would lack empathy, and his thinking would be distorted. It's obvious he has a dislike for females and probably doesn't see them as humans at all. Murderers find killing easier when they dehumanise their victims, as they believe it's OK because they're not human. He was most likely rejected as a youngster. No doubt, somebody in a position of trust, such as a teacher in your case, had taken him in but then let him down. That teacher would have been female. He also defiled her sexually just before he killed her. He clearly has anger towards females. And that ties in with the stabbing of the stomach. Other than transgender women, most females have wombs. Everything your culprit did was designed to attack her femininity. But if your culprit had issues with femininity, he could have killed anybody he considered female. He didn't. He killed a teacher."

"OK, so what you're saying, Mark, is that our culprit picked Erika out as his target because she was a female teacher?"

"Exactly. He may have even done something to that original teacher from his childhood. Or maybe he was having an affair with Erika, and this was his first kill. But I don't think so."

George felt ill. "Wait. What you're saying is that you think he's done this before?"

"Oh, yes, from what you told me about the lack of forensic evidence, it's almost certain," Mark said. "And if you don't catch this guy, Erika won't be the last."

"So, we have a possible serial killer on the loose?" DSU Smith was going to have a field day with this.

"I believe so." Mark wasn't smiling now.

"And this is based on what?"

Mark leaned forward. "Let me tell you about the patterns we talked about earlier." The pub had become steadily busier during their conversation, and Mark had to drop his voice as a group occupied the table next to them. "You'll have learnt this during your training."

George nodded.

"Your culprit probably started with a crush on a teacher, and maybe something happened where she either couldn't or didn't want to form a relationship with him. He took that as rejection. Maybe she got with somebody else. Maybe he was her student?"

George listened closely, thinking of the story Ms Mitchell had told him.

"So, he followed her. Watched her with her new partner.

The rejection he felt grew."

George nodded again.

"Now he would have fantasised about her, probably about having sex with her, or harming her, or doing both at the same time. But he may not have had the courage to act upon that at the time. But the thing about fantasies, George, is that they can become obsessions. Maybe one day, he threatened her."

"Would he have killed her?"

"Probably not. But as that obsession with her grew alongside the rejection he felt, he may have planned to kill her and then carried out his plan. Once he realised how satisfying it was, he would have wanted to do it again. And he would have picked someone just like her. They probably look alike. Or have the same or a similar name. His obsession wouldn't have stopped because he killed her, you see. Nor would the rejection he felt."

"Oh fuck," George said. "So, this guy... He's definitely done it before."

"Of course. But killing teachers is risky, so he most likely moved around a lot to stay off the radar. He would have made a new home somewhere and then killed nearby. Rinse and repeat. I do a lot of geographic profiling, and killers usually kill very close to home."

"So, we're looking for murdered female teachers around the area?"

"I would expand the search to the north of England first, but you may have more luck looking across the UK."

George tapped the table, his anxiety through the roof. If Mark was right, then this was huge. It wasn't a personal attack as he had first thought, but it could end up being a nationwide serial killer hunt. He thought about DSU Smith and the press. Both would be in an uproar. "How many times do you think he's done this?"

Mark shrugged. "It's difficult to say, George. Three, at least. I'd go with four, including Erika, but it could be more. This is an educated guess, remember? Most killers aren't serial killers. They find their victims through opportunity. They have no plan, it just happens, and they shit themselves and try to cover it up. The crime scenes are messy, with lots of evidence."

"This guy's not like that at all," said George.

"I know." Mark gave him a hard stare. "Your guy had been planning Erika's death for a while. He knew her routine inside out. He'd made sure of that. My guess is that he's already got his next victim in mind." George made a mental note to get a DS to check recent reports of other women in Yorkshire who reported being stalked. With any luck, they would find a female teacher who had reported something. Maybe stop this fucker before he could kill anybody else.

"The best advice I can give you is to rule him in or out of cold cases by looking at the MO. Then look for victim selection. Look back ten years in the north of England, first. Then spread out your net if you find nothing. The key to this, George, is finding his first kill. It'll have a similar MO, but the scene will have been sloppier. He wouldn't have been as forensically aware. Find that first murder, and you find your killer."

Chapter Fourteen

"I need everybody working on cold cases," George told his team that Sunday morning at the squad meeting. He'd spoken with DSU Smith at his house last night, explaining what Mark Finch believed about how their culprit probably moved around a lot to avoid detection. He wasn't too happy Finch believed it was only a matter of time before the killer struck again.

"We're looking for anything with the same MO. Look for female teachers, too, but put them on a separate list. Start out with Yorkshire and then move steadily out, but it doesn't matter where it is as long as we stick to the north of England for now." He looked towards DS Wood, the only person other than DSU Smith to know about Finch's profile, who nodded. "This guy could have moved around."

"Sir, what about us? Shall we stay on CCTV?" Dan, the CID detective constable he assigned to Yolanda, wanted to know.

"Please. At the moment, CCTV is paramount to the investigation. I have a strong feeling that's how we're going to get an ID on this guy. Do your best to catch him on camera." Dan looked tired, having spent most of the night at the station working overtime. In fact, they all did. The overtime wage bill was going to be staggering. "From interviews with Erika's close family and friends, he followed her around for weeks. He must have messed up. All we need is just one clear shot of his face."

The public appeal had resulted in hundreds of new leads, which Wakefield's new DCI, Jennifer Wilson, was sifting through before passing on. He couldn't help but think that if he didn't find something soon, she would end up taking over the case.

Back at his desk, he logged into HOLMES to update his own reports when Wood knocked and hovered in the entrance to his office.

"We've found a cold case with a similar MO."

George gestured for her to sit. "What have you got for me?"

"Five years ago, in Cleethorpes, North East Lincolnshire, the body of a young woman was found in Weelsby Woods. The post-mortem confirmed she'd been strangled whilst she'd been raped. But that's not all, George. The woman was stabbed repeatedly in the stomach."

George sat up straight. "Was she a teacher?"

Wood shrugged. "The report doesn't say. It's just a similar MO."

"I wouldn't call that a similar MO, Wood. It sounds to me like it could be our man. Who was the SIO?"

"A DCI Brown, Humberside Police. They never charged anybody. I've printed the file." She handed it over.

"This is good news, Wood. Have you spoken to DCI Brown?"

"No, he was away from his office. They wouldn't give me his number, but they've left him a message to call you."

"It's Sunday afternoon. He's probably gone home." George tapped his fingers incessantly on the table. He desperately needed to be out investigating. "Fuck it. Fancy a trip to the

CHAPTER FOURTEEN

seaside?"

"Do I ever. I'll drive," DS Wood said.

* * *

The journey to Cleethorpes took just under an hour and a half. Traffic was light at that time on a Sunday, and they cruised the eighty miles with no problems. Whilst Wood drove, George spoke to the desk sergeant, who spoke to DCI Brown.

The desk sergeant called back within ten minutes, directing them to a Starbucks on Cleethorpe Road, where DCI Brown would be waiting.

DCI Brown explained that Liz Anderson was murdered in a park, and a dog walker found her body. She was naked, lying on her back. She'd been strangled and raped. His team looked at the usual killers, like the fiancé and family, but they all had alibis.

They also found out that Liz was a secondary teacher at the academy on Chatsworth Place in Cleethorpes, and like Erika, the fiancé mentioned that one dad from school had taken a liking to Liz.

As DCI Brown said goodbye, he added, "If you catch the bastard who did this, let me know, won't you? Liz managed to scratch the bastard, so we have a DNA profile on the system, just waiting for a match. You let me know, George, because this murder still keeps me up at night. It's her face that wakes me up. I've seen pictures of her when she was alive. Yet instead of those cornflower blues, I see grey husks that sink into her skull, her blonde hair withering away to nothing. She's like a ghost. Find that bastard and get him to confess. I don't think I'll ever sleep easy after seeing her like that, but at least I'd know that he's off the streets."

A teacher with blonde hair and blue eyes. Beaumont and Wood looked at each other.

* * *

They walked back to the car, a delicate mist of rain spraying them. "A similar MO, but not the same," Wood said.

George opened the passenger door and shrugged. "It's too similar for it to be a coincidence. When I spoke to Mark, he said that killers perfect their MO over time. Liz was killed over five years ago. Maybe he's altered it. Improved it?"

"What about the fact that DCI Brown believes it was an opportunistic attack?" DS Wood got in and turned on the engine. "Our culprit planned his murder. They had tied Erika Allen up. Liz Anderson hadn't. It's similar, but also very different, George."

Mark's words echoed through his mind: 'Most killers aren't serial killers. They find their victims through opportunity. They have no plan, it just happens, and they shit themselves and try to cover it up. The crime scenes are messy, with lots of evidence.' "Fuck!" he said aloud. "Maybe you're right, Wood. Maybe this trip has been a waste of time?"

Wood ran a hand through her hair and poked her tongue between her lips. "I haven't been to the coast in a while. Even if I can't see it, I can smell it. Brings back memories. I don't think it's been a waste."

Her eye contact was intense, yet George didn't feel uncomfortable. There was no doubt that he was strongly attracted to the bright, brunette detective sergeant. The feelings he felt had been immediate; he was confident that she had felt them, too. The inside of the car was dark, and they were sitting very close together up front. He could smell her perfume mixed with coffee.

"Mark said that this guy has probably killed someone before. Erika was probably his third or fourth," George thought out loud in an attempt to break the silence. He twisted in his seat and stared straight ahead. "The culprit didn't use duct tape to bind her hands and feet. He strangled her with his hands. This is both very different to our culprit. But yet the fact that the victim was a teacher with blonde hair and blue eyes, and a similar age to Erika when she was murdered, is significant."

Wood was still staring at him, but when he said nothing, she turned the car around in a wide arc. "Maybe she was his first kill. His victim selection became specific enough that it set up the next two victims. If Erika was his third, then we need to find the second. We need to find another murdered blonde-haired, blue-eyed female teacher in her mid-twenties. That's if the teacher theory is accurate."

"And not only that," George said, a solemn look on his face. "We need to catch this bastard before he can find a fourth. I think we should alert the local schools tomorrow."

Wood shook her head. "Are you sure? Because I think that'll cause a panic. And from the profile Mark gave you, he was explicit that he thought the culprit would move away after a kill. I was thinking about calling up local estate agents and checking for people who are moving away."

"Sure, Wood, you may as well make sure. And you're right. First and foremost, we need to treat this as a single murder case."

Wood turned to him as she braked for a red light. She looked upset. "I'm sorry, George. I hope I haven't overstepped."

George smiled and shook his head. The light turned green, and she set off. "It was planned, George. The way he killed Erika and where was too perfect. He might start stalking again, and I know you've got DC Scott monitoring any new stalker or harassment reports, but for him to kill again, and so soon, it just doesn't bear thinking about. Think about it, George. That would mean that he's already chosen and is monitoring a new victim."

Chapter Fifteen

They'd spent the entire Monday checking and double-checking CCTV for images of their stalker. It was all too easy to miss something; the work was slow and tedious. Yolanda Williams had volunteered to work overtime again and run her facial-recognition software on the files, but the footage they had was dark and grainy, and with no full image of their killer, they weren't any closer than they had been when they started.

Tuesday morning, George was the first one into the office and put on the coffee pot before making sure he set the Incident Room up. As the coffee dripped into the empty bowl below, George looked through HOLMES 2, checking the additions from yesterday. A new entry, posted by DS Wood, had been listed detailing another cold case with a similar MO. George clicked on the file and was about to read through it when a booming Geordie accent made him freeze. "DI Beaumont, I'd like to see you in my office. Now."

Shit.

He poured two mugs of coffee before heading to DSU Smith's office. "Morning, sir. I didn't know you were in," he said, handing over a mug before sitting down.

Smith stared at him, a look of indifference on his face. "Is there anything you'd like to share with me, DI Beaumont?" he asked, offering a printout to him.

"No, sir?" The papers contained a list of names and numbers that equated to the overtime accumulated since Friday night. George placed the sheets gently on the table and lowered his eyes. He'd screwed up. It had been an enormous mistake not to get permission from Smith for any unauthorised overtime. Whilst he was the senior investigating officer on the case, he knew better. And instead of trying to justify his error—a significant one judging the high numbers on the sheets—he knew he had to take responsibility.

"I have no excuse. I'm sorry, sir," he said, knowing that sorry wasn't good enough.

"The public has already slammed us for the 10% increase in the precept for Council Tax, and I have to justify these figures to the chief superintendent. I've been accused of wasting public funds because I've tried to justify these man hours, but looking again, I was bloody foolish."

"I should have asked you, sir. And I'm sorry. But these hours were valuable."

"I need to know now, Beaumont. How long is this going to take?" Smith said, gesturing to Yolanda's Incident Room.

"We've been targeting CCTV to get an ID on the killer," George said.

"And what have you found so far, because HOLMES isn't telling me much? I've been here since five, Beaumont, trying to justify the figures. And all I can see is that you have footage of the culprit covered up. Has this expensive CCTV operation given you any leads?"

George shook his head.

Smith frowned and rubbed the spot between his eyebrows,

above his nose. He'd been very supportive of George, and George knew that. He'd even given George this case instead of the other two Detective Inspectors that were available. "We're already under threat from Wakefield. You have no leads and no results. That, along with an increased wage bill, will mean it's only time before they take over," he said. "Is that what you want?"

George shook his head. "We have a lead. And we have DNA, sir. We're following every line of inquiry we can. I understand that you're annoyed at me because of an increased wage bill, but don't tell me we're not getting closer because we are."

"I'm trying not to be dismissive, George, but your suspect may as well be a ghost. A teacher has been murdered, and when I'm asked what we're doing, I have to be vague because all I can say at the moment is that we're staring at computer screens all day, splashing the cash!"

"With respect, sir, that's modern police work. If there isn't a team concentrating on CCTV, then I'm doing my job wrong. Isn't that why the council puts up the cameras? For reasons like this?"

Smith nodded, drained his mug of coffee, and said, "Beaumont, keep your CCTV team working, but you are under strict orders to stop all overtime."

"What if I have a lead for you by the end of the day?"

"Don't push it, Beaumont. I'm ordering you to cease all overtime. Now, I've got a lot to do, so if there isn't anything else, don't let the door hit you on the way out."

* * *

George shuffled back to his desk, feeling like a naughty schoolboy. He looked around, grateful the rest of his team hadn't arrived. At first, George had considered making an excuse during his conversation with DSU Smith. But he knew that he would have lost his boss' respect. It was a shocking error, one that George should never have made. He wondered why, for a moment, and conceded that his relationship problems had seeped into his work. For George, that was unacceptable.

Trying to forget his earlier error, George thought about Smith and his speech about not mixing work with family life. If only he could follow in the DSU's footsteps. A slip like this could cost him everything, everything he had worked for, and everything he was working towards, and now it wouldn't help to have the added burden of DSU Smith on his back.

The nagging doubts festered. George knew the CCTV footage was a long shot, but he also knew that humans made mistakes. The murderer went to great lengths to keep himself hidden, but unless he lived in the area, he'd need access to a vehicle or public transport. The culprit would need to get to the school and presumably get home. How did he do that? The conversation with Smith had struck a chord. It had helped him to refocus and reiterated how valuable CCTV could be.

He knew they were still waiting on the ANPR for the car Edith Jackson had seen in the school's vicinity. It had private plates, plates not registered to the DVLA. But the bollocking from DSU Smith had helped to clear his mind somewhat. George fired up his laptop and searched for bus routes around both the area of the school and Erika's home in Middleton. All buses had CCTV cameras on them. They were like dash cams and of decent quality, too. His idea was that they could plug in the images of the registration number of the car into the facial-recognition software and see if they could get a hit. He fired off a separate email to Brad Fox at Wakefield, who confirmed five minutes later his plan would work.

George composed an email to DS Williams, copying in DS Wood and DSU Smith, asking her to contact the bus company for any CCTV footage of the bus numbers he had isolated. He explained his plan and advised her to check footage for the rest of the day with her team.

The email made him feel good, and George poured himself more coffee as he watched the rest of the team arrive at work. At first, he'd been paranoid that his team knew about his fuck up, checking for signs in their body language that they knew, but it soon became apparent he was being paranoid.

Despite having worked all weekend, Wood was looking fresh. "What's the plan, George? Are we sitting in front of our screens all day, sifting through CCTV?"

"No," George said. "Whilst I think CCTV is the way forward, I have a different job for you. DSU Smith is pulling the plug on our operation, allowing only Yolanda and her team to continue. Check your emails. It will explain what I've asked Yolanda to do. I need you for something else."

She raised her eyebrows and grinned. "What do you need me for? Something good, I hope." He thought she was being flirty. He hoped she was being flirty. She was gorgeous, and he feared he fancied her.

* * *

Practically everything that could have been done had been done. Now it was a waiting game. The DNA from the cigarette butts should come through any day, and Yolanda and her team were syphoning through the CCTV. He called DS Fry in to check in on the ANPR results. The detective gave his apologies and explained that they couldn't find anything to match the plates. They'd triple-checked all the footage and decided that the culprit instead arrived on public transport, parked in a different car park, or came in an unfamiliar vehicle.

George slammed down the receiver, the sound reverberating around his office.

DS Wood was currently going through Erika's joint account statements, but so far, she advised everything looked normal. They set all their bills up to be paid automatically, and there were enough funds each month to more than cover everything. They rarely withdrew cash. Despite this, DS Wood advised she would keep looking and let him know.

It was strange for George to be cooped up all day in the office, almost like a peculiar type of torture. He was used to being ordered about, following lines of enquiry, and talking to people. He had his team on it, and delegation was the key to being a competent SIO. Yet it didn't feel right. He stood up and went for a drink, the heat from the radiators adding to the suffocating atmosphere on the Homicide and Major Enquiry Team floor. There were too many people milling around, and he desperately wanted to get out of the station.

Chapter Sixteen

The hooded man watched as a young woman left her house. She lived in a very popular area of Middleton in the New Forest Village. She was dressed in her running gear and was his next target. He hadn't known her as long as he had Erika but liked her enough. The man shivered with excitement, butterflies jangling around his belly. He always got this way at the beginning of something new.

He'd waited outside her house at six that morning, watching. Then he had to attend work, but as soon as his shift had finished, he went straight back. She attended church most Tuesday evenings at St Mary's in Middleton on Town Street, but it wasn't a dead cert. It started at 7 pm, and finished anywhere between 7.30-8.15 pm. After, she would walk home and go for a run. He knew that. He had done his research. In fact, the young woman had confirmed the times herself, so he knew the information was correct. He had struggled to keep his composure when he spoke with her, afraid and almost excited too, that she would figure out who he was, that she would remember him. The face mask helped.

She left the house at 6.30 pm, and he sped off in his car, wanting to get a seat near the back corner so he could watch her.

Ten minutes later, the man pulled up his car at a blind spot between the two CCTV cameras situated between St. Phillips Avenue and Moor Flatts Road, and with his hood up and head down, walked down Town Street and into the churchyard. He removed his hood and entered the tall wooden doors. The scent of lit candles blasted his nasal cavities. He put on his mask, both to protect him from the scent and to protect his identity. The smells took him back to his first memory of visiting a church. That memory was his first and his last.

He didn't believe in God and hated the religious insinuations people had used to ridicule his and Eve's relationship. The man thought that people who believed in God were suckers, people who were followers. He was a leader, not a follower. That bitch, Erika Allen, was religious, though, and so was the bitch before. The one from Lincolnshire. They'd both had it coming, those pretty blonde whores with tight bodies and firm tits. And the next would have it coming, too. She was the same, if not worse. But this time, he knew he needed to be careful. He'd seen the forensic team outside Beeston Park Academy. They had taped off the area where he had watched Erika, no doubt trying to collect evidence. He'd been stupid; he knew that, scoping out the area so close to her death. It had been his cockiness that had worked against him, and he was sure that the police would connect the dots to Elizabeth. He'd made a mistake with her murder, too. She'd scratched him. She'd been tough, more formidable than he realised. So they'd had his DNA on file for about two years, which was unfortunate, but he had been lucky and wasn't on any police record. In fact, he had had no run-ins with the cops since—well, since Eve.

The man knew that whilst he needed to be careful now, he knew he was safe unless the pigs pulled him over or into the station for anything, and they took a sample. Then it would all be over, and he didn't want that; he was having way too much fun. He knew that if he was careful, then he could continue, and he was just getting started.

The church was empty, and he sat in the back left corner, facing the pulpit. Parishioners, mostly older women, began shuffling into the empty pews. He didn't recognise any of them, nor did he see his mark. He checked his watch. It was still early. He knew she would walk up St. Georges Road and then cut through the District Centre. Then cross the main road, cut through Shelldrake Drive and onto Town Street. The annoying thing about his next target was that she was never really early for anything. She simply showed up exactly on time. Erika had been different.

He'd planned the attack on Erika meticulously, following her for weeks, watching her get a lift to work, watching her walk back through the woods. He'd accompanied her to the supermarket; he had even followed her to Wakefield, where she had met her mother for coffee. He'd left nothing to chance. A heat spread through him as he thought about how perfectly he'd performed his plan.

But that heat soon became too intense, and a more profound need replaced it, a dark desire that he struggled to control. Then she arrived. And the hunger he had for her, the extreme need, was suddenly controlling him.

Pulling his hoodie over his groin, he turned his attention back to the parishioners, making sure that there were none he recognised. It was too dangerous, but the danger he'd put himself in only made him more aroused.

Five minutes later, the priest made his way to the altar. This priest was older than his parishioners, a man nearing the end of his life, his movements slow and measured. He'd love to kill a priest and show the world that God wasn't to be feared, but it wasn't his MO. He knew that. Once he'd satisfied his conditions, he would stop, and nobody would know it was ever him.

How long he'd stop for, though, was anybody's guess.

After the service, the man knelt and pretended to pray as Emma passed by him on her way out. He knew she would take another thirty or forty minutes to get home and changed for her run. He had plenty of time.

* * *

He watched as she jogged at a leisurely pace up St Georges Road, her blonde ponytail bobbing as she moved. Emma Atkinson, her name was. Miss Atkinson to her students.

A keen jogger, she ran around the estate every evening around eight, but every Tuesday and Friday, she ran extra miles, taking a lap around the Middleton Woods Nature Reserve. The sun had already set, and there wasn't much light, but it was still light enough to determine the gravel path around the edges. Dog walkers were rare so early in the spring, but they would flock to the area once summer began. Emma didn't care about the failing light; she usually wore a light attached to an elastic band around her head and a HI Vis jacket.

She had a nice, round ass in the leopard print leggings she was wearing, her black running top struggling to contain her bouncing breasts. She'd pay, just like the others. He was already hard thinking about it.

Keeping in the shadows, he followed her on foot until she turned left off the main road. He wasn't concerned. She usually did this and would weave back up in around five minutes. By that point, he'd be waiting for her near the gate to the reserve, hiding.

It would be easy. With his mask on, he wasn't a man people noticed. He blended into wherever he was, invisible. It wasn't the same when he was younger. He'd never been invisible then; he was always somehow part of somebody's jokes. He'd spent years becoming the invisible person he was now, knowing that one day, the skills could be used to his advantage. A predator is what he was, one that could easily blend in, one that was patient until it was the right time to strike.

He felt butterflies in his stomach as anticipation built inside him. Tonight, Emma would pay for Eve's betrayal, just like Erika had, just like the others had. He wouldn't stop until he'd finally destroyed every woman who reminded him of Eve.

Like a horse's tail, her hair swished back and forth as he watched her jogging towards him up the path, the light on her forehead not yet on. Tonight she wasn't wearing her HI Vis jacket. He took that as a sign from the universe that tonight was the night. In a couple of minutes, she'd run right past him and swing left through the gate and into the reserve.

He turned his back as she passed, but he was in the shadow of a wide chestnut tree, so she wouldn't have noticed him. No one ever noticed him.

Once in the reserve, she ran down the northern dirt path. That was perfect for him, as it meant that Emma would come back on the southern road, parallel to the beck. It meant he could wait for her, hidden in the trees, ready to pounce.

It was another sign.

He'd been studying her route for a few weeks now. He'd studied all their routes for weeks, in fact. The man had his next two victims already lined up. She rarely ran the south road first, but it did happen, though not tonight. It would take her five minutes to get to the junction at Fenton Gate, where she would head north. Emma would have a drink and stretch; then, she would turn around and head south, then east, around the nature reserve. This part would take her twenty minutes, past the pond and through the trees. Away from the houses and their occupants looking out of windows, running parallel to the beck was the darkest section of her run. Tall, wooded areas would flank her, the place where he would wait, ready to pounce.

The man took the southern path and strolled leisurely along the dirt path as if going for an evening walk. He reached a densely wooded area. He looked around. There was no escape.

He felt in his woollen jacket pocket for the duct tape, the end already neatly folded back so he could rip it off at a moment's notice. This area was much more populated than the woods, so he couldn't afford to waste time. He'd triple-checked the tape earlier, making sure he could easily find the end. A quick look down at his watch told him that there wasn't long to go now.

As dozens of insects scurried about looking for food, he stood silently behind an enormous tree trunk. He trod over acorns that crunched beneath his feet, but he wasn't too worried because she wore headphones. They would drown out any noise he made.

He heard her footsteps first before he saw her, a light but regular patter approaching him from up the slight incline. Invisible in the darkness, he pulled up his face mask, making sure his hood was tight and peered out from behind the tree. The bright moonlight meant she hadn't put her headlight on, but luckily, the moon was behind her and not him, so he was still invisible. He heard her heavy breathing as she got closer; became entranced by the rise and fall of her swollen chest. He knew from experience that she used the downward part of this section to gain momentum to get back up the steeper incline behind him.

He stepped out and, with a gloved fist, punched her in the throat. His thick, heavy fist knocked her down hard, her legs buckling underneath her. She landed on the dirt path, and for a fleeting second, the man thought that he had already killed her. He stopped and listened intently, hearing the short, wet gasps coming from her crushed throat, the result of his surprise attack.

The man looked around. It had been too easy.

Despite his blow crushing her larynx, she still attempted to make a strangled crying sound as he dragged her by her ponytail into the trees. He wasn't worried about anybody hearing the mewling noises. There wasn't anybody around.

Once in the trees, he gripped the end of the tape and, with a practised move, wrapped it several times around her wrists to prevent her from doing what Elizabeth had done to him. She opened her eyes, those cornflower blues wild with fear.

This was his favourite part.

He was already waiting for her with a section of tape in his hand when she opened her mouth to scream.

The man pulled down his jeans and walked toward her.

"Now, now, Miss Atkinson," he told her in a soft voice. "Lay still, and it'll be over for you soon."

Chapter Seventeen

It was early that Wednesday morning when George arrived at the crime scene. DS Wood was already there, and despite the early hour, she looked beautiful. He was struggling with the way he was beginning to feel about her, wanting desperately to stop thinking about the way she smelled or the way she flicked her hair behind her ear when she needed to concentrate.

Mia was still giving him the cold shoulder. Her indifference towards him had only strengthened his feelings for DS Wood, yet he knew it shouldn't have been that way. As George lay there last night, he desperately wanted to message Wood and ask her if she was still up. He wasn't sure he even knew why. Did he only like Wood because Mia was being indifferent? He wasn't sure why she was the way she was, either. So after an hour of facing away from her, he got up and slept on the sofa, dreaming about Wood for a solid six hours. He'd woken up and scolded himself, knowing that fantasising about your colleague was not great, especially in the middle of an investigation.

George knew the Middleton Woods Nature Reserve because he used to go jogging around it when he had lived in the Heritage Village five or six years ago. He'd do a few laps five days a week, amazed by how difficult the terrain was on his ankles, the swapping between running uphill and downhill exhausting. Unlike himself, the nature reserve still looked the same, as if unchanged by the years. The sun had risen only half an hour ago, its light not yet warming the air as George gazed into the slight mist that was suspended above the bushes. It was how the place looked when he used to jog here those mornings many moons ago, and he felt a sudden longing for those days when the world didn't fight back. He ran around the reservoir when he got the chance, hoping that there wouldn't ever be a murder there to ruin it for him.

"Over here, George," DS Wood called, walking ahead towards the crime scene.

He walked along the dirt path, a beck bubbling away to his left in the shadows. The birds were tweeting, oblivious to the horrific events of the night before. Soon, the cold drew in, and the sun disappeared as he reached a densely wooded area. DS Wood was standing at a break in the trees and leaving the dirt path; George walked towards her. Underfoot, tons of insects scurried about, searching through the dead acorns for food. He carefully stepped over them to get to the police tape that indicated the common approach path. Ahead was a blue forensic tent that had been erected to both protect the victim's body and preserve the crime scene.

"Morning, DS Wood; what's the situation?" he asked, putting on the protective coverall handed to him by a police officer guarding the tape. Wood was already dressed in hers. He then placed on his shoe covers.

"Another young, blonde female. Found by a dog walker about an hour ago." The look in her eye told him she thought it was connected. After signing in, they stepped through the tape and headed towards the tent, standing on the stepping plates leading towards the blue forensic tent. "Looking at her outfit, she was a jogger. No ID. I got a hundred per cent scan on the lantern, but it looks as if, like Erika, she isn't on the database. MO looks the same as our guy."

The flap of the tent dropped behind them as they entered, immediately suffocating George. He fought to regain control and, without speaking, took in the scene that lay before him. The Crime Scene Co-ordinator, Stuart Kent, was bending over a slim, blonde-haired woman who was lying on the ground. He could see from the angle he was at that the culprit had taped her wrists behind her back.

The culprit had also sliced her black running top open, causing her breasts to be exposed, and her stomach was a bloody mess. She was wearing no underwear, and it looked as if her leopard print leggings had been cut and rolled to just below her knees. Her ankles were also bound with the same black tape.

A crime scene photographer took in situ shots and was accompanied by another SOCO, clipboard in hand.

Unlike Erika Allen's, the victim's face wasn't bruised, suggesting there wasn't much of a struggle. However, there was little doubt that she had been sexually assaulted; he could see bruising and dried blood on the inside of her thighs.

He rubbed his head frantically and averted his eyes. "Christ," he muttered. He moved closer and looked at her face. "Blonde hair and blue eyes. She's young, too." She was tall and thin; she could easily have been a model

"Mid-twenties, I'd say," Kent said. "She looks very similar to your last victim." George was thinking the same. "Similar MO, too. There's a slight variance from last week. But I'll know more from Dr Ross later."

"What? Something's different?" George asked.

"Yes. Whilst I'd say the cause of death was asphyxiation and that your culprit strangled her with his hands—"

"She wasn't punched in the face," DS Wood interjected, confirming what George had also noticed.

"Yes, it looks like he subdued her with a blow to the throat this time," the Crime Scene Co-ordinator confirmed. "Yes, there is some bruising—"

"Unlike Erika Allen, she didn't seem to put up much of a fight, despite the small amount of bruising," mumbled Wood.

Kent glanced at her. "Perfect, DS Wood. Because of that, we can get a clearer look at the bruising just above her clavicle where your suspect had his hands around her neck." He pointed to the black and purple mess around her throat. "Marks indicative of strong fingers."

"High chance then that it's the same guy?" George asked, not expecting an answer. "What are the chances of getting any DNA off that tape?"

Kent carefully unwrapped her feet and wrists before gently peeling it off the victim's mouth and inserting it into a clear, plastic evidence bag. "No rain. It was cold, though, and so the body was damp. It's possible." He secured the plastic bag and handed it to the crime scene officer. She marked it off on her clipboard and dropped it into an evidence box. "Sometimes habits are hard to forget. I often tear the tape off with my teeth, even when I shouldn't. It's like it's ingrained. Maybe you'll get lucky."

"Lucky? I hope so. But you're right; this guy has to slip up, eventually." George knew they solved most cases from evidence left by culprits making mistakes. As awful as it sounded, new victims meant more contact, more sightings, and more chance of a transfer of DNA.

The crime scene photographer continued taking pictures, taking orders from the pathologist, whilst the officer with the clipboard continued taking notes. Every piece of evidence was first photographed in situ on the victim before being bagged and noted down.

"Is there anything else I need to know, Stuart?"

His eyes widened as if he was trying to remember something, but then he shook his head and said, "No, DI Beaumont. It's clear that she was raped and killed in the same way as Erika Allen. There are some differences, but nothing major. The pathologist will be able to look more thoroughly when I get her back to the lab."

"Fair enough," George said. He knew he'd have to wait for the post-mortem. "Thanks, Stuart."

As George left the tent, he let his eyes linger over the defiled body one last time. "Do we know whether she's been reported as missing?" he asked Wood, who had followed him out and was gazing at the ground. She had her arms wrapped around her body and was wearing no coat under her coverall. He almost offered her his but stopped himself. Mia would smell her perfume for sure. It wasn't worth an argument.

"She was jogging, so she had nothing on her, no ID, no phone, no purse. Uniform's going to get back to us."

George remembered his past. "She must be local to the area if she was jogging out here. Unless she lived alone, a partner or a parent would have reported her missing, right? Especially when she didn't return from her run?"

Wood nodded as her phone rang. She listened intently. When she hung up, she said, "That was Uniform. Somebody reported

CHAPTER SEVENTEEN

a missing person last night at about half eleven for a local woman named Emma Atkinson."

Chapter Eighteen

E mma Atkinson's partner lived in an impressive three-storey detached house in the New Forest Village, overlooking a park, with its own private gated car park. The area was relatively new, or so it felt that way to George.

The two detectives left their vehicles blocking the front of the gate and pressed the buzzer. The gate opened, and they slipped inside. Inside the car park were three cars. "Nice place to live, George. The guy who lives here's obviously doing well for himself," DS Wood remarked. "How the other half live, eh?"

It wasn't a professional athlete who opened the door. They'd barely had time to knock before a short, squat man wearing a suit was standing in front of them. The large door, and the void it created whilst open, dwarfed him. From where he stood, George looked down on him and saw signs he had shaved his head. Poor guy had all this money yet was bald, short, and fat.

The man looked up at them. "I am Ryan, Emma's partner. Please come inside."

They followed him up a flight of stairs and into an open living room with wooden flooring and brightly coloured furniture. The colour of the curtains matched the pair of armchairs—where Ryan asked the two detectives to sit down—and was held open with gold rope, allowing the sunlight to light up the white walls. A glass coffee table that had been sprayed gold stood in the centre of the room. Atop that was a tall, curvaceous white vase containing an enormous bunch of hot pink tulips. The colour matched the fireplace surround, a striking focal point below a 75-inch Samsung TV. Ryan sat on the crimson-coloured leather sofa, it groaning under his weight. To his right was a floating shelf, the doors painted sunflower yellow, and above that was a diamond-shaped mirror. It was overall a modern living room brimming with colour, yet Ryan didn't look overly comfortable.

As requested, George took a seat on the cyan-coloured armchair to the right, leaving Wood to sit on the other, bathed in glorious sunlight.

"I take it you are here about Emma?" Ryan asked in an unrecognisable, bland accent. He wasn't from Leeds, probably wasn't even from the north. Yet there was a tone to his voice that suggested he was used to giving orders.

"I'm sorry to say this, Mr Jenkins, but we found the body of a female this morning, and it matches your description of Emma."

"A body?" He stared at them and stood up before sitting back down again. "You found my Emma?"

George nodded and gave him a moment to understand.

After a moment where tears streamed down Mr Jenkin's face, he said, "You found her body? Where?" He continued to sob after getting his words out.

"The Middleton Woods Nature Reserve," Wood advised.

"I'm very sorry for your loss, Mr Jenkins." Cathy, the FLO, was so much better at this than he was, but when he had called for her, he was told she was tied up in another case. With it being their second murder in less than a week, the detectives came alone, not wanting to waste time waiting for another FLO to be allocated. Cathy would come tonight, introduce herself and regularly keep Mr Jenkins informed of the murder investigation.

"How can you be sure it is her?" Ryan said. A soft, gasping sound punctuated each word. After, there was a painful silence.

"From the description, you gave when you reported her missing," Wood said.

George added, "If possible, we'd like you to identify her. You let us know when you're ready, and we'll set it up."

"Identify her? Now? But I have—" Ryan looked down at his shoes. He was dressed for work. He surprised George by nodding. "Yes. I want to go now. I do not want to wait. How did she die, detective?"

"She was attacked," George said and hesitated, not wanting to explain that she'd also been sexually assaulted whilst being strangled.

Ryan dropped his head into his hands and wept. Wood met George's eye, wanting to continue the explanation, but George gave a slight shake of his head. Ryan didn't need to know the rest. Not yet.

Leaving a blotchy, wet imprint, the accountant removed his hands from his face. "How did this happen, detective? I wondered whether she had met a teacher colleague for a drink or something when I got home and she was not here. It is rare with how busy she is, but she does not always tell me."

George and Wood shared a look. They had another murdered teacher.

"Go on," Wood said.

"It's not uncommon for her to change her running route and

CHAPTER EIGHTEEN

get a coffee up at the Leeds Urban Bike Park café. But then you said they found her in the reserve?" Both George and Wood gently nodded. "Do you know who did this to my Emma?"

"We think it's the same man who killed a young woman in Middleton Park last week."

Ryan nodded. "Erika Allen? Yes, Emma mentioned her. Emma worked as a teacher at Middleton Park Academy. Both schools are part of the Park-Academy-trust. The teachers work together regularly, and Emma was rather upset about her death. There is a third school, actually. Hunslet Park Academy. The teachers get moved around a lot to cover."

George knew the school well. It was where Mia worked. But Mia had never mentioned working with Erika Allen at Beeston Park Academy, nor had she mentioned working at Middleton Park Academy.

"Thank you for that information, Mr Jenkins," said Wood. "We're following several lines of inquiry, and it won't be long before we have something."

"Emma had many admirers that included staff members, parents of the students, and, I dare say, some students themselves. She called it an occupational hazard. It was, I suppose. Both Erika and Emma were teachers." His deduction impressed George. "But she was funny, was Emma. She had a way about her, a dry sense of humour. Yet she was cheeky. I miss her already."

It was weird how similar Emma and Erika's lives had played out, both being teachers and having stalkers who were their student's fathers. "Did Emma ever mention anything about anyone following her or watching her over the last few weeks or months?"

The killer had known everything about Erika, even down to

what routes she took home and when. All the bastard had to do was wait for the right moment. It would make sense that he did the same with Emma, which was why they had a DC working through stalking reports at the station.

"Actually, detective, now that you mention it, Emma told me she thought someone was following her. It was over a week ago. When she told me at the weekend, I must admit I thought she was being paranoid, and I told her as much."

"Was she usually a paranoid person?" asked George.

"No, not at all. We should have reported it," he said, rubbing his eyes. He wept again. He obviously thought he was responsible, telling her she was paranoid. "This is my fault, is it not? We should have reported it, and then the bastard would have backed off. Correct? But then..." He went silent again.

"But what, Mr Jenkins?" DS Wood asked.

"I initially thought she had been mistaken and that her stalker was not a stalker at all. She told me a guy followed her from St Mary's church to the District Centre last Tuesday, but then she saw him again outside the house when she got home. That was the part that, to quote her, 'freaked' her out. It was also why she suspected he was following her. But she could have been mistaken, right? It was dark. She didn't go running that night. She had been too afraid. I told her it would have been a different guy. I was correct to do that?"

George was sure it had been the same guy but didn't say so aloud.

"Do you have CCTV?" asked Wood.

Ryan shook his head. "There is CCTV on the estate, however. I believe a call to the council will get you access. It was last Tuesday. The service starts at 7 pm on a Tuesday. She would have been home no later than 8.45 pm. I understand there is

CCTV on Town Street, as well. Emma was the kind of person to arrive exactly when she was supposed to arrive, so she would have left here at 6.30 pm. I expect those times to have been accurate as well yesterday."

"Thank you, Mr Jenkins; we will look into that," George said, text messaging DS Williams, who was back at the station. Whilst they had a lot to look at already, they might get lucky.

"Did she mention what this guy looked like?" Wood asked.

"Only that he was thin, of average height, and wore dark jeans and a hooded top. Sounds like a chav to me."

George met Wood's gaze before she turned back to face Ryan. "Mr Jenkins, did she get a look at his face?"

"No. She found it strange that he was wearing a face mask if I am being honest."

"A face mask?" asked Wood.

Ryan nodded. "It was a dark one, with red on it. She was not close enough to see the details."

"OK," George said with a sigh. It was the same story, and the same description, with no way to identify the guy. "Sounds like our culprit. We'll check on the CCTV for those dates and times you provided."

There was a long, awkward pause before Ryan said, "Is this guy the same guy who killed Erika?"

"We believe so, yes. Too many similarities."

His face dropped, and he said, "Emma told me that whoever killed Erika had also raped her."

There was no point in putting a spin on it, so George gave him a frank stare and nodded.

Ryan sobbed once more. His voice trembled when he asked, "Why my Emma? Why would anybody target her?"

George wasn't ready to share Mark Finch's ideas, but he

acknowledged the question. "We're not fully sure," he said. "But we have some links, especially regarding the women. We're working tirelessly."

Wood caught his eye and raised her eyebrows. George said, "OK, thanks. Listen, this may be difficult, especially with the grave news we've given you, but I have to ask you this question."

"Go on."

"How was your relationship with Emma?"

"Fine."

"OK, thanks. I need you to tell us what her schedule was like the past two weeks so we can locate her and the guy on CCTV."

Ryan looked out of the window. "I usually leave for work before her, so I am unsure what time she leaves. I work in the city centre, you see."

"Anything else?" DS Wood asked.

"Sorry, no. Can I go and see Emma now?"

Chapter Nineteen

There was good news for George when he arrived back at the station.

"Inspector Beaumont, this came in whilst you were out," Samantha, the office manager, said, handing George a phone number on a sticky note. "The lab called with their results. Amanda Hammond was her name. She said you can call her and has emailed over the details."

"Thanks, Samantha."

George turned to his laptop as the office manager disappeared and logged on. He scanned through the email from the lab before rereading the document to make sure he'd missed nothing. As he'd expected, the DNA samples found at the site were numerous. The development of forensic detection in the last few years has made it near impossible for a killer to avoid leaving any traces at a crime scene. Despite this, none of the DNA found on Erika matched anything on the PND, the Police National Database. He cursed aloud, understanding that it meant the killer didn't have a DNA record on there. There were some hits for her colleagues, but they'd already been cleared from the investigation.

He uploaded the report to HOLMES 2. Regarding the second body, the only positive was the ability to match any DNA found at both scenes. Obviously, it meant little if there was no valid suspect to test, but it was a start. They would get the DNA analysis from the cigarette butts probably tomorrow.

The wait for results was getting to him, a restless, dull feeling set deep within his bones, and he felt useless until Samantha Fields, the office manager, put a call through to him from the editor of the local paper, South Leeds Live.

Johnathan Duke was a six-foot-five American man. He was nearly as wide as he was tall and jolly, too, when George had met him on a few occasions. Duke was an indulgent man, and on those few occasions, he'd never seen the man without a cigarette or a drink in his hand. George said hello, and when his unmistakable accent replied, George, regretted picking up the phone.

"Ah, Inspector Beaumont, how are you, my friend?"

The way he spoke was too regular for it to be an act as if he lived every second, as if Johnathan was an actor on the stage and every person he spoke with was a patron in the audience. George found it annoying, yet he knew Duke was the best-connected person in the city. "Forgive my manners, Mr Duke, but I don't have time for pleasantries. How can I help you?"

"Now, now, George. You know to call me Johnathan. And I do hope you're well," he replied. "Especially considering—"

"Thank you, Johnathan," he cut in. "I'm good. How are you?" He thought it would be best to play along.

"I am well, Detective Inspector. It's a pleasure to speak to you. In fact, it's why I'm calling you. I have something I think you need to hear, and I was wondering if you would care to join me at your favourite coffee spot along with an employee of mine? It won't take long."

"Whilst I'm happy to tell you I'm intrigued, Johnathan, I am busy."

"Of course, Inspector. Erika Allen's death has negatively influenced everybody. I think you'll like what my employee has to say."

"I'm guessing you mean Paige McGuiness?"

"Right you are. I guess that's why you're the detective, and I'm not. Meet us there in half an hour?"

George nearly scoffed down the phone at his attempt to butter him up. It didn't take a genius to figure it out. George had been avoiding Paige's calls since they'd gone public about Erika's death. But it intrigued him, hoping it wasn't just a bluff on their end to get an interview. What was it she needed to tell him? "What's it about, Johnathan? As I said, I'm swamped."

"Naturally. Miss McGuiness is working on an article about Erika Allen and Emma Atkinson. She's the best journalist I've got. She's very talented despite being in her tender years."

He knew the vultures had been circling, that it wouldn't be long before they found out about Emma. "If you need information on Erika Allen and Emma Atkinson, then I have to insist that you go through our press office."

"Oh, forgive my manners, Inspector, but this could hardly wait. Or would you prefer to read about Paige's theory in the paper? I could send you a copy if you like?"

George closed his eyes and counted to three. "I hope you aren't threatening me, Mr Duke."

"Absolutely not. Settle down, my boy. I'll give you a tasty morsel, but I'll let young Paige tell you more. She has a theory about why your teachers were murdered." George let out a long sigh down the phone and heard Johnathan Duke laugh. "You don't have to trust my words, Inspector, but from what I hear, you don't really have any other option."

"OK, Mr Duke, I'll be there soon."

* * *

Johnathan Duke was waiting for him at a table in the corner of the Starbucks. As George approached, a broad smile formed on his face, his rich American accent bellowing across the room. "Detective Inspector Beaumont, welcome, welcome! I'm sure you already know Paige McGuiness. Do sit, do sit. Would you like a drink?"

George ignored him and held his hand out to the journalist. He'd never met Paige before but knew her by reputation. She had an air of confidence about her, yet she was relaxed in his presence. He knew from experience that people froze around police officers. She was young, early twenties, not long out of university, yet she didn't dress that way. He had expected her in jeans and a jumper, yet she wore a tailored business suit and heels. "It's nice to meet you, George," she said.

The usage of his first name slightly took him aback, and he hoped it didn't show on his face. His rank deserved respect, and he nearly said so. "Likewise, Miss McGuiness."

Duke snapped over a barista cleaning tables and ordered drinks for them. "I usually like mine Irish, but this place is a little too PG-13. I'll make up for it later," Duke said, putting his fingers to his lips. The man was obviously craving a cigarette. There was a no-smoking sign on the window behind them. "I'm still not used to the rules," he explained. "I miss the days you could have a cigarette and a drink inside. It's bloody ridiculous. Now I eat, instead, and I don't mind telling you that my waistline has suffered because of it."

George tried to hide his smile. He'd been as large now as he had ever been, as had his personality. Nothing had changed. An older woman drinking from a steaming mug gave them a dirty look every time Duke spoke.

"So, what can I do for you?" George said, turning to the journalist, who was unusually quiet. He'd heard other detectives mention her from time to time. He'd even listened to some of the higher-ranking officers compliment her, sarcastically suggesting she should become a detective herself.

Paige glanced at Duke, who nodded before retrieving a picture from her handbag. She placed it in front of George without speaking.

George glanced at the image and then raised his eyebrows at the pair. "Other than images of the two deceased women, what am I looking at?"

"You're the detective, George," she said. "Why don't you tell us what you see?"

He ground his teeth together but said nothing.

Duke broke the silence. "Come now, Inspector. The lady asked you a question."

"One picture of Erika Allen and one of Emma Atkinson?"

Paige retrieved two smaller pieces of paper, each with a name on them, from her handbag and placed the names under the pictures. "What do you see now?"

He saw one picture of Erika Allen and one of Emma Atkinson, each with their name beneath. "You're going to have to tell me."

She reached into her handbag and took out four smaller pieces of paper. She used them to remove parts of the women's names. "Care to comment?" asked Paige.

George glanced at the remaining letters below the images. E for Erika and A for Allen showed on the left, and E for Emma and A for Atkinson showed on the right. "Their initials are the same? So what?" he asked. "Do you know something I don't?" He stood up, fed up with their games.

"Tell him, Paige," Duke said.

"There's a pattern. Your guy is killing female teachers with the initials E and A, and I'm going to publish this pattern. Not one other newspaper has mentioned this yet. But they will."

George wasn't sure what troubled him most. That the journalist had worked this out, or the fact that he and his team didn't.

When George said nothing, Duke said, "Sit. Please sit, Inspector. We could have posted about this without speaking to you."

"I understand that Mr Duke, but if you print an article about this, you're going to curtail the investigation."

"The residents of South Leeds have a right to know," interjected Paige.

George rolled his eyes. The journalist knew that this was a story she could sell. The public loved a gimmick. He was surprised Paige and Duke hadn't named their killer the Teacher Terminator or something ridiculous like that. "I disagree. I think it's too early to let the public know, Miss McGuiness. All I can say is that their initials are a theory we're working on at present." He hated lying and was desperately hoping it wasn't showing on his face. "Releasing this to the public would be highly irresponsible."

"Could you at least provide something I can use to delay my findings?"

George had dreaded the question even though he'd expected it. "No. This is an ongoing investigation, Miss McGuiness."

Paige raised her eyebrows at Duke as if she understood the lie

CHAPTER NINETEEN

in George's response. Duke drained his mug of coffee and put his fingers to his mouth, his displeasure at not being allowed to smoke a cigarette all too clear on his face. "I assumed as much, Inspector. But I believe it would be unfair of you to leave us with nothing. Now to business. I believe we can come to an arrangement?" Duke said.

"An arrangement?"

Paige took over and said, "I won't publish any information for now. But George, I want something in return."

"Go on."

"You deal with only me. I want the story. I expect you to contact me and advise of any developments on the case," said Paige. "I want the story. Otherwise—"

"Otherwise, you'll fuck my investigation up? This is more blackmail than an arrangement." It sounded to George as if the journalist was happy there had been another death.

"I'll repeat what I said on the phone, Inspector Beaumont. You don't have to trust my words, but from what I hear, you don't really have any other option."

George nodded. "OK. We have an arrangement in place." He stood up without saying goodbye.

It was important that this information wasn't public knowledge, and George was happy to arrange for the time being to stop that from happening. The agreement meant very little to George, as he had no intention of updating the journalist beyond occasionally answering her calls. It also meant that they could investigate the idea of his victims having the initials E and A, especially as the woman murdered in Cleethorpes, Elizabeth 'Liz' Anderson, had the same initials.

Chapter Twenty

He rang DS Wood and updated her on both the DNA and his meeting with the journalists. She was at Middleton Park Academy, speaking with Emma Allen's work colleagues.

DSU Smith had ordered George into his office to inform him that because of the second murder, the chief superintendent had allowed extra resources. All leave had been cancelled, and Yolanda's CCTV team had been bolstered. Whilst George had visited the journalists; their floor had begun to overcrowd with borrowed CID officers. Smith told him all concerns about overtime had vanished, with a slight twinkle in his eye. This double murder case was now a priority. "Let's find the fucker before he can commit serial murder," DSU Smith's Geordie accent boomed.

Requests from media outlets had been high, with George's phone being continuously off the hook. They were out for blood. The suburb was already trending on Twitter, yet nobody other than Paige had made the connection between the two murders.

More officers meant more CCTV footage was being looked at. It also meant that DS Joshua Fry had assistance with the enormous job of syphoning through the ANPR cameras looking

CHAPTER TWENTY

for their green car. This meant they soon had a hit.

Preston Blake was a thirty-year-old male who owned the car. The green vehicle they had been looking for was a Ford Fiesta with private plates and had been caught by an ANPR camera travelling on the M621. They contacted the council and used CCTV to follow Blake, where he got into a second car, a silver Vauxhall Astra. That was registered to him, and so by accessing the files from the DVLA, they managed to get both his picture and address.

George immediately sent DS Brewer and DC Scott to the address. They came back empty-handed an hour later. Blake hadn't lived at the address for over two years, and the current occupants didn't know of him or where he now lived.

Samantha Fields slid a newspaper across his desk, momentarily distracting him from the footage on his laptop. "The evening paper, sir."

The West Riding Evening Post had pictures of the two dead women on the front page. George folded up the newspaper and chucked it in his bin. He didn't want to read inaccuracies. But there was something he could do. Experience told George that he now had two options: get annoyed with the press or use them. He chose the latter, calling Paige before anybody could change his mind.

"Hi, George," said the journalist, as if he hadn't just seen her hours before.

"Paige, have you seen the Evening Post?"

The line went quiet, and he thought she had hung up on him. But she soon answered. "Yes. Annoying, isn't it?"

George could have bypassed Paige and gone straight to the national papers, but she obviously had contacts in the area, and she had Duke on her side, too, so he felt it better to have her on his side as well. "This is about our arrangement, Paige. I have an image I need circulating. Preston Blake, aged thirty, from Beeston. His car was repeatedly seen in the area during the night of Erika Allen's murder. We ran facial recognition software to confirm it was him. He doesn't have his DNA on the database, but we found DNA on cigarette butts we are confident the killer had smoked. He's our number one suspect. You said you wanted to release your paper tonight? You can do so with my blessing as long as you circulate the image I have of Blake."

There was a fumbling sound as if she had put George on speaker. "Can you email it over to me now? Thanks for the exclusive, George. I really appreciate this."

George hung up, wondering whether he had made a mistake, and questioned how much the journalist's appreciation was worth.

A moment later, DS Wood knocked on his door and entered. "Let me send this email to our internal PR department, and then I'll be right with you," George said. He clacked at his keyboard for a minute or two before looking up. "What is it, Wood? We need to be next door in two minutes. I'm giving a briefing."

"One of Emma's colleagues, Andrea Small, told me that Emma had complained to her about a white van that had kept following her both to and from work."

* * *

"Can I have your attention, please?" George stood in front of his team in Incident Room Four. They had two dead bodies now instead of one, and the pressure was starting to show. About thirty tired faces stared back at him. Yolanda's team looked the worst. The late nights and relentless sifting through CCTV footage were beginning to show. They desperately needed a lead soon.

"As you know, a second victim, Emma Atkinson, aged twenty-eight, was found in the Middleton Park Nature Reserve this morning. From what we have found out, the MO is the same as our other victim, Erika Allen. We're very confident this is the same guy." He paused and looked at Wood, who was sticking a blown-up photograph they'd got from Emma's driver's licence to the whiteboard. He didn't look at the other two. "She was also a teacher. Young, blonde, and had blue eyes. Now, that is rather one hell of a coincidence, or it is victim selection."

There were a few nods and murmurs of agreement.

"We also have a suspect. Preston Blake, aged thirty from Beeston." DS Wood tacked up a blown-up photograph they'd got from the DVLA on the whiteboard. "This image is a few years old, but he looks the same. We've located him in the vicinity on the night of Erika Allen's murder. I need three of you to check the CCTV footage on St. Georges Road on both the night of Emma's murder and previous days and weeks, too. Use the facial recognition software to find both Blake and either the green Ford Fiesta or the Silver Vauxhall Astra." Wood tacked up images of the cars with their registration numbers below. "We need to tie him to the scene. DS Williams is checking the local CCTV for sightings of Blake. It's imperative that we find him."

Nods all around.

George continued. "I've also managed to get his picture in the local paper asking to contact us if they know his whereabouts. I expect a lot of calls, but DSU Smith has Wakefield and DCI Wilson on it. We don't have a motive for Blake yet. We're not even sure whether he's our culprit, but we need to follow all lines of investigation. But after speaking to Emma's partner, Ryan, DS Wood and I have got some more information on Emma's movements. It turns out she told him she thought someone was following her, somebody wearing jeans and a hooded top." The room went silent. "Yeah, but you guessed it, he was wearing a face mask, and she never saw his face."

He could hear murmurs of frustration, feel the place deflate. It had been a hive of energy before, but all that energy had now dissipated.

"Now, with this being our second teacher, our killer's victim selection is all but confirmed. There must be something in this guy's past. Maybe he was divorced or dumped by a teacher. Could he have had a crush on one as a teenager and was rebuffed? Maybe his mother was a teacher, and she abused him. DC Scott, this is your shot. I need you to head up a three-person team and look into this. Any volunteers?"

Two female detective constables put their hands up and moved to sit with DC Scott.

"Emma Atkinson went to church the night she was murdered. St Mary's on Town Street in Middleton. From what we know, the sick bastard likes to follow his victims before killing them," George added. "I know CCTV is tedious work, but it's important. Somebody once told me it was what modern police officers did." He winked at DSU Smith, having told him the same thing just yesterday. "Yolanda, I need officers to check the CCTV footage on Town Street. Start at Erika's house and work your way down. You're looking for five things. Preston Blake, Emma Atkinson, the green Ford Fiesta, or the Silver Vauxhall Astra. Blake may have worn his disguise, so you need to be looking out for that, too."

DS Williams nodded. "I have two officers I can spare."

"Great."

"There aren't any other active murder cases," DSU Smith cut in, "so feel free to expand into the other Incident Rooms. It's getting rather crowded."

"Jay has also started mapping out Emma Atkinson's movements for the two weeks before she was murdered. Her partner told us she never took it when she went running, but it should show her going to work and back. We can use that information to check the CCTV in detail."

"I'm nearly finished with that, sir," DC Scott said.

"Thanks, Jay. Now," he said, turning to face the room. "DS Wood has questioned Emma Atkinson's colleagues this afternoon, and one of them mentioned a white van that was possibly following Emma to and from work. When looking at CCTV, note down any you find. I need dates, times, and registration numbers. I know it's extra work, but I promise it'll be helpful. One of you could find the link to identifying the bastard."

An enormous cheer erupted from the back of the room.

"OK, that's all the updates I have for you. Dismissed."

His team filed out in silence, a feeling of deflation in the air that George figured was down to sheer exhaustion and fading interest. He hoped it was neither, but it was probably both. Despite having Blake as a solid suspect, they weren't really getting any closer to the killer, and they now had two bodies instead of one. If DS Wood was right, and this bastard had killed Liz Anderson, then the killer was escalating; he was getting greedy. Two bodies in less than a week. Even though he dreaded admitting it, he very much feared they wouldn't have long to wait before they had another body.

He turned to Wood, who was the only person left in the room. He found she was always there when he needed her. "We've got to stop this guy before he escalates further. There's got to be a link other than them being teachers and sharing the same initials. Somehow, Wood, we've got to find it."

Chapter Twenty-one

By early next morning, they'd found Preston Blake. Or, to be more accurate, Preston Blake had found them. George walked over to Samantha, and the room fell silent.

"Preston Blake is just being processed by the front desk," Samantha said.

George followed her to find a six-foot beanpole who must have suffered from severe acne as a teenager.

"I saw my photo in last night's paper this morning. I knew it would be best to come and see you," Blake said with a smile. The smile that formed was one that showed amusement rather than nerves, which George found odd.

"I'm DI George Beaumont. Thank you for coming here, Mr Blake. I assume you're OK with answering a few questions for us?" Blake nodded. "Set up an interview room for us, please, Samantha. Can I get you a drink?"

"I had one before I left, but I'm happy to answer a few questions. I need to be at work soon. Please believe I just want to help."

George nodded and asked him to follow Samantha. DC Scott followed them closely. "The suspect coming to us? That's new. I wish the job were always this easy," DC Scott whispered to

George.

"What I want to do, Jay is interview him alone. But, I want you to watch the video, see if you spot anything that I don't," George replied. "Get DS Fry in with you as well. I want to make sure everything's being recorded properly."

Blake stood as he entered interview room two, hand extended. George smiled and offered him a seat instead of shaking it. He sipped from the glass of water in front of him, a scowl on his face. George noted in his book that Blake didn't like to be ignored, nor did he enjoy being disrespected. Not that George was trying to do either, he just wanted to make sure he didn't interfere with the forensic swabbing they were going to ask permission for at the end of the interview.

"I just wanted to start by saying thank you for coming to see us so soon, Mr Blake. I can only imagine it must have been a huge shock to see yourself in the papers."

"It was an enormous shock, Inspector—"

"Before we get started, Mr Blake, I wanted to advise you that this interview is being both audio and video recorded and remind you of your right to legal representation."

Blake waved the suggestion away. "Stop with the Mr Blake nonsense. You can call me Preston," he said. "I know why you wanted to speak to me. I watch a lot of documentaries." The earlier smile that had been tinted with humour faded and was replaced by excessive eye contact.

"Go ahead, Preston."

"I've been having issues with my girlfriend, Penny. She lives opposite the school. Last week, we had quite a row, and she kicked me out. On Thursday, I was in the area around the school a lot. I was driving up and down the road because I thought—" George smiled, keeping silent to allow Blake to

CHAPTER TWENTY-ONE

speak. "I thought Penny had been cheating on me. There was a white van parked up near her house. It had been there for a while. It was there Wednesday, too. I know because I was doing the same on Wednesday." He looked down into his hands, embarrassed.

"So just to clarify what you just said, Preston. On Wednesday and Thursday evening, you repeatedly drove up and down Gipsy Lane? What time would this have been?"

"Between six and seven on both nights. I work different shifts, and I knew I needed to be at work for seven. The van had come and gone, though."

"What do you mean?"

"Well, the van was facing one way on Wednesday and the other on Thursday. So it had been driven."

"What kind of make and model was the van, Preston?" George asked, thinking of what Emma Atkinson's colleague had told DS Wood.

"I don't know, a Ford?"

George sent a text message to DS Yolanda Williams, their CCTV expert, to check the footage they had to see if they could identify a white Ford van.

"Let's go back to the Thursday night in question. Do you smoke, Preston?" Preston nodded. "For the record, Preston nodded at my question. How many cigarettes do you smoke on average a day?"

"Is this important? Am I in trouble over smoking? I don't understand the relevance."

"Every detail matters. Do you know that a teacher was murdered in the woods close to where you were driving? Driving up and down repeatedly is odd behaviour, don't you think?"

"I told you about that. I was watching Penny's house."

"I have a witness who said they saw you in your car. They stated that 'he drove up again about five or six times whilst I was out there. Although this time, whenever the car went past me, it slowed. It scared me. It never went into the school. But yet for an hour, the car kept driving up and down.' Is Penny's house on the main road?"

"No. But I can see her house from the junction. My car is easily recognisable. It's green. I didn't want her to know I was watching, so I kept slowing down and looking through the fences. There's a streetlight outside her house. It's easy to see."

"Does Penny know you were checking on her on those dates?"

He sniffed and pulled a handkerchief from his pocket. "Sorry," he said. "I'm homeless now. I've been sleeping in my car. My friend let me use his shower this morning. He offered me his sofa, but he has kids and stuff. I didn't want to impose."

"Does Penny know you were checking on her on those dates?" George repeated, keeping his tone light.

The man shrugged and continued with his intense way of looking at George, his eyes never leaving his. "She said she saw me turning around using the junction. I told her I was going to hers to collect some stuff. It was a lie, I guess. I don't want to collect my stuff because I want to sort it out, you know?"

George found he did know. Mia had been asleep again last night when he got home, so he had spent the night in the spare room again.

"I understand. Penny would collaborate with your story?"

"Of course."

There was a break in the conversation, and Preston Blake looked uncomfortable. If Blake wasn't their culprit, then he may have seen who was on the night he murdered Erika Allen. "Preston, where were you between the hours of 6.45 pm and 10 pm?"

"I told you already. I was driving up and down Gipsy Lane until I had to start work at seven. So around 6.45 pm. I would have been on my way to work as I start at seven, and my shift ends at three. I was there. Both nights."

"Where do you work, Preston?"

"I'm a warehouse operative. I work five nights on, two days off, and then five days on. Would you like the address?"

"Thank you," George said, handing him his notebook and pen.

He wrote an address and then smiled as he handed George the notebook back. "Is that everything, Detective? I need to be at work by eleven. I take over from the 3 am shift. We have three shifts per day, you see."

George understood that there were three lots of eight hours in a day, not that he gave a shit. This guy could be the break they needed. They'd keep him as long as necessary.

"What clothes were you wearing?"

"What does that have to do with anything? I need to be in Stourton soon; otherwise, I could get the sack."

"I understand, Preston. Let me help you, then. I could call work for you now and explain that you're involved in a murder enquiry? I'm sure they'll be understanding."

"No. It's bad enough that my picture is in the paper. I want it removed. I've come to you. You understand?"

George smiled. "Sure. Now answer my question."

He stood up and twirled on the spot like a model. "I was

wearing exactly this, but with gloves. It's what I always wear. It gets cold."

Whilst Preston was wearing boots, dark jeans and a black wool fleece, George noticed the logo on the jacket. They'd had plenty of eyewitnesses, but not one of them had mentioned any logo. It was large and in your face. They wouldn't have missed it. It would have also been easily seen on CCTV.

Fuck.

"Did you see anybody loitering on Gipsy Lane? Perhaps they were smoking a cigarette? They wouldn't have been too far from the junction into The Links."

Blake kept eye contact with George as he considered the question. "No. I don't believe so. As your eyewitness mentioned, I slowed down repeatedly so I could see Penny's house. The streets were deserted."

"Have you spoken to Penny about the van?"

Blake lowered his gaze, and George noted a flicker of hesitation. His eyes narrowed, and he paused before answering. "Yes. She told me she knew nothing about it other than noticing it being parked outside her house. That's when I accused her. I shouldn't have, really. I don't think she's ever going to forgive me." He sniffed once more and blinked a tear from his eye. "I tried to see her on Saturday during my day off. She wouldn't answer the door. I noticed the van wasn't there."

The interview was slowly dying. If Preston Blake was telling the truth, then they were following a dead end. He would ask Preston for a sample soon and finish up the interview, but he wanted clarification on the private plates and the ownership of two cars.

"Tell me about the Fiesta's private plates."

The man was slick. He barely reacted. "It all comes down to

affordability. The car's insured, believe me. I didn't even know they were private when I paid for the car. The MOT showed up as the car having a different reg. I just can't afford to put new plates on it yet."

It sounded to George like an excuse, one that he'd rehearsed. "I have an eyewitness claiming to have seen a silver Vauxhall Astra following Erika Allen in the days before she was murdered. You have a silver Vauxhall Astra. Is that a coincidence?" It wasn't exactly a lie, but it wasn't a fact either. It had been reported by a member of the public and added to the report DCI Wilson had sent over. They'd decided it wasn't worth checking, but sometimes he needed to see the reaction of the suspect.

Yet George got the reaction he was hoping for as a small crease formed on Blake's forehead. "This wasn't just a friendly chat, was it, Inspector?"

The question had changed the dynamic of the interview, and George knew he had to be careful not to lose him; they had no evidence they could use to keep him at the station. "Of course it is. But there are certain lines of enquiry we are following. Have you ever been to Cleethorpes, Preston? It's a seaside town in North East Lincolnshire."

"What does that have to do with anything?"

"Answer the question." The death of Liz Anderson may or may not be connected to the two murders here in Leeds, but George knew a break in the questioning about Leeds might get Blake to let his guard down.

"Of course, I have," Blake said. "My grandma had a caravan there. I spent practically every holiday there. Why?"

"What about recently?"

"Sure. I go every year. But I only tend to go for the day. The last time I went was with Penny last summer."

"And the year before?"

"I don't recall."

"You only go for the day? So you drove there?" Blake nodded. "For the record, Preston Blake nodded. Tell me about the Astra. It's registered to a place where you aren't living. As is your driver's licence."

George saw a flicker of unease on the man's face. "Is that what this is all about, Inspector?" Blake asked, smiling. "You're going to lock me up for having both my licence and my car registered at the wrong address?"

George matched his smile. "That's not my job, Mr Blake. You made it harder to find you, that's all. But you're here now. Voluntarily. Why do you have two cars?"

"Is it a crime to have two cars?" Preston asked just as George's phone pinged.

He ignored it for the moment and continued questioning. "Of course not, Mr Blake, but when that same car is seen around the time Emma Atkinson was murdered, it begs the question."

"I don't know anything about Emma Atkinson. I only heard about it this morning."

"So then you'll have no problem telling me where you were between the hours between 5.30 and 10 pm last night?"

"I worked the 11 am to 7 pm shift. It's why I need to be at work like I said."

"And after?"

George saw a faint flicker of unease on the man's face; a glimmer Blake masked exceptionally well. "I was at a friend's house. We left work together and got a takeaway. He's the one I mentioned before. I slept on his sofa last night. You want his name and address?"

"Please," George said, sliding his notebook and pen across

the table. "Tell me, though. Did you sleep at your friend's house last night or not?"

Preston Blake wrote a name and an address below the one provided earlier and then smiled as he slid George the notebook back. "I just told you, I slept there."

George looked down at his notes. "You said, 'My friend let me use his shower this morning. He offered me his sofa, but he has kids and stuff. I didn't want to impose.' Which is it, Mr Blake? Were you at your friend's, or not?"

George looked at the address Blake had provided and recognised the area. His friend lived near where Emma Atkinson had been killed. It would explain why his Astra was seen around there. He was frustrated by the answers. If his work and friend could alibi him, then this certainly was a dead end. He was about to message DS Wood to get her to check the alibis when he noticed the message that his phone had notified him of was from DS Wood.

The background check on Preston had come in. When he was seventeen, he'd been in trouble with the police for stalking a teacher by the name of Miss Eleanor Adams. He'd driven his car up and down her street, and she was afraid to leave the house.

"I was confused, detective. With no home, it's been difficult."

"I understand, Mr Blake. But as I said before, minor details matter in an investigation like this." He looked back down at his phone. It was a risk to include this in their conversation, especially having only just found out about it, but everything about Blake had been calm and rehearsed, so he felt the need to try to throw him off guard.

"Tell me about Miss Eleanor Adams." Initials E and A again.

Adrenaline surged through his veins.

He couldn't tell for sure if it worked. Preston Blake shrugged. "Who?"

"Miss Adams. The teacher you stalked when you were seventeen. The one who wouldn't have sex with you. The one you threatened? I'm sure you remember?"

As if he was about to ask a question, Blake's mouth opened slightly. He stayed silent.

"As you may know from your documentaries, we often do background checks?" George said.

Blake's frown was laced with irritation, a slight undertone of anger in his voice. "Of course, I know that. But I wasn't aware that I was a suspect."

"You're not. I believe everything you have told me. But as you know, I am required to check everything. A teacher was murdered in an area where you were sighted. Tell me about Miss Adams."

"No comment."

"No comment doesn't help me or you, Mr Blake."

"No comment. Check your old files. I'm not here to rehash the past. I came here to help you."

"So help us."

"I have done my best. If that's everything, then I have to get off to work." He stood up.

Sensing Blake's attitude towards the interview had turned, George turned off the tape. He stood up and walked over to the door. He said, "We would like to take your fingerprints and a DNA sample, if that's OK, Mr Blake? It's just procedure."

Blake scowled as he answered. "I only came in here to clear my name. To try and help you with the investigation. You said this was just a chat, that I would be answering a few questions, yet you're treating me like a criminal."

George got to his feet as the door opened and DC Scott entered. "As I said, Mr Blake, this is purely procedural. We like to clear people from crimes, as I'm sure you're aware from watching the documentaries. I'm sure you wouldn't want to implicate yourself in any way by refusing a procedural forensic sample?"

Chapter Twenty-two

Blake was taken to be processed by DS Jason Scott. At the end of the interview, Preston Blake no longer displayed any anger or hostility. Instead, a smile appeared on his face as he went along with DC Scott. Despite not knowing what to make of the man, George found his response to his question about Miss Eleanor Adams revealing, as if asking the question had offended him as if he took it as a personal attack. George was intrigued by the change in behaviour. Before that, he had been a calm and respectable interviewee, if not slightly overconfident. Yet on account of the anger shown, George suspected Blake's earlier performance was a front. The revelation of his background had rattled Blake, and George was convinced he was withholding information from them. He looked at the clock and cursed. The post-mortem was just starting.

The post-mortem was being conducted that morning at precisely eleven o'clock, but it was gone half past by the time George got there. It was the same pathologist that Wood had seen before. Dr Ross. He flicked the speaker switch on.

"Sorry I'm late, Dr Ross," George called from the viewing gallery, his voice sounding tinny. He hated autopsies. The body of Emma Atkinson lay on the metal table, her sternum sliced open to the stomach, her insides on display. Rather than on the corpse, George focused on the doctor's face. "What have you got for me?"

"As the deceased was raped, I started with an internal inspection," the pathologist said, looking across at George through floor-to-ceiling glass. "It's exactly the same as Erika Allen. She has dried blood and bruising on her inner thighs. There's some internal damage. I've taken swabs, but I wouldn't hold out much hope of any DNA. I could smell the lubricant that had been on the latex."

"Guy wore a condom?" George asked.

The pathologist nodded. "Yes."

"Cause of death?"

"Asphyxiation."

"Stuart Kent, the Crime Scene Co-ordinator, suggested the same."

The pathologist nodded. "There's clear bruising around her neck. She was hit with a blunt object directly to the throat. I say blunt object; it could have been a fist. I can see a rounded indent in the trachea."

"Despite that, do you think the two killings are related?" George questioned.

"I would assume so. The MO is similar. I would also say the wounds on her stomach are similar." This guy was consistent, George thought if nothing else. Patterns, as Mark had said.

"Do we have a chance of any DNA from under her fingernails? Or on the duct tape?"

"I've sent the samples to the lab. If he's left any DNA on that duct tape, we'll get it."

"I bloody hope so," George said.

* * *

The killer sat at his desk and stared at the newspaper. He was alone, but the silence was deafening. The police had found Emma Atkinson and would have linked the two murders by now. He'd been careful the other night but had taken a risk by going to Mass first, and the thought of him being captured by making a mistake made his stomach lurch. Other than the priest, not one person acknowledged his presence. Yet he knew that because of that, he would be picked out. He was a stranger in a mask, wearing gloves. He doubted they could identify him, but between them, there was a chance they'd come up with some form of a description of him. And now, with officers ramping up their investigation, he knew that time was running out. He would need to kill the next two as soon as he could.

* * *

"Blake's gone," said DC Scott after George returned to the station. "He was still reluctant to give a voluntary DNA sample, but in the end, I convinced him. I told him what you basically said, that we could look at clearing him from the case if he did. Otherwise, unlike voluntarily walking in today, he'd be in an interview room with us treating him as a suspect."

"You watched the interview as I requested?" He nodded. "Good."

"Thank you, sir. He didn't like it when you mentioned the teacher. It has to be more than a coincidence, sir? The two women were both teachers and around the age Eleanor would have been when Preston Blake was seventeen. The initials fit, too."

CHAPTER TWENTY-TWO

The inspector nodded. "It's our job to prove it's not a coincidence, DC Scott," George said, but in truth, he wasn't sure he believed Blake had murdered either Emma or Erika. He was six-foot tall, yet the killer had been of average height. The man had also attended the station of his own accord and had been helpful. DS Wood was back from her job of interviewing the parishioners and was speaking with the company Blake worked for, who would instead confirm or deny his alibi. Other than the crimes relating to his licence and the two cars, they didn't have a reason to pursue Blake further.

He could already hear Smith's regurgitated thoughts, those of the chief superintendent Sadiq. Without a direct link, Blake was impossible to pursue. They had to work harder and faster and find something that would break the case wide open.

George knew that odd feelings and hunches had no place in police work, but something was off. George was an expert interviewer, and he knew when to use his gut. His interest in Blake was still high. He was hiding something, and he owed it to the three women and Liz Anderson, the woman from Cleethorpes, too, to keep going and find out what it was.

The focus of his briefing later that afternoon was all on Preston Blake. "We need to find out everything we can about this man, and I mean everything. Everything from his past to his present. DC Scott, I need you to focus on the teacher stalker link. Josh, how long before we get the bank statements?"

"Should be here within the hour, as far as I'm aware," said DS Fry.

"Great. Look, I know it's a lot of work, but I need the rest of you to trawl through the CCTV images once again. We need to find the owner of this white Ford and a link between Blake and the two women."

* * *

After a briefing updating his team on Preston Blake, DSU Smith called him into his office. George followed him in. He was paranoid that Smith was going to take him off the case now that some of the more senior investigators had been freed up from their court cases.

"We have a problem, Beaumont," he said. "I've spent all day fielding phone calls from the press."

"I've spoken with Paige McGuiness, and she has agreed to—"

"This has nothing to do with that damn McGuiness woman. The press is on to us. They're particularly apt at putting two and two together. Two women, two identical murders. Both teachers. Same initials. We can't keep the investigation hidden any longer; otherwise, they will lose faith in us. We're going to have to issue another statement."

George met the DSU's gaze, who smiled. "You mean I'm going to, sir?"

Smith sat down and offered him a chair before he sighed and rubbed his temples. He looked tired, which was out of character. George was concerned and frowned as he asked, "What are you not telling me, sir?" He didn't sit down.

"It's Wakefield. And DCS Mohammed Sadiq. He's insisting on sending DCI Wilson over to assist with the case. I've told him we can handle it, but he doesn't want to hear it. I'm on your side, Beaumont, but if we don't have a suspect by Sunday, DCI Wilson will be here on Monday."

"Why? If you've told them we can handle it, which we can, then why are they being insistent?"

"Two women, George. Two bodies. Don't get me started on

a third. This must not turn into a serial case. It'll be bad for my heart, which also means it'll be bad for you. You're lucky they aren't taking over in the morning. That's how much respect I have for you. I fought for you, George. Don't let me down."

George sank into the chair opposite Smith. It was inevitable, really. According to Finch, this guy had already killed before. If they could link the cold case to the two in Leeds, then they were looking at a serial killer already, not that he said that aloud. But there had been two women murdered in less than a week. What did he expect? The case was snowballing, and now it was bigger than him, more important than his team.

* * *

The awful news George had received from DSU Smith was compounded by the fact that Mia was ignoring him. Again. He'd called her a few times and left messages, but she hadn't answered or called him back. He had no missed calls and could see that she had read his messages.

Juliette Thompson, the press officer, had prepared him for the press conference, and without DS Wood to stand by his side, she opted to assist him instead. He confidently outlined the details of the second murder and, like before, kept it short. George answered no questions and provided only the facts. He ended the press conference by asking anyone that had any information to get in touch. He knew Wakefield would be overwhelmed with a fresh bout of callers over the next twenty-four hours, and whilst there was always a chance someone had seen something, he would not rely on it. George knew both murders had occurred in isolated locations, in places that were devoid of lights and CCTV cameras. They were committed late enough at night to almost guarantee there were no pedestrians. Not one person had noticed someone assaulting a woman in the bushes.

He thought about that for a while, twirling a pen around his fingers as he sat at his desk. George looked up at the clock. It was getting late.

* * *

Later, George uploaded a few reports to HOLMES 2. DS Wood had worked through the list of parishioners given by the priest. George was intrigued as he read the accounts from three elderly women about a lone male who had attended. The women had never seen the man before, but it was the most promising lead they had. The women were to visit the station in the morning for a face-recognition questionnaire arranged by DS Wood. He was surprised that DS Wood hadn't told him directly, but then, he'd unfortunately seen very little of her that day. He didn't like how that made him feel. It was strange, but they'd worked so closely together for the past week, and he missed her.

Identifying the man would allow them to look for more eyewitnesses and perhaps even catch sight of him on the CCTV cameras in the area.

An hour later, George left, the day's events leaving him feeling physically drained.

George wanted to go straight home, to grab Mia and collapse into bed. He wanted to sleep the memories of the day away. Yet, despite his tiredness, he made a detour, travelling through Beeston. On autopilot, he drove to St Mary's Church in Middleton. He parked outside the glare from the streetlights

CHAPTER TWENTY-TWO

harsh in his eyes. He got out and walked through the gap in the low wall and followed the uneven paving flags towards the church entrance. DS Wood's report had said there were eight people at last night's service: the victim, six older women, and a lone man. George pictured the women shuffling out of the church into the darkness, looking at the stranger who was in their midst. He needed more information from them. From anybody. Had the culprit driven to the church? Did he live locally? Why had he risked his identity by going to church? It made little sense to George. It was pitch black. There were no cameras. Why hadn't he assaulted her here? Waited outside for her to leave and pounce? A shiver ran down his spine as he imagined the stalker hiding behind a gravestone, watching him.

George exited the churchyard and took a right up Town Street towards Erika Allen's house. He looked up and down the streets that filtered onto Town Street, looking for any signs of CCTV.

His team had exhausted the area already, fully aware of the blind spot between the two CCTV cameras between St. Phillips Avenue and Moor Flatts Road. If it were the killer who had been present the previous night, it wouldn't have been easy for him to slip in and out of the church unnoticed, as there was only one way in and out of the churchyard.

Other than the blind spot, the rest of the area had extensive CCTV. It was a residential area, and it would only have taken one neighbour, whether that be them shutting their curtains, or taking out their recycling bins, to spot someone they deemed suspicious. George knew it was often these small chance events, events that couldn't be accounted for, that helped them to identify perpetrators. Yet, the residents had been canvassed today, and they had been told nothing.

They hadn't known about the lone man at mass when they had canvassed that morning. So on his way back to his car, he emailed DSU Smith, insisting that officers repeat the canvassing again in the morning, paying specific attention to the lone man at the church.

Chapter Twenty-three

"How's work?" George asked Mia later that night. He'd tried to bring Chinese takeaway home, Mia's favourite, from the bottom of Middleton Park Avenue, but despite it being a Thursday, they were shut. He'd opted for fish and chips instead. They were sitting at the kitchen table, sharing a pot of tea when he asked.

"Work's not going so well, to be honest, George. This killer of yours is scaring people. Everybody's wondering who's next. They keep pleading with me as if I somehow have the capability of catching him. It's your fault. It's because you're the SIO."

A headache was brewing. "I wasn't even going to bring up the case. But I understand why your colleagues are scared. I'm going to catch this killer. I promise you."

The annoyance turned to irritation, and she raised a brow. "The killer. You mean the Miss Murderer?"

George paused. "What? The Miss Murderer? Fuck me, is that what they're calling him?"

She nodded. "That's right. That's what they're calling him in all the tabloids. Janine showed me today. That's two unmarried teachers killed within a week. Some of the teachers were joking about getting married so that they wouldn't be targeted. Or colouring their hair."

"Colouring their hair?"

"Yeah, both teachers were blonde. I hope I'm not next, George."

George Googled the Miss Murderer and found she was right. He tapped his fingers on the table rapidly. "Trust the media to label him," he said. "I bet that fucker's gloating. Bet the sick bastard is happy about his nickname. I'll catch him. Hopefully, it'll make him more reckless and more prone to mistakes. You're safe, babe, trust me."

Mia bit her lip and grabbed his hand that was on the table. "This killer's definitely killing unmarried female teachers, right?" George nodded. "You need to catch him before he kills a friend of mine."

"Don't be silly, Mia," he said, not denying her theory. His team believed the fact that the teachers were unmarried was a coincidence. They were convinced he was selecting young teachers with blonde hair and blue eyes. Most young teachers were unmarried. They'd kept victim selection back from the press release.

She stared at him. "How does he know they're teachers?"

"He stalks them before he kills them." They'd kept that back from the press release, too. "But it's not common knowledge, so don't mention it to anyone, OK?"

She nodded and smiled. "So, why teachers? Doesn't he think our lives are hard enough as it is? I've got so much planning to catch up on. And it'll be parents' evening soon. Then it's reports. It's never-ending."

George knew she struggled with parts of her job. She loved teaching but hated the paperwork and the politics most of all. She'd nearly quit last year, but her colleague, William, had convinced her to stay. Not that he had any proof, George had been sure they had started an affair. She'd stayed late at work and went out at weekends, opting to stay out and sleep at her friends' houses instead of coming home. It was one of the reasons why he'd proposed. To test her. He regretted that now, especially with how indifferent she was being. Maybe she seeing William again?

He shrugged. "You knew what you were getting yourself in for, but if you want to leave and do something else, I'll always support you." She pulled a face, got up, and unscrewed a bottle of red. "It's Thursday," he said.

"As if I give a fuck. What are you, my father?" She winced as she said it. "Well, you might not be him, but you're certainly emulating him. He abandoned me, and now you are too."

George got the impression that she'd wanted to argue right from him walking in that night. Fish and chips with a pot of tea weren't good enough for her. She wanted him to take her out to the fantastic Italian restaurant on Leeds Road. The day had exhausted him, and the last thing he needed was a fight.

"Please, Mia, that's not what I meant."

"Of course it is. It's not my fault you have a stupid pact with your mate from work, George." She drained the glass. George watched her throat gulp down the liquid and was almost aroused. He had an irresistible urge to do the same. One drink. How bad could that be? Mia, sensing his craving, offered the bottle to him. He almost took it, then shook his head. "I've had a stressful day, and I need this. What I don't need is you stressing me out even more. Do you understand, George?"

George nodded. She offered him the bottle. He shook his head and poured another drink of tea. She shrugged and carried on drinking. "I know your job is hard, George, but spare a thought for me, too. It's difficult being a detective's partner. My mother went through it. And I don't want to say that I regret it, but I just wish you were at home for me. It's why I'm always out. I'm lonely."

George rubbed his forehead. He understood. She still struggled with the loss of her father. It had also been the direct cause of her mother's suicide. She despised everything about his job. "I know you think I don't understand, Mia, but I do. I had this job before I even knew you. It's how we met, remember?" he asked with a smirk. He tried to grab her hand, but she pulled it away.

"Well, George, I hope you understand then when I say you need to sleep in the spare room again tonight so I can be fully rested and ready for my long day at school tomorrow."

Chapter Twenty-four

"I think we should break up, George," Mia said that Friday morning as he was about to leave for work. "I'm serious, and I'm moving out." She was dressed for work and had her hand on the telescopic handle of a suitcase.

"Wait, what? What do you mean, you're moving out?" George had opened the front door to leave and had stopped in his tracks, letting in an icy blast of the April morning air.

"You're never here, George," Mia said, her tone serious. "I'm scared. I don't want to be the Miss Murderer's next victim. Living by myself isn't what I signed up for. And as the days go by, you're starting to remind me more and more of my dad. It's difficult being with you."

"But we can get over this, Mia. My work has never bothered you this much before. Aren't you happy with me? I'm exactly what you signed up for." He pointed towards the ring on her finger. "You said you would marry me."

"Are you deaf, George? I'm unhappy. I have been for a while. Why do you think I'm always out? I choose to spend my time with other people."

"If this is about work, then you know once I've caught this guy, everything will go back to normal. Babe? I'm sorry. You know I'm busy."

She didn't answer him, so he closed the door and closed the distance between them. "This isn't about your work," she finally said. "This is about you. And me. But mainly you."

"What about me? If it isn't my work, then what's the problem? Come on, Mia, there's nothing wrong with us."

He came towards her. She stepped back. "I've been seeing somebody else." He could tell by her voice she really meant it.

"You're telling me you're having an affair?" Was it William she was seeing again?

"Yes, our relationship is over. It's too late, George."

"How long have you been seeing this guy?" he asked, closing the distance. She didn't react; she didn't even move away. He had to touch her arm before she responded. "I can't believe you've done this to me. What did I do wrong?"

"You said it yourself, George, you're a detective. You can give me the affection and attention I need until you get your next case. I just decided one day that I didn't want to be with a detective any more. I tried to make it work. I made mistakes, but I'm lonely."

She was right, but it didn't stop how he felt inside: hollow, numb. How could she leave him at such a crucial time? Didn't she know what he was going through, how much stress he was under? Didn't she care? "Is it William again? Or somebody new?"

She didn't even flinch at his name, nor did she answer his question. "As far as I'm concerned, George, it's over, both this conversation and our relationship. Teagan is picking me up in ten minutes. I'd appreciate it if you left, so I can finish packing."

"Fine." He took a deep breath. "But before I go, I at least deserve to know his name and how long it is that you've been seeing him. I know you were seeing William late last year. I also know you ended it with him to stay with me. Who is it?" Overcome by a sense of sadness, he gazed at her beautiful face. The woman he loved was leaving him.

She turned around and marched upstairs without replying. She wasn't being fair. He had done nothing wrong and, other than working hard on his career, he had nothing else without Mia. He desperately wanted to know the kind of man she had thrown away their relationship over. Was he better than him? If so, why? What could he give her he couldn't?

He wondered briefly if he should go after her. He even followed her to the foot of the steps but then decided against following her up there. Her voice hadn't wavered. Nothing he did now would change anything. With a sigh, he closed the door softly behind him and drove to work.

* * *

George struggled to believe what had just happened to him. He'd known for a while that during the second half of last year, Mia was having an affair. He was sure the man was named William and had convinced himself they had stopped seeing each other.

Yolanda came out of Incident Room Five, having been holed up in her makeshift CCTV studio, and looked to George like a mole who'd just popped up from her fortress. She scanned the detectives in the office.

"Yolanda, are you looking for me?" George called. He was by the coffee machine. A deep groaning sound that sounded as tired as George felt emanated from the machine as it dripped away.

Yolanda came over. "Yeah, we think we've got something on the culprit."

He left his mug by the machine and followed her back into her burrow. It was stifling in the dimly lit room, with too much heat and too little air. Yolanda pointed to the screen in front of an empty chair.

"Sir, this is CCTV footage from outside a takeaway in the Middleton District Centre on the day that Emma Atkinson's partner mentioned."

The footage was frozen, showing a lone female on the screen. Yolanda sat on the chair, leaned forward, and pressed a button on her keyboard. The video played, and George recognised the woman as Emma Atkinson, dressed in jeans and a coat with toggles at the front. She walked through the centre and past the bargain shop on the corner. There was nobody else in the shot, so Yolanda paused it again.

"She travels past Iceland, the carpet shop, and the gym before making her way past the St George's Centre. We lose her as she heads into her estate, but shortly after walking past the takeaway, a man in a hoodie follows her."

Not wanting to miss anything, George stared at the screen without blinking. In less than a minute, a hooded man passed in front of the camera. The man followed the same route as Emma and then disappeared from the footage.

"Is that everything you have, Yolanda?"

"Nope," she said with an impish grin.

George mirrored her grin. "Holding out on me, are you?"

"You're going to love this, sir."

Yolanda pressed play and sped up the footage until they saw the hooded man again. This time, they got his back as he travelled into the car park with what looked like a key in his hand. George raised his eyebrow and spread his hands in question. "Are you teasing me, DS Williams?"

"No, sir, I wouldn't dream of it." He hadn't seen this side of her before. They'd worked together a lot, but nothing of this cheeky nature, and certainly nothing of this magnitude.

She pulled up another video from a camera that must have been placed up high on one of the floodlights as it showed their hooded man and a quarter of the car park. The hooded man fumbled with something in his hand, and the lights of a white van flashed. George met Yolanda's eyes and grinned.

George inched closer to the screen, the footage too grainy and too high to make identification of the vehicle possible. The same went for their culprit.

The pair saw their culprit walk towards the van, pull the door open, and look around. The man then pulled down his hood and pulled down his mask.

Whilst they couldn't see the details from the front of his face, such as his nose or eyes, they could make out a shadow at the bottom of his face. The man had a beard. He had light brown hair, as had been mentioned before.

"That's great, Yolanda. Great work, well done. It's more than we've ever had. It's not only helped us to confirm that he has short, light brown hair, but now we can confirm he has a beard."

"I thought so too, but I was wary. The beard could be an attempt to disguise himself in the chance he gets caught on camera," Yolanda suggested. "The guy eludes all camera activity and then conveniently gives us a shot of his face with a beard." George understood; those cameras were high up but were hardly hidden.

"Point noted, Yolanda. Maybe you're right; maybe he's

hoping to throw us off. Did you get a reg on that van?"

She shook her head. "I tried following the van, but I lose it on every camera. The footage is too grainy, and the van is quite dirty. Maybe we'll get lucky. Maybe our culprit gets pulled over because his reg isn't clearly visible?"

George knew they would need to be extremely lucky for that to happen. Most officers wouldn't bother with that kind of thing: too much paperwork, too little budget.

"I'll speak to DSU Smith, see if he can get a forensic imagery analyst to help. They're invaluable in a case like this. And as for our culprit, if he insists on wearing that hoodie, we'll catch up to him, eventually. It's as if he's wearing a uniform, one that's easy to spot. It's Ironic, Yolanda, but that's probably how we'll end up catching him."

"We haven't finished all the cameras yet, and I know Mr Jenkins said Emma saw the man outside her house. I'll keep going and see if any of the other cameras pick him up."

"Great stuff, thanks, Yolanda. Can you make a digital copy of that image?" He pointed to the picture of their culprit, his face exposed. "I figure we put out another appeal, see if anybody recognises him. I want the image sent out to all schools in the area, too. He could be a parent." George thought back to what Ryan Jenkins had said about the father and son who had both professed their love for Emma. The school had provided their details, but they had moved out of Leeds because of the attention they had received. DS Wood had traced them at an address in Wales, but so far, every attempt to contact them had failed.

"Sure thing, sir," Yolanda said, tearing him away from his thoughts.

Deep in thought, George went back to his desk. He could

feel it. They were getting closer. The more the hooded man escalated his activities, the more he was exposing himself, and it wouldn't be long before they had him.

* * *

Later that morning, Wood perched on George's desk. The eight days of closely working together meant they now had a close familiarity. It helped Wood broke down barriers between people without realising, a charm most people didn't have. He was under her spell already, as were some of his team. He found that it made him jealous.

"I might have found something else, George," DS Wood said, tapping a pen against a clipboard.

"What have you found?"

"Ten years ago, a woman was found dead in a nature reserve in Greater Manchester. She'd been raped and murdered."

George stuck his tongue between his lips and raised his brows. "Was she strangled?"

Wood nodded. "It was a mess. According to the coroner's report, to which I only have access to partial information, there was a lot of damage to her body and a lot of blood at the scene. The victim suffered before she died, George. I need more information, but this looks personal."

"Have you called through to see if anybody can see us?"

She nodded. "A PC Flint is available today to help us. Could she have been his first, George?" she asked. "Girl Zero?"

"That's what I was thinking, Wood." He checked his watch for the time. They'd be back for the mass. "Fancy a trip to Manchester?"

Chapter Twenty-five

After spending two hours on the M62 in George's Honda Civic, the two detectives were grateful when they pulled up in the car park of a nature reserve.

PC Flint introduced himself as they exited George's vehicle. They walked east for about half a mile, following the river through the undergrowth.

"This is where the body was found." PC Flint shouted to be heard above the weather. The rain was hammering it down, and both detectives were drenched. They were standing beside a fast-flowing river that continued through the trees like a serpent's tail. "We got the call from The RRC, who was in the area on a field trip." George must have looked confused because Flint elaborated. "The RRC is the River Restoration Centre. They had an interest in the river Irk and conducted a site survey. It's a good job, really, because who knows how long it would have been before she was found. As you can see, it's rather off the beaten track. But I'll never forget detectives. I was the first officer on the scene. I was young and inexperienced. Those memories never left me. The poor lass. I remember she was naked and just completely mutilated."

George frowned. "What? She had no clothes on at all?"

The PC shook his head. "No, none whatsoever. The culprit

had covered some of her body up with dead branches, and I don't know whether that was done intentionally to get her to blend in. But then..." He shivered. "Her face was looking up at you. Haunting stuff, believe me."

"Do you remember the name of the person from the RRC who found her?" George squinted against the wind, his eyes watering. The salty water from his eyes added to the rain.

"It'll be in the report. Come on, let's go back to the car. DCI Roberts is waiting for us at a café not too far away."

* * *

They got back to the Honda and followed PC Flint to the local shopping centre.

They went into a small café, a Brazilian chain George wasn't familiar with, that reminded him of Costa. The glass cabinet at the front housed a multitude of delicious-looking muffins, and he suddenly realised how hungry he was. Wood, however, moved directly towards a table at the back corner, where PC Flint was standing, waiting. Sat down was a grey-haired man wearing a black fleece. In front of him were a cup of coffee and an untouched muffin. His stomach rumbled, but food would have to wait. George followed behind Wood.

PC Flint introduced them. "DCI Roberts, this is DS Wood and DI Beaumont from Leeds. They're here about Eve Allgood."

Roberts stood briefly to shake hands. "Retired DCI, actually," he said. "Please, take a seat."

A waitress appeared to take their order as soon as their bottoms touched the seats. George ordered a large latte, hoping the caffeine would give him a boost, with Wood ordering the same. PC Flint ordered tea. George eyed up the DCI's muffin but thought it would be better if he didn't order one.

"Now, detectives, what can I do for you?"

"Tell us about the case, sir," Wood said with a smile. "We want to get the facts directly from you."

The retired detective offered a smile in return, clearly having warmed to her. George wasn't surprised. DS Wood seemed to have charm in substantial supply. PC Flint's surprised expression suggested Roberts didn't thaw very often. "Certainly. I mean, it was a decade ago, but it struck a chord with me, and I remember it as if it were yesterday. Eve Allgood was killed the day before her thirtieth birthday. I remember because I'd been invited to the party."

"You knew Eve Allgood?" Wood asked.

He nodded, a poignant look in his eye. "Yes, I was friends with her mother. I have been since we were kids. The family moved back to Greater Manchester because of a bereavement. Eve's father. He passed away a few years before Eve did. I feel for Marie; I really do. She buried not only her husband but her daughter, too."

Wood gave a compassionate nod but said nothing, allowing Roberts to continue at his own leisure.

He continued. "As PC Flint has shown you, she was found at the Alkrington Woods Nature Reserve, in a grove of trees by the side of the river Irk. She was naked and had been raped and strangled. Stabbed, too." He looked down at his lap and shook his head. "It was awful. But in a place like Greater Manchester, these kinds of crimes have a way of blending in, you know? She lived here, in Middleton, and practically the whole place came out in mourning. Eve worked at a local bakery. No one could believe it. The death of a popular young woman. It was a terrible ordeal. But it barely made national news."

CHAPTER TWENTY-FIVE

DS Wood made eye contact with George. Eve wasn't a teacher. Did that mean she wasn't connected? George had been aware of a Middleton in Greater Manchester, but was this a coincidence? "You made an arrest?" George said. It wasn't really a question, but the retired DCI had gone quiet again.

"Yeah, she'd been seeing a guy called David Clark, a local lad from Newton Heath. He could have been a pro footballer for City but ended up getting into trouble with us quite a bit. Hated the dibble, or so he said."

"The dibble?" George asked.

Roberts laughed. "That's right, cock, the dibble. The police. You. Me. Her. I'll be honest; David was a little shit. He got kicked out of school and arrested once for grand theft auto, though he claims he was innocent. It's what fucked it for him with City. PC Flint's father had a run-in with him once or twice. You're about the same age, right lad?"

"Went to school with him. He was a sound guy, actually. But yeah, always in trouble. Once threatened my dad. Said he'd knock out his Newtons." Flint grinned with his own Newtons, ones that suggested he smoked at least twenty a day. George had heard the Mancunian rhyming slang that Newton Heath were teeth.

"I'm sure I hauled him in once for hitting windows with rocks. He said the person deserved it." He sighed. "David had a proper temper on him, but I never took him for the murdering kind. The lad was always in a bit of mither, but murder? I was as surprised as anybody."

"What kind of evidence did you have on him?" Wood asked, beating George to it.

"The irrefutable kind. Eve's clothes were found in the rubbish bin outside his house, and DNA extracted from her hair was found in the boot of his car, as were the boots she was wearing. They were found lodged in the section of his boot where his spare tyre was."

"Sounds pretty damning." Wood looked at George and frowned.

"Yeah, forensics had a field day. One of her shoes was found in a ginnel outside his flat."

"What sort of guy was he?" Wood asked. "Intelligent? Or was he a bit dense?"

"By all accounts, he was intelligent. Went to uni. He told my dad that once his footy career was over, he needed a proper job to fall back on. He was a maths wiz." PC Flint added.

"Then why would he leave evidence to be found?" George asked. "The report suggests she was killed by the river, so he could just as easily have left her clothes at the scene to be found."

Roberts shrugged. "Who knows? Maybe he wasn't thinking straight? I can't imagine a murder helps. The pressure must be enormous." George thought back to Erika and Emma. Their murders had been planned and carried out efficiently. He doubted whether this was going to help. "According to the pathologist, she died at least twelve hours before she was found. That puts the time of death at around eight o'clock the previous evening. Clark said he was home alone watching footy on TV, and because he was alone, no one could vouch for him."

"Where did he say Eve was?" Wood asked.

Roberts thought for a moment but stayed silent. George could see the cogs whirring. "I can't remember, but it'll be in the report. I want to say something about being at her mum's house, but I don't want to give you any false information.

Sorry," Roberts said with a slight shake of his head. "I know it made him even more suspicious in our eyes that he couldn't account for her."

"So, he raped and strangled her?" George said this more to himself than to anyone else. "I hate to ask, but was the rape pre- or post-mortem?" More silence from Roberts. George added, "What was the cause of death again?"

"Stabbing. She was stabbed repeatedly in the stomach. We first believed the stabbing happened post-mortem. But the pathologist confirmed it was the cause of death." Roberts took a long drink from his cup and pondered how he was going to phrase his next words. "The pathologist suggested Clark was having sex with her whilst strangling her. She also said Clark must have stabbed her to near-death before forcing her on her knees. They found a lot of muck and dirt within her stomach wounds. A specialist was called in who confirmed she was killed by the river, as you said. We knew that . David denied everything."

George scratched his spiky chin. Wood was watching him. "What are you thinking, George?"

"That this was different. Personal. I know our murders are personal, but they were planned and carefully carried out. This feels different as if the culprit was upset like he wanted to hurt her." He kept going back to his victims and Liz Anderson of Cleethorpes. Their deaths were planned and calculated. This was different. It felt different. Yet it felt the same. Almost as if their culprit killed Eve first, then Liz, and then killed Erika and Emma in Leeds. Her initials matched, too. But Eve wasn't a teacher. Was the teacher theory a dud?

She nodded her eyes understanding. "I agree. I feel as if he was punishing Eve." She leaned forward towards Roberts.

"Did you ever establish a motive for David Clark? Why would he want to punish her? Brutally stab her. Then rape and strangle her. Why?"

"That's it. It's why she was at her mum's. Clark had admitted they'd had an argument earlier that day. He'd denied murdering her, of course. She'd left at dinner time, and he claimed he hadn't seen her since."

"What were they arguing about?" Wood wanted to know.

He straightened up again. "To be honest, I can't remember. I think it had something to do with her mum. I know she didn't like him much. She didn't think he was good enough for her little girl. It turns out she was right." He nodded towards PC Flint, who placed a manila folder on the table. "My memory isn't what it was, so any questions you have should have answers in the report."

Wood gave him another smile. "Thanks for this, sir."

He pushed the folder over to her. "My pleasure."

They finished their drinks, and Roberts pushed his chair back, scraping the metal legs against the tiled floor. George shivered at the sound. "I hope it helps both of you. From what PC Flint said, you have something similar in Leeds?"

George was looking through the report. "There are definite similarities."

"Well, David Clark is serving a life sentence at Strangeways, which I reckon makes for a pretty decent alibi." He chortled at his own little joke.

HMP Manchester, or Strangeways as it is still commonly referred to, was a vast prison just north of the centre of Manchester.

George checked the receipt and placed some cash down on the table. They walked out together, past the counter and through the door. "Were there any other suspects in the case, sir?" George asked. "Anyone who may have held a grudge against Eve, for some reason? An ex-boyfriend, perhaps? Anybody stalking her?"

"Why?" Roberts' tone changed.

"Just because the evidence seems too perfect. Everything was there for you as if it were placed there."

"Are you saying what you think I'm saying, Inspector Beaumont?"

George stopped dead. He didn't like Roberts' tone. Their eyes met, and George noticed Roberts' expression had darkened. "Excuse me, sir?"

"Are you suggesting we got the wrong guy?" PC Flint tried to move the group outside, but Roberts squared up to George. "You remember what I said, Inspector? The forensic evidence was irrefutable. He didn't have an alibi for the time of the murder. The jury took just fifteen minutes to convict him. It was him, all right. The judge believed it. The jury agreed. I've never seen a case so clear-cut. It was a crime of passion, Inspector, a one-off. And we caught the bastard. I can't believe you're questioning me—"

Wood put a hand on the retired detective's arm. "That's not what anybody is saying, sir," she whispered. DS Wood smiled. "DI Beaumont is just being thorough. As an extremely experienced detective, I'm sure you've done the same?"

Roberts grunted but returned her smile. "Thorough? That's all we were. Very thorough. We prosecuted David Clark based on the evidence."

George stood there, stunned.

"Exactly, sir. Which was, as you say, irrefutable," Wood smiled once more, removed her hand from the retired detective's arm, and allowed Roberts to hold the door open for her. "Before we go, sir. You mentioned that Eve and her mother had moved back to Greater Manchester. Where was it they moved from?"

"Oh, York. But they moved to York from up your end," retired DCI Steve Roberts said. "Ironically, a place called Middleton in Leeds."

Chapter Twenty-six

"What?" Wood said, grinning at George. "What is it?"

"Is there anyone immune to your charms?" George asked as he headed north to reach the M62 that would get them back to Leeds.

Wood grinned. "Yeah, I'd say one or two are immune." They made eye contact for a brief second before George had to check his mirrors. "I try my best, though. I think I'm getting there. But this charm of mine, it comes in handy during cases, you know?"

"I think I'll start and leave the talking to you in the future," he mumbled, causing her smile to turn into a laugh. "It must be my accent. It throws people off."

She raised an eyebrow. "Accent? What accent? Maybe I'm just sweet, and you aren't."

She was probably right. He smiled and shook his head.

The radio was on, and whilst George hadn't received the news he was hoping for, the journey back to Leeds was steady, and he concentrated on the road ahead while Wood read silently through the case file.

George pulled off the M62 at Birstall and made his way towards the Plantation Services. He'd seen an advert for their cinnamon rolls. They'd be able to follow Gelderd Road after and get back to the station.

"Speaking of something sweet. How about it?"

Her eyes lit up. "Only if it's your treat."

George chuckled and parked the car. They entered and, after ordering, sat in the corner. Wood had brought the folder in with them.

"I've read this from cover to cover, and there are a few things that make little sense," she said to him whilst he was inhaling a rather large cinnamon roll.

"Yeah?" he finally said, choking as he did so.

"Yeah." She nibbled her own roll. "Clark's alibi is rubbish. If he had killed Eve, then he would have lied and made up a better alibi. He was an intelligent man, apparently. It doesn't sit right with me."

"Excellent point." She was correct; the alibi was rubbish. Usually, the culprit made sure someone had seen them around the time just before or after the murder to give their alibi some credibility. It would place doubt in the jurors' minds. Yet Clark had instead been stupid or too honest.

"And as you pointed out to the retired DCI, why all the evidence? The report explains that Clark was a petty criminal. He should have known better. He left evidence for the police to find. It makes no sense. And to be honest, the fact that Eve was killed in Middleton rather than in Newton Heath, where he lived, strikes me as odd. Most killers, especially first-time killers, kill closer to home."

"That struck me as strange, too." George was glad she'd questioned it too. *Why Middleton?*

Wood continued, "The pieces fit too easily. The evidence is too good. The fact that the jury took fifteen minutes proves it."

"Are you thinking the same as me?" She raised her brow. "Thinking that Clark was set up?" George drank the rest of his coffee.

She sighed. "Yeah. That's exactly what I think. It makes total sense because if our killer wanted to get away with murder, then what better way to do it than to frame someone else?"

"But why Clark? And why Eve? What's so special about them? If Eve is girl zero, then why?"

"Maybe she was in a relationship with our culprit, and she left him for Clark? Maybe she cheated on him with Clark? Eve was blonde with blue eyes, so think about what Mark Finch said."

He shook his head, not comprehending. It felt like he'd seen Mark months ago, yet it had only been a week.

"Finch said a 'serial murderer selects his victims,' so it means victim selection is key. And from what I gather, our culprit's selection criteria are extremely specific. E and A for initials. Blondes with blue eyes. Females. Teachers. Under thirty?"

He nodded. Everything she said made sense. "So Eve isn't one of ours?"

"There's something else, too."

George raised both his eyebrows. "Go on."

"I've just had a message from Josh Fry, who is working on Eve Allgood's background check. Roberts was right. She was a Leeds girl, born in Belle Isle before moving to Middleton." George grinned. "She qualified as a teacher from what is now Leeds Trinity University. It says she was fired in 2007 due to an investigation. The records show little more than she was barred from working with children and vulnerable adults. But it makes sense why she worked in a bakery in Greater Manchester."

"And it makes sense why they moved away."

"I really believe there's a connection to our culprit and Eve Allgood. I really believe she's girl zero." She nibbled the roll and sipped her coffee. "Maybe he was jealous of her relationship with Clark? Maybe she wouldn't date him? Preston Blake was accused of stalking a teacher when he was seventeen. She wouldn't have sex with him, either, so he threatened her. We still haven't fully ruled him out. Maybe he travelled to Greater Manchester to kill Eve? If it's not him, though, it could be somebody like him."

George met her gaze and nearly became lost in her eyes. He started nodding frantically. "So we have our culprit, who is underage and wants to have sex with this teacher. She rebuts him. He threatens her. Does he possibly stalk her? And what finds out she's moved on?" She could see the cogs whirring. "Wait, wait. So what you're saying is, what better person is there to frame other than a man who had a relationship with Eve?"

"Exactly."

It made sense.

"I think we should check it out, George, don't you?"

He nodded furiously, a broad grin on his face. "You've cracked it, Wood. As you said, if it's not Preston Blake, it's somebody similar. The stalking and threatening of that teacher. I need to speak with the headteacher from Beeston Park Academy. A witness named Edith Jackson told me that Eileen Abbott had worked at the school for years. Does it say which school Eve Allgood got fired from?"

Wood shook her head. "Maybe she... Eve was born in Belle Isle, right? That suggests a few secondary schools she could have worked at, but only if she had stayed in the area. Maybe Eileen Abbott will know about it. This could blow the case wide open, Wood. Also, let's pay David Clark a visit on Sunday and see what he has to say for himself."

Wood nodded with a huge grin on her face. "I think we should go and see Eve's mother, too. She still lives in the Middleton in Greater Manchester."

* * *

Only standing room was available by the time DI Beaumont and DS Wood arrived at St Mary's church. Despite the pair arriving earlier than they expected, they were forced to stand at the back as Father Denton led a procession between the pews of St Mary's. George watched as an altar boy marched behind their priest, taking in the faces of every visitor, wondering whether the killer was there, too. Both Ian Kennedy and Ryan Jenkins were in attendance and were sitting at the front.

"Is it always this crowded?" George asked as Father Denton approached the pulpit.

The smell of incense was making Wood dizzy, and she wished there'd been an empty seat. "I doubt it," she said. "That group over there are Erika's colleagues."

George cast an appraising eye over them and nodded. They were all clean; all had an alibi for the night Erika had been murdered.

Although the Mass had been arranged, it had also been informally assigned as a tribute to both Erika Allen and Emma Atkinson, whose funerals had been suspended because of their investigations. George knew that not knowing when they could bury their loved ones was difficult for the families of the victims and made a mental note to speak to FLO Cathy Hoskins more. She'd visited the grieving partners more than once, even travelling to Scotland to see Ian. He'd made the trip back.

George swept the congregation once more, and the diversity surprised him. The elderly ladies they had interviewed were present, but so were many younger people, families, and individuals gathered to mourn the deaths of the well-loved teachers.

Despite attending church as a child, and knowing that Father Denton was going to be giving a eulogy for the late teachers, George was surprised by his words.

"We're assembled here today to share our grief and to celebrate the lives of Erika Allen and Emma Atkinson," Father Denton said. He looked around the church to nodding heads, his words punctuated by the sounds of sobs and snorts. The sounds of crinkling tissues penetrated Beaumont's facade. "Both women were kind, generous, and well-loved by both their peers and their students."

"As well as a teacher, Erika was a gymnast, an All-Around British Champion, as well as a local dance teacher who gave up what little spare time she had to the community. Emma Atkinson, a keen runner who raised tens of thousands for charity, and regularly volunteered many school holidays abroad, supporting local educators. Both magnificent women kept children safe and secure, passing on their knowledge, and safeguarding their futures."

He looked directly at George.

"So how is it we are here today?" The eye contact was

intense. "We weren't there when they needed us. We didn't listen to the warning signs." The priest didn't blink once. "So, today, in celebrating their lives, we also have to admit that some of us failed Erika Allen. Just as we failed Emma Atkinson." Father Denton looked down at the bible on his pulpit. "Mark 12:31 tells us, 'Thou shalt love thy neighbour as thyself.' If we are not a community of neighbours, then we are nothing. Somebody here knows something that can bring peace to both Erika's and Emma's families. I implore you to speak up."

"And finally, during these, the darkest of times, we have to do better."

Many members of the audience wept openly at Father Denton's words. George felt like an outsider, the residents' disapproving gazes matching Father Denton's, the crowd not afraid to express their dissatisfaction at two police officers interrupting their Mass, nor their anger towards the detectives for their lack of an identified suspect.

The firm words from the beginning of the eulogy influenced George. What should have been a celebration of the deceased's lives had turned sour, and he didn't feel the joy he had expected to. He understood. The suburb was mourning Erika and Emma, but they had only a hooded figure to blame. Instead, they transferred the blame to him and DS Wood. He should have expected it but hadn't. He made a mental note to check into Father Denton's alibi further and question him again. After all, he had been the last known person to have spoken to her.

George turned to Wood and saw she was attempting to compose herself. Tears glistened, but at the recognition of George's glance, she hastily brushed them away. He desperately wanted to comfort her but knew that it was both currently professionally and personally wrong.

Chapter Twenty-seven

"I'm sorry, George, I'm not sure what came over me in there," she sniffed, turning away. They walked side by side down the paved path, receiving glances from the crowd who had stopped to shake Father Denton's hand.

George stopped and looked at her sympathetically. "There's no need to apologise, Wood." She nodded and continued, and he followed behind her at a short distance.

The inside of the car was still warm. He turned to face Wood before turning on the engine. "Are you OK?"

"Not really," replied Wood, "but I will be. I don't normally find this side of the job difficult. But as the words left Father Denton's mouth, it hit me. The victims were people with lives and families. I'm aware it's difficult not to feel that way. Most times, I switch it off to make sure it doesn't affect me. It was unprofessional. Forgive me."

"It was far from unprofessional, Wood," George said sympathetically. "Look, I get it. As detectives, we can't let these feelings overwhelm us because they can prevent us from doing our jobs. But Wood, you wouldn't be human if you felt nothing, trust me. An important part of the process is that we keep the victim and their family in mind at all times. It's that compassion and empathy that enables us to execute our jobs to the fullest. Erika and Emma are, unfortunately, no longer with us. It's our job to give them a voice. We've got to figure out what took place and use it to bring both themselves and their families justice."

Wood nodded before she smiled. He desperately wanted to grab hold of her hand and squeeze it, desperate to comfort her in any way. "You're doing great, Wood. We've got a man out there killing women your age," George whispered. "I will not pretend to know what's going through your head, but if it were me, I'd be terrified. The women of South Leeds are frightened. I don't blame them. You only get one life, and so who wouldn't be afraid to die when there's so much to live for? Morality sucks, Wood; it really does. But it's precious, too. And it's our job to protect that morality."

Wood flashed him a grin, a grin George thought was the sexiest grin he had ever seen. "You know, Inspector Beaumont, I always thought that brooding exterior of yours was a front. You can't hide it from me. I knew deep down you were a sweet, sensitive guy." She placed her right hand on his left, which rested on the gear stick, and squeezed.

Wood kept it there until he turned on the engine. "Come on, let's get back to the station. We've had a busy day. I think we both could do with an early night to start tomorrow fresh." George didn't mean it and hoped she would disagree with him.

She did. Wood sat up in her seat and smiled. "I'm starving. Fancy a burger or something?"

* * *

The pair stopped at a McDonald's drive-through in Hunslet to grab a bite to eat and drink more coffee. He appreciated Wood and her ease of where they could eat. Mia would never have stepped foot in a McDonald's. She'd rather go hungry than eat fast food. George often wanted a simple KFC, while Mia had wanted roasted chicken with risotto and caramelised onions or chicken Provençal. The food had never tasted bad, but it hadn't quite hit the spot. He mused for a moment, believing it had been a perfect metaphor for their finished relationship.

"You know, Wood, I'm going to have to eat healthier." Famished, George chewed his burger. "This is becoming a habit."

Wood chortled as she unwrapped hers. "I get what you're saying. My diet flies out the window when I'm on a case."

"You don't need to be concerned," he answered rather hastily. As soon as the words left his mouth, he regretted it. She paused, and he frowned. Had he crossed the line? He'd purposefully kept his growing feelings for her to one side. He grimaced.

"Thank you, George," she mumbled after taking a nibble. Her words calmed him down. "However, I have a secret."

"What secret?"

"I have a treadmill. It allows me to stay in shape and relax on the nights when I can't sleep."

"You struggle with sleep too?" Insomnia came with the job. Mia had never understood.

She nodded, stuffing her face with fries. Wood was a breeze to chat to; their conversation flowed whilst they finished their food. She told him she had a psychology degree from the University of Leeds, which, in George's eyes, explained everything. It had taken her several years to know what she really wanted to do with her life, and she wished she had studied criminology instead. Wood told him how criminal profiling really interested her, and they spoke about Mark Finch for a while before she changed the subject.

"How did you end up being a detective, George?" she said after they got back into the car.

"I didn't really know what I wanted to be when I was young, so I screwed around a little after leaving school," he said. "I worked for a sandwich shop, a baker; I even collected glasses. The money meant I could travel a little, but then I ran out of money and ended up going off the tracks. It was boredom. I had no focus. I got a job at a bar, got in with the wrong crowd, and started drinking. Next thing you know, I get into a couple of bar brawls with idiots. I was never pulled by the police, but something about those idiots just got to me. And then I realised what it was. They were all dealing drugs, putting people's lives at risk, and fighting a lot. They had knives and guns, too, I'm sure. I was lucky because I'd seen the knives, yet they didn't kill me during those frequent fights. But I couldn't tolerate how they were acting, and it seemed obvious I needed a way to channel my anger. So first, I started boxing, and then I joined the police."

Talking with Wood felt like breathing. It just happened. He didn't need to force it. George wanted to tell her about how his father was a piece of shit and the last person anybody would ever want as a role model. He'd never spoken about his father to anybody before—not even to Mia—and he wasn't sure why he was doing so now.

"It was Mark Finch who advised me to join the police force. He'd just finished university and was rejecting job offers left, right, and centre. We used to box together regularly, and I thought he was insane at first. I remember thinking, what would the police want with an arsehole like me? But he'd bring it up during our sparring sessions. I signed up six months later, and it was the best decision I ever made." He turned the car out of the car park, deciding to drive the long way back to the station. "It turns out that it was a nice fit after all. I spent a few years in uniform before applying to CID. Then I joined the Homicide and Major Enquiry team." He gave a wry smile. "Being a Uniform was fine, but I wanted to work on more important cases and wanted to solve crimes. I seemed to have this ambition that I'd never thought possible. I'll tell you the truth. It took me by surprise. It also helped to get rid of the red mist I usually spent my life living in, you know?"

She took a long sip of coffee, her eyes bright in the car's darkness. "Have you lived in Leeds your entire life?"

"Yeah, pretty much." He explained about moving down to Leeds from Scotland when he had been younger. He also explained about his mum divorcing his dad and their year in Wakefield. "I classify myself as a Leeds lad. I considered moving down to London after becoming a detective, thinking there would be more crimes to solve, but I got into my job and was promoted pretty quickly to DS. That's when I moved to Elland Road. It was an opportunity, and I believed the change would be beneficial."

"And you're happy, George?"

"Yeah, I am." He pulled into the parking compound at the station. "What about you, Wood? What was it that inspired you to become a detective?"

A brief silence ensued. "It's hard to explain. I was obsessed with serial killers as a teenager, always watching documentaries or reading books. I wanted to get into their minds and find out what makes them tick. It was a morbid fascination, I guess. I studied psychology as an option for my GCSEs. Then

CHAPTER TWENTY-SEVEN

I did my Psychology A-Levels, too. It made sense for me to go to university and study it. As I said, I should maybe have studied criminology. My dream is to meet David Wilson. Have you heard of him?"

"Absolutely. I'm a huge fan."

She smiled. "But that's it, really. Once I earned my psychology degree, I decided I wanted to catch serial killers."

George felt as if she wasn't telling him the entire story, but he was OK with that; she'd shared more than enough with him. He'd never asked Mark why he'd gone into the profession but made a mental note to ask him one day.

"You can't catch a killer if you don't know how they think. Or so I was told. Once I left university, I applied via the West Yorkshire Police's fast-track recruiting programme, and here I am six years later. I've had an incredible time so far." He'd never asked her age before, but from working it out, she'd be about twenty-nine.

"Pretty career driven then, Wood?" She laughed as he parked his car next to hers. "What about family?" he inquired. "Do you want to get married and have children?"

"You offering?" she asked, her face straight.

He didn't know whether to take her seriously or not, so he didn't answer, and soon, the silence was deafening. He was about to break the awkward silence when she burst into hysterics. Between little fits of giggles, she managed to say, "When the time is right, I do, George. How about you?"

He could see, even in the dim light, that she had turned red. He hoped it was a telling look, hoped she fancied him as he did her, but he doubted it, thinking it was probably the laughing that had made her turn crimson.

George shrugged. "I'm into my career at the moment. I want

to be a DCI. Having children would make me want to be home with them, not at work. There are days I really want to settle down, but other days where I want to be out solving crimes."

He'd never managed to have the child talk with Mia again. Maybe it had been a sign, after all. She had been purposefully ignoring his phone calls recently and was refusing to reply to his messages. The relationship was over. He knew that. His frequent calling and texting wasn't anything to do with trying to get back with her. He simply wasn't pleased with how they'd left things. It didn't seem right. She may have broken his heart, but there was still a killer on the loose, and he still cared about her.

"Never say never, George. I guess that's rich coming from me, but I guess you'll never know." She gave him a wide grin. "Life is full of unexpected twists and turns."

Later, when the pair parted, and George watched as Wood drove away, he knew he'd wanted to spend more time with her but hadn't been quite sure how to put it into words.

Chapter Twenty-eight

George shot up out of bed, the sound of his alarm clock deafening that Saturday morning. The trip to see retired DCI Roberts up in Greater Manchester had exhausted him. That, and the events of the church, and his meal with Wood meant he had been out like a light. He stretched and glanced at the spot next to him where Mia usually lay. They were finished. There was no way to repair their relationship. He wasn't sure he even wanted to.

As George walked downstairs and flicked the kettle on, he thought about the case. The upcoming trip to the prison in Manchester excited him, but it meant going against Steve Roberts. It didn't excite him that there may have been a gross miscarriage of justice, but it did that David Clark was possibly innocent. DS Wood had arranged for the both of them to visit David at Strangeways, the category A men's prison in Manchester. They'd then swing by Marie Allgood's house later that day. He was itching to go that morning, but Eileen Abbott was more important. George needed to know why Eve Allgood had been banned from working with children.

Both Erika's and Emma's phones were still missing. They'd got the data from the phone companies after having promptly provided them with warrants. DC Scott and DS Fry had worked late into Friday night, checking their last movements, tracking their mobile phone data and analysing their calls. But he had had no calls or texts updating him.

He'd work extra hard today, knowing full well he couldn't possibly work any harder, but at least he wouldn't have Mia breathing down his neck. The thought made him feel guilty, but now that she wasn't there, George had no reason to give her an explanation nor an apology.

He made a quick coffee, downed it, and showered. After brushing his teeth and getting dressed, he headed directly to work, denying his craving for a Double Sausage & Egg McMuffin. The spring morning was crisp, the sky the same colour as Erika's and Emma's eyes, and everywhere he looked, he saw their dead, bloated faces, the ones from his nightmares, looking back at him. He wondered how many more would die before he caught the killer.

None, he hoped.

He strode into the squad room. "Morning," he called. He glanced around. The detective superintendent wasn't in. He didn't work weekends, usually, but he thought he'd remembered something about Smith coming in 'specially'.

"You're in early," Wood said, taking off her coat.

"Last night didn't sit well with me, Wood. That bloody priest. I know I lectured you, Wood, but I wanted to get a head start on what retired DCI Roberts told us yesterday. Any extra info from Eve's background check yet?

"Not yet," she said.

"OK, as soon as everyone's in, we'll have a briefing."

* * *

CHAPTER TWENTY-EIGHT

George updated his team on what they'd discovered in Greater Manchester. "We don't know whether the murder of Eve Allgood is related yet to our murders," he told them, "but Wood and I are going to HMP Manchester on Sunday to have a chat with this David Clark."

"Good idea," barked DSU Smith. "But I'm worried, Beaumont."

"Sir?"

"David Clark was tried and convicted for the murder of Eve Allgood. I've heard of DCI Roberts. He has a great reputation and was considered one of the brilliant detectives of the north. I'm not saying he's right about Clark, but if he isn't and we have to step on his toes, we're going to have to come up with some pretty compelling evidence."

George nodded. He was in complete agreement. Retired DCI Roberts had undoubtedly made himself clear he wouldn't look too kindly on them opening the case again. He just wondered why that was. Was it because he had caught the right guy, or was it because if he were wrong, then his reputation would take a hit?

"Let's keep this between us for now," DSU Smith ordered to the room. "If I hear about any of this in the news, I'll know the only place it could have come from was here. Understood?"

The team nodded.

George stood forward. "Yolanda, do you have any news on the CCTV footage of the white Ford van?"

She shook her head. "Sorry, sir. We're struggling to find anything new for you."

He bit his lip. "Shit. Right, OK, we knew looking for the van without a reg was a long shot anyway. What about the phone records?"

DS Joshua Fry also shook his head. "The records that come back are normal, sir. No calls or texts out of the ordinary. Without their actual phones, it's more difficult."

"OK, keep at it." George looked at Wood. "Anything back about Eve's background?"

"Not yet. Nothing on the PNC that we don't already know. As soon as I have more, I'll let you know."

"Right, thanks everyone."

* * *

Despite working sixty hours per week as the headteacher for Beeston Park Academy, Eileen Abbott volunteered for the Middleton Elderly Aid every other Saturday morning. It was only for four hours, eight until noon, but the staff appreciated it, and Eileen enjoyed it. Eileen was a woman in her late forties, but rarely did she look it. In spite of the sixty-hour work week and the extra hours volunteering, Eileen found the time to work out. She looked good, and the hooded man couldn't wait to get his hands on her.

An hour before her shift was due to end, the man parked his Ford up at the curb opposite the charity shop where she volunteered. He was hungry and waltzed into the café that was four shops up. He was a regular, and the owner greeted him by name. There were a couple of older men drinking cups of tea, talking about the rugby league that had been on last night. One of them reminded him of his own grandad, and a sense of melancholy came over him. He understood why. Once he had finished his mission, he would soon again be saying goodbye to the place that was the only home he'd ever known.

Once he'd finished his salad, he paid with cash, leaving

the waitress a big tip. He left the place, surprised to see Eileen Abbott leave the charity shop thirty minutes before her shift usually ended. He voiced his surprise, and she squinted towards him, her hand raised against the sun. For a short period, they were staring at each other until he broke the spell by re-entering the cafe. She'd raised her hand in greeting as he pushed open the door. He asked to use the toilet and hoped she hadn't followed him in.

Eileen Abbott's house was a detached bungalow a half-mile walk from the shop. He gave it five minutes and left. She was nowhere to be seen. He wouldn't fret over it, but he wondered why she had left the charity shop early. If he had been any later out of the café, then he'd have missed her.

In the safety of his van, the hooded man waited for her to arrive home. Once he saw her, he'd planned to park his van in the blind spot between the two CCTV cameras. After, he would walk his way back to the end of West Farm Avenue where she lived.

The hooded man put on his disguise. From experience, he knew there was only one way into the cul-de-sac and one way out. It was dangerous. But because it was dangerous, it was also exciting. As he walked down the street, his only thoughts focused on finding an alternative escape route, so much so that at first, he ignored the car pulling up outside Miss Abbott's house. His attention only returned as a man got out of the car and walked up the pathway to the Abbott house.

The man shook and balled his fists tight. He'd seen the man before, a few times on the television after he'd killed Erika Allen. It was the man in charge of the police investigation that was hunting him.

Detective Inspector George Beaumont.

Chapter Twenty-nine

Detective Inspector George Beaumont yawned as he rapped on Miss Eileen Abbott's glass door. Eileen's house was a beautiful detached bungalow just off Town Street in a pleasant area of Middleton. George had looked at a few properties in this area himself before settling on East Ardsley. The prices had been eye-watering at the time, and he imagined they were now even more expensive.

A slim woman with a wedge of blonde hair answered the door. "Eileen Abbott," the woman said after George introduced himself. She gave a confident smile that stretched from ear to ear. The woman wore no makeup, and for her age, George thought she looked good. He, himself, had been neglecting the gym recently.

She led George through to a kitchen at the back of the house. He noticed she had many framed photos, some situated above the fireplace and others that littered shelves and units. "Yours?" George asked, pointing to a cluster of pictures of two blonde girls with matching pink dresses.

"No." He thought he saw something behind the look she gave him. "They are my nieces and not that little any more."

"Do you see much of them?"

"No. Please take a seat."

CHAPTER TWENTY-NINE

She'd already given him verbal consent for the recording of the conversation, and so he placed his Dictaphone down on the table.

George accepted the offer of tea and thought small talk might get her to open up. "Have you lived in Leeds your entire life, Miss Abbott?"

"No, why do you ask?"

"The accent."

She smiled. "No one usually notices," she said. "I guess that's why you're the detective. I was born in Scotland. My father moved us to London when we were young. I moved to Leeds when I earned my teaching degree—been here ever since. It's been mentioned I have a posh Yorkshire accent. But that's all."

"You say you've been here ever since you earned your degree?" She nodded and took a sip of her tea. "How long have you been teaching at Beeston Park Academy?"

She raised her brow and smiled. "Come now, Detective. I think we both know that you've done your research prior to coming here." George mirrored her smile but didn't answer. "I've taught at Beeston Park Academy my entire career. I started when I was twenty-two and never left. Is that what you want to speak to me about?" said Eileen.

The woman was still smiling, but the confidence had decayed. George had seen this type of smile before, one that was devoid of warmth, one that held many secrets. He wasn't sure why her attitude had changed since greeting at the door, but whatever the reason was, he needed to know. "As I said on the phone, Miss Abbott, I'm investigating the deaths of Erika Allen and Emma Atkinson. Erika was an employee of yours, but I believe you knew Emma, too?"

"What happened to those young women was tragic, just absolutely tragic," she said, shaking her head. "It's terrible what's happened to the community, too. But to answer your question, yes, I knew both Erika and Emma."

"In what capacity did you know them?"

"Erika, as you already know, was one of my teachers. She completed her training at the school. She was a local girl, and I took to her immediately. I offered her an interview for an opening, and she accepted. This year would have been her fourth year of teaching for me."

"And Emma Atkinson?" asked George.

"Like Erika, she completed her teacher training at Beeston Park Academy. She was good, very good at what she did, actually. She accepted a position at an academy in Lofthouse. I was disappointed, but it was easier for her to get to. She didn't like the place and, after two years, called me up asking if there were any vacancies. We became a multi-academy trust while she was at that other school, and whilst we had no vacancies, the newly created Middleton Park Academy did. I won't lie to you, Detective. I was waiting for a teacher to leave my school so I could get her transferred over to me. Emma was a wonderful teacher and a wonderful friend. She was quite the talent, being able to not only command respect but hold the attention of teenagers. Her students doted on her. As did Erika's."

A lull in the conversation began to happen. It was normal. He took his chance and spiced it up. "For both victims, were there ever any issues you can remember?"

"Issues?" She frowned.

"Any disgruntled pupils or parents?"

Eileen shook her head, her eyes darting towards her drink, then back to George. "Nothing that I can recall. They were outstanding teachers and talented women, but no matter how great of a teacher you are, there are always issues with parents. As you can imagine, there are some who tend to interfere. There are those that don't get involved at all. As head, I have to work with my teachers to manage parents' expectations. Those were hard conversations. And many parents have unrealistic views about their children. But to my knowledge, there were no issues. Is there anything else you need to know?"

George sighed, sensing a dead end to the conversation. He only had the Eve Allgood questions left. "In your years as a teacher in Leeds, have you ever heard of, or come across, a teacher named Eve Allgood?"

Eileen opened her mouth to say something but hesitated. The grave look was still there. She'd turned white. "I'm unsure. The name sounds familiar, but that's all. Why?"

"Forgive me for asking, but you're forty-eight, right?" She nodded. "Eve would have been about eight years your junior. She was born in Belle Isle and was a secondary school teacher. She was barred from working with children and vulnerable adults during the time you've been at Beeston Park Academy. Are you sure you don't know her?"

"I've already said, haven't I?" Eileen stated a sour look in her eye. "I've worked with a lot of teachers over the years. I could easily have worked with Eve Allgood."

George thought about Edith Jackson and what her daughter, Janice Mitchell, had told him. "Do you recall anything about a teacher at Beeston Park Academy ever being sacked for having an affair with a student?" George saw her flinch and was sure she was hiding something from him. She said nothing. "It would have been about seventeen, eighteen years ago?"

"Yes, a teacher was sacked for having relations with a minor. A young boy and a female teacher."

George kept his gaze on her. "Do you remember her name?"

"That's where I know her name from. It was Eve. Miss Eve Allgood."

George raised his brow, surprised by her honesty. "Do you remember the young boy's name?"

She shook her head.

"No?"

"No."

He was beginning to lose his patience. "What can you tell me about the relations?"

"Not much, Inspector. I was there whilst it happened, but I was only a teacher, not a head like I am now. It was obviously a very long time ago now, and my memory isn't what it was. I wasn't privy to those conversations, you understand?"

The atmosphere in the room was becoming strained, and he knew there was nothing else he could get from Eileen Abbott at the moment. He thanked her for her time and got to his feet. He'd send Wood to question Eileen again Monday. From experience, giving people time to consider the implications of their answers meant they usually remembered more.

Eileen showed George to the door. "Thank you for leaving your voluntary work early to see me. I'll be in touch," George said, handing her a card. "Please call me if you can think of anything else that may help."

"Yes, Inspector, of course."

As he stepped over the threshold, he decided to take one last punt. "One thing before I go," he said, turning around to face Eileen. "You may have noticed, but Erika and Emma were very similar. They were both unmarried, young, blonde teachers with blue eyes. One of our lines of enquiry is that our culprit is selecting his victims using these identifiers."

"OK," Eileen said, her eyes narrowing.

"Could you think of anybody else at Beeston Park Academy who may fit our victim selection?"

George noticed Eileen pause before answering. "Other than the obvious?"

He wasn't sure what she meant and furrowed his brow.

"Well, I don't consider myself old, Inspector. I look after myself. I'm an unmarried teacher with blonde hair and blue eyes. Are you saying I need to be worried?"

George kept his gaze on her and shook his head. She was a beautiful woman, but he thought she was too old. "I don't think so, no. No disrespect, but the age of the victim is key. Mid-twenties to early thirties. It may be nothing anyway, but thank you. Can you think of no one else?"

She shook her head and smiled. "Is there anything else?"

He mirrored the shake of her head, turned and walked down the drive towards his Honda. Like everything else she had told him, the information felt incomplete, and he was convinced Eileen was keeping something from him. She was being defensive, but he understood answering questions from the police could be intrusive. It only made him more determined to find out what she was hiding from him.

Chapter Thirty

Having initially recovered from the scare of seeing the detective, the man went back to his van, removed his disguise, and waited at the end of her road, pretending to talk to somebody on his phone. He looked anonymous in the suit, just a businessman having a chat. A few of the neighbours had looked out of their windows at him, but he simply smiled back and pretended to walk up their drives. Who didn't hate cold callers?

He tried and failed to understand why the detective would want to interview Eileen Abbott. It had to be more than routine because he knew both Eileen Abbott and Erika Allen's colleagues had already been interviewed. As far as he knew, they had all been excluded from the investigation, so why would he go to all the trouble of visiting her at her house?

Every way he looked at it, the man came back to one thing. The detective must have made a connection. The detective left the house, and the man watched him make a call. They looked roughly of similar age, and though not by much, the detective was taller than him. He had sandy blond hair with a matching, closely cropped beard—a professional with an air of confidence. The murderer began to panic.

The moment the detective had driven off, he walked up a

nearby empty drive, hoping no one was home. He knocked on the door and was torn between two options: to stay and pay Eileen her last ever visit, as he'd planned, or to leave and try another day.

He'd chosen the former mainly because he'd been meticulous. The man knew it could have all been a trap. Maybe the detective had arrived to warn her of impending danger. If that was the case, then the police knew his selection criteria. If so, he'd have to bring his next kill forward. Was he ready? Only time would tell.

As he walked back to his van to change, the man felt helpless and was disgusted to find himself on the verge of tears. He'd been so careful during all of his kills. Before seeing the detective, he'd felt so positive, yet now all he felt was chaos.

His plan was now a risk. What did he do next? Did he keep to his plan as he had promised himself earlier, or did he bail? He was amazed what a five-minute walk did to add doubt.

The man took a deep breath, counted to three, and pulled up his hood. All he had to do was walk down the road, knock on her door, and pounce. The detective's arrival had unnerved him, but he thought the best plan of action was to continue. Within the confines of her house, he could take as long as he wanted with her. Maybe he'd interrogate her on what she spoke to the detective about first?

The killer knocked on Eileen Abbott's front door before he changed his mind.

"Hello detective, did you forget something?" she said as she smiled in that false way of hers. Her lips did the usual movement towards her ears, but her eyes showed no warmth as she did so. But, the smile soon turned to a look of confusion as she realised it wasn't the detective. She stepped back as she tried to recall where she'd seen him before.

"Hello, Miss Abbott," he said, noting the split second of recognition and fear as she realised who he was.

He punched her in the nose, which helped to get her inside because she stumbled back before he hastily stepped in after her and pulled the door closed.

Miss Abbott was out cold, and the hooded man placed her on her side before dragging her down the hallway. He hefted her onto a chair in the kitchen and used the tape to bind her arms and feet. She awoke as he was cutting off her skirt, her blouse already open, her breasts exposed. "What do you want?" she asked in a daze.

"Send my regards to your colleagues, Miss Abbott," he said, placing a piece of tape over her mouth.

* * *

After interviewing Eileen Abbott, he'd called the station asking for an update on Eve Allgood's background check. Unfortunately, they'd found nothing more. George raced back to the station, desperately wanting to find a link.

Whilst searching through HOLMES and the PNC, George kept thinking about Miss Abbott. She was hiding something. But what. Then the background check came in. Eileen had been hiding a big secret. So he decided to question her again, without notice this time.

It was darker than George expected when he left the station. The traffic was horrendous on the A6110. He desperately wanted to get to her house and thought about cutting up Millshaw and on to Beeston Town Street. He could see flashing lights and the wail of a police car siren. George called in to

CHAPTER THIRTY

find out there was a road traffic accident at the White Rose Shopping Centre roundabout.

Everybody had the same idea he had, and he followed a pack of slow-moving vehicles up Millshaw hill and onto Beeston Town Street. George cursed himself, knowing he should have travelled to Eileen Abbott's via Wesley-street. They continued at a slow pace down Old Lane, his stomach rumbling as he passed a local fish and chip shop. He'd had nothing to eat since a slice of toast at the station that morning, but there was no time now. They only had the rest of today, and the whole of tomorrow, to get a solid suspect, and the thought of Wakefield taking over banished all concerns of hunger.

The traffic was getting worse, and so he was stuck for another twenty minutes at the Tommy Wass traffic lights before the traffic began to relent as he headed up the Ring Road.

With no available parking spaces along Eileen's road, George was forced to park at the bottom of New Lane. As he locked the door to his Honda, the clouds let loose their bounty. A freezing wind mixed with the battering rain, and George was drenched by the time he reached the house.

Cursing himself for not wearing a coat, he knocked on the front door, only to find it was already open.

* * *

After the killer had taped her mouth, despite being bound, Miss Abbott struggled and, at first, had put up quite a fight. After somehow taking a knee to the nose, a red mist had descended over him, and the memory of the following ten minutes was still clouded. He'd obviously retaliated, knocking her over in the chair where she'd fallen and smashed her head on hard kitchen tiles.

It meant the killer had to wait for her to regain consciousness. He wanted her to be alive when he fucked her; he wanted her to feel everything as he choked the life from her. He considered allowing her to die by his blade instead but soon changed his mind. Only Eve needed to die by his blade. The rest were just tributes. They were nothing. Yet, discounting Eve, who was the most special of all, compared with the other lives he'd taken, Miss Abbott was special.

She was special because everything led back to her. She had started this. Everything had been her fault. Miss Abbott had been the one to raise concerns with the school about their relationship. Yes, he had only been sixteen at the time, but he loved her. Miss Allgood. She was his, and he was hers. Miss Abbott had taken that away from him. He remembered the events well. Miss Allgood had turned twenty-three in the April, and he had been sixteen the September before, the oldest in his year. He had a month left at school. A month and their relationship would have been legal. Yet that woman, that fucking degenerate, Miss Abbott, got involved.

At first, the man thought she'd been jealous of their relationship. He didn't look sixteen. He'd grown a beard, both because he could and because he wanted to hide it—to hide the embarrassment. Hide the shame. It had worked well for him over the years. He'd shaved that beard off last night, preparing himself for today. But she hadn't been jealous of their relationship, only suspicious.

If he hadn't tried it on with Miss Abbott, too, then he and Miss Allgood would have been together now. He knew that deep within his loins.

CHAPTER THIRTY

And because of that, he knew Miss Abbott needed to pay.

In the end, he'd waited long enough for Miss Abbott to awaken on her own and searched her house for anything he could use. Under the sink were ammonia smelling salts, which he used to arouse Miss Abbott to consciousness. He removed his hood and his face mask so that she knew who he was. She screamed in protest as, realising he'd been there too long, rolled her on her front and sliced down the back of her tights. A bead of blood welled just above her tramp stamp, and his penis hardened immediately. Then, he used his blade to remove her thong. As he had done with her bra, he pocketed it, taking her mobile phone, too.

Then, as he had done with Eve, Elizabeth, Emma, and Erika, he entered her from behind and enclosed his hands around her throat. As he thrust with his hips, he heard her screams as they found a voice through the tape across her mouth.

He shuddered as he came and tightened his grip even more. Once she was dead, he rolled her over and laid next to her. His signature move was next, and he wanted to enjoy it. There was something about a woman bleeding that turned him on.

In the end, he hadn't asked her anything about the detective that had visited her. He'd just wanted to get it over with. But he couldn't drag himself away just yet. Despite thinking that the police could already be on their way, he lay there exhausted.

It was the sex. It had extinguished his strength. His thrusts had been so powerful, so he waited.

When he was ready, he gripped his knife and began his attack, an attack so frenzied that the knife covered in Miss Abbott's blood became slippery, and he cut himself with his own blade. He spent the next few minutes in the kitchen on his haunches, the images of Miss Abbott fresh in his mind, his skin and clothes still slick with her blood.

* * *

The smell of blood hit George as he edged through the door. He had no gun, no pepper spray or an extendable baton. No vest, either. After entering, he'd stepped back outside and called his location in. There were no lights on in the living room, and wary that the killer could still be around, George slowly headed towards the only light he could see, the one in the kitchen. A slight wind buffeted him as if a door was open somewhere. George shivered, already drenched from the freezing rain outside.

It took a few seconds for his eyes to adjust to the light as he stepped into the kitchen. The bright kitchen lights illuminated not only the blood-splattered corpse of Eileen Abbott, her bloated and lifeless eyes staring at George, but a hooded figure knelt on the ground, furiously mopping up blood with a tea towel.

George stopped dead, surprised by the figure looking up at him. He looked exactly like he did on the CCTV footage, exactly how eyewitnesses had described him, and it made him hesitate. The killer didn't. "Stop! You're under arrest." The hooded man grabbed his knife with his right, and with his left, a bag filled with blood-soaked towels. Instead of charging at him as George had expected, the killer turned and fled through the already open patio door.

He sped after the killer, keeping a wide berth between himself and the body, crashing out into the deluge that was typical of England during April, and saw the masked man clearing the fence at the back of the garden.

CHAPTER THIRTY

Clearing the fence himself, he looked left and right to find no sign of the killer. He had, however, graciously left them his bag filled with the soaked towels. He jumped back over the fence, cursing himself for not reacting quicker.

George didn't encroach any further into the crime scene, tracing his steps back to the entrance to the living room. He scoured the room, trying not to dwell on the mangled mess that used to be Eileen Abbott. Chances were the killer was long gone, but he crept slowly back to the front door and ascended the staircase, all the time convincing himself that the killer hadn't come back for him.

He secured the rooms of the upper floor, pausing on the landing as he heard the front door creak open.

Chapter Thirty-one

The killer pulled away in his van seconds before the wailing sirens turned on to New Lane. He admonished himself. It was as if he'd wanted to be caught. What the hell had he been thinking? They had his DNA anyway, and with him not being on the database, he needn't have worried about cleaning up.

As he cruised his way down Belle Isle Road, he thought about the DNA he'd left at other scenes, knowing they could use it to tie him to those murders. Did that matter? Were those murders a secret? Not really, but he'd managed to put the blame on someone else and didn't want them going free.

All he knew was that a part of him wanted to enjoy the sensation of thrusting sharp metal through flesh again. By losing control, he'd put himself in jeopardy.

At the end of West Grange Fold, under the shadow of a growth of trees, the killer reversed his van so that there was just enough space to open the rear doors. He climbed into the back of the van and changed, tossing his clothes and boots into a black bin bag. Two other matching bags already stuffed with blood-soaked clothes were waiting for him to dispose of. He'd do that at work once he took his last Leeds victim. The back of his van had taken on a now familiar coppery smell, and he savoured it, knowing he'd have to calm his actions after killing Emilia. The bundle of clothes he'd wear for her were still in their wrappers, waiting.

The rain was still falling as he exited the back of his van. He'd put the suit back on he wore earlier, as well as a wig and a fake beard. It would be no good if somebody from the houses nearby recognised him. There were no council cameras here, no private cameras, either. It both worried him and elated him that no one in their right mind would be out in this weather. It meant people were off the streets, but it also meant they were in their homes, bored. And bored people looked out of their windows.

He locked the van and, using a rag, cleaned the muck from his number plates. His car was parked around the corner on Old Run Road, which wasn't unusual, for it was close to his place of work.

* * *

His baton extended out in front of him, DC Scott entered through the door. He announced his presence as George walked down the stairs. "Don't go into the kitchen, Jay," he said, causing the DC to jump.

"Jesus, sir, you scared the shit out of me. What's the situation?"

"One body through there," he said, pointing to the kitchen. They stepped outside. "Stay here and secure the front door. I don't want anyone else in here until the SOCOs arrive."

He walked a hole in the ground whilst waiting for Uniform to show up. Within minutes, the area was shut down, with police cars and ambulances lining the street. George's clothes were already soaked, and he didn't care that it was raining any more. He was just glad he left the house when he did, appreciative of the fresh, bitter air.

The magnitude of the situation hit him when he saw DSU Smith pull up. He'd only been to Eileen Abbott's that morning, and just an hour later, she was dead. How close had he been to catching the killer? George squatted down and let out a cry. If only he'd taken Wesley-street instead of the A6110. He would have arrived easily twenty minutes earlier. Then what? Would he have been able to arrest the killer successfully, or would he have been killed, too?

"George. How are you?" Smith asked, handing him the umbrella he was carrying. He called a paramedic for a foil blanket.

"I don't know. I feel guilty, sir. If I'd have just got here earlier."

"Don't blame yourself, George. He could have easily added you to his body count." Smith hesitated before continuing. "Why were you here anyway?"

"After receiving more information about Eve from her background check, I wanted to question Eileen further. I wanted to ask why she lied," he said, studying Smith's reaction. It was an arduous task because of the rain, but there was no hint of anything other than concern. "I'm getting closer to the killer, sir. Eileen's death suggests our theory is correct. Though now, I feel as if he's trying to kill potential informants. From what I've seen in the kitchen, the MO matches. He was wearing exactly the same clothes as he was on the CCTV. He was also mopping up blood, which struck me as odd. Maybe he'd made an error somewhere? I think it's because we're putting pressure on him."

CHAPTER THIRTY-ONE

Smith nodded but said nothing more. He strolled inside the house to study the crime scene.

* * *

In all his time as a policeman, George had never seen any station so crowded. Uniform, HMET and CID swarmed the main reception area. He recognised some of them from his floor, but most of them were strangers. Somebody had set the heating on full, and intense blasts of heat struck him as he signed in. That, along with the large number of people, meant the atmosphere was both hot and stifling. The smell of sweat lingered. Whether it was his, or the people in the building, he wasn't sure. But that smell, mixed with the coppery remnants of Eileen Abbott's blood, made George nauseous. He just wanted to get naked and take a long, scalding shower.

The Incident Room was just as busy. As he approached, all eyes turned to him, reminding him of a time when he was little, and he'd been accused of breaking his mother's prized vase. His parents and grandparents had looked at him with a mixture of amazement and sadness. He was even sure his mum had been angry with him. It was probably why he had, other than the incredible memories of his time with Mark Finch, an indifference to his Scottish heritage. His father had beaten him black and blue that night.

Ignoring everyone, George shut the shutters in his office and changed into his spare suit, his skin itching from the temperature change.

He'd stayed at the Abbott house until the SOCOs were done documenting, following which he and Crime Scene Co-ordinator, Stuart Kent, had examined the body. This attack was different, his onslaught post-mortem more ferocious. Eileen was also murdered in her house, which was something new. Other than that, Eileen's death followed a similar pattern to both Erika's and Emma's. Her phone was missing, too. George's only other question was how the killer knew Eileen's address.

Chapter Thirty-two

George's thoughts were on Mia during his drive home, and so he called her. She wasn't answering. As luck would have it, George had Teagan's phone number saved on his mobile. Teagan was the woman Mia had temporarily moved in with, so he called her. She answered on the first ring and told him Mia had gone out with some of her work colleagues. By her pensive tone, George got the impression Teagan wanted to be out, too.

The cocktail bar she was at was in Morley, just on the outskirts of the centre. George knew it well, having met Mia there several times when they had first got together.

George parked up by the entrance, got out of his Honda and entered. The bar had character, and whilst George had never admitted it to Mia, he actually liked the place. It had once been a home for the Lord Mayor of Morley but had been redesigned and refurbished to create a luxurious environment. He spotted Mia and her colleagues immediately. Drinking and laughing, they were sitting on plush yellow chairs against the windows. He felt a momentary flash of annoyance that she complained about him not being home yet was out with her friends as if George had done something so terrible. He had worked his arse off the past two weeks, yet all he had received from her was abuse.

He recognised one or two of her colleagues, but there was a man sitting next to her who he did not know. George watched as he offered her a taste of his cocktail. He frowned as Mia put her crimson lips around the straw and sucked. She maintained eye contact as she did so, and a fire raged within him.

George approached the table. Mia spotted him and, eyes wide with shock, let the straw drop from the corner of her mouth. "George. What are you doing here?"

Without smiling, George said, "Hey, Mia. Teagan told me where you were. I was worried when I couldn't get in touch, so I thought I'd surprise you."

Mia stood up. "Well, you were successful in surprising me, George." The man whose drink she shared looked up at George with interest. He had a noticeable cleft lip scar, and George stared at it for a moment longer than he wanted. Her friends stopped talking, as did others in the bar. "Look, George, why don't you join us? Have a drink?" She tried to grab his wrist to pull him over, but he dodged it. She frowned. It made him angry.

"Mia, I came all this way to see you. Could I have a quick word?"

She excused herself, and George noticed she patted the man's hand. He was wearing gloves, which was odd considering they were inside. As she glided over to him, the smile had vanished from her face, as did the smile from the guy watching. The two men made eye contact. It was intense. Neither man wanted to look away, but George did because Mia spoke. "You've embarrassed me in front of my friends, George. Don't you think you could have given me some warning?"

"I tried calling, Mia. I know we're not together any more,

but do I need to warn you before I see you?" The man looked back at him. He had stood up and closed the distance slightly. He wasn't tall, about average height, with mousy brown hair.

"A warning would have been nice."

"Why? Is that so you don't get caught with other men?"

Her eyes narrowed. "What are you talking about?"

"Him." George pointed toward the man with the cocktail. "Is that William?"

"Don't do this, George. Not here."

"Don't do what? Is that William?"

"George—"

"Answer the question, Mia."

She shrugged petulantly. "Why? What do you care? It doesn't matter who he is, though if you must know, then yes, that's William from work."

"William," he said from behind them, offering his gloved hand. He'd managed to sneak up on them.

George looked him up and down, focussing on the cleft lip once again. He wore a navy suit with brown winkle pickers. "Detective Inspector George Beaumont," he replied. "I'd like to talk to Mia in private if that's alright with you?" William frowned, and George felt a sense of déjà vu.

"You're being rude, George," Mia hissed.

"Of course. What did you do to your hands, *William*?"

"My hands?" He held up his right hand to look and shook his head. "Nothing. Poor circulation. My hands get cold and stiff easily. I'm wearing socks if you'd like to check."

"Fair enough. Do you mind, *William*, if I have a quick word with Mia? Thank you."

William raised his gloved hands as if in surrender and grinned before turning and walking away. George breathed a sigh of relief. "Look, I'm sorry if I overreacted. You break up with me and then tell me you've been seeing somebody else. What was I supposed to expect when I see you out with another guy, Mia?"

She sighed. "I don't have to explain myself to you any more. And anyway, I'm not doing anything wrong. We broke up, remember?"

"So that's William is it? The guy you were seeing last year? He's the work colleague who got you to stay? No fucking wonder!"

Mia gazed at him for a long moment; then, she nodded her head. "Yes, George. I'm sorry we had to end the way we did." She tried to embrace him, but he pulled away and sighed.

"You should have just spoken to me, Mia, instead of cheating on me," he snapped, feeling the anger from his youth return. His blood was boiling, and he could feel it in his ears. His fists clenched on their own. He needed to calm down and work through the red mist.

Despite trying to hide it, her lips went up in a smirk. "This can't be easy for you, George. So go home. You're being rude anyway. I saw the way you looked at him, the way your gaze lingered on his facial scar."

She was being totally unreasonable. "No, don't you dare do that, Mia. Don't make me out to be the bad guy. Does he even know who I am?"

"Of course he does," she said. "But he isn't to blame for anything, George. You are."

"Now, who's being ridiculous? I'm not to blame for your cheating. You are."

"Whatever, George. I'm going back to my friends," she said as she spun on her heel. He got a hint of her perfume, the perfume that still lingered on her pillow. "We're through. I don't want to see you ever again."

* * *

The killer watched as Emilia Alexander left the cocktail bar and said goodbye to her friends. He could tell by the way she wobbled on her heels that she was slightly tipsy. After his mistakes earlier that day, he wondered if he should take her now. The alcohol had dulled her senses. It was dark. She was vulnerable, and it would have been so easy.

All he had to do was get her alone, but he decided against it. It wasn't the right time.

As he had done with every kill, he followed behind her at a short distance, his hood pulled up and head bent down to avoid the cameras. It was apparent they were looking for him. He wouldn't be surprised if he were currently on every police officer's most wanted list. And most areas in Leeds were now littered with CCTV cameras. With both council and private cameras, there was no privacy any more.

Detective Inspector George Beaumont, her ex-fiancé, was in charge of the case. He'd seen George earlier that day as he fled from Miss Abbott's house. He looked bigger on the television, more commanding. In life, he was nothing. Taking Mia from him would be child's play. It shouldn't be, though. He'd expected more reassurance patrols, leaflets to be distributed, press conferences telling women not to walk alone after dark. As a Yorkshire man, his idol was the Yorkshire Ripper, and as his body count increased, he knew he was feeling the same euphoria Sutcliffe must have felt.

He shivered in excitement. Sometimes he couldn't quite

believe he'd managed to become a serial murderer. He'd carried out what Sutcliffe had done all those years ago. And like Sutcliffe, the press had even given him a nickname. The hairs on his arms prickled in anticipation. *The Miss Murderer.* It felt like a dream come true.

He watched as Mia went into a taxi rank. Instead of opting to sit inside, she stood unsteadily on the pavement, her heels buckling with every step. She was an attractive woman with an incredible body. He knew he must have it soon and was looking forward to making her pay.

A taxi arrived, and she leaned through the window to ask if it was hers. She flirted with the guy, and the hooded man's eyes were drawn to the way her denim skirt rode up the back of her thighs. The thought of slicing that from her body sent shivers throughout his entire body. Like all straight men, women made him weak. They knew what they did to men. The way they teased them with the clothes they wore or the way they used touch, or a lack of it, to entice. He'd been a victim of it his entire life. They were in control, and he knew it.

The only way he knew how to wrest back control was to slide his cock inside them whilst his hands tightly squeezed their necks.

The taxi driver nodded, and she opened the back door and climbed in.

The Miss Murderer vanished into the shadows. He didn't need to follow her because he knew where she was going. "It'll soon be your turn, Miss Alexander," he whispered to himself as he watched the taxi drive away. "Just you wait."

Chapter Thirty-three

Thanks to the conversation with Mia and the resulting restless night, George arrived at work early. He'd had unsettling dreams about Mia and the murderer. George couldn't get the image of the hooded man bent down in Eileen Abbott's kitchen, knife in hand, out of his head. The picture he had was monstrous, a caricature rather than an accurate representation. Yawning, George went to make coffee, only for him to decide he wasn't in the mood for the cheap shit at the station. On his way back to his own office, he glanced towards Smith's and saw only darkness. That struck him as odd. The DSU was usually the first one in. it was Sunday, though, and he usually didn't work weekends. Maybe that was why?

He'd wish he'd stopped by Starbucks on his way in and bought himself a coffee, but it meant using the drive-through, and the drinks there were usually hit and miss. Being early, his preferred place inside the cinema was closed. George needed coffee, though, so he got in his Honda and drove to McDonald's. After ordering a bacon roll with brown sauce and a large black coffee, he doubled his order as an afterthought, assuming Smith would be in when he got back. George appreciated his boss for how he pacified DCS Mohammed Sadiq and kept him as the SIO.

"Thanks for having my back yesterday, sir," George said, offering up his bounty. Despite there being a serial killer on the loose, Smith seemed surprised to see him there.

Smith raised a brow and laughed. "Bribing me, Beaumont?"

George placed the items on Smith's desk. "No, sir. Just showing my appreciation. Thanks."

George turned to leave but turned on his heel when Smith said, "My pleasure, George. You're doing a good job. How come you're here so early on a Sunday? You got a new lead or something?"

"Same could be said for you, sir," George said with a laugh. "But no, nothing new. I—I couldn't sleep, so I came in. Thought I'd go over the reports on HOLMES."

Smith nodded before giving him a long look. "The case getting to you?"

George hesitated, and Smith raised a knowing brow. "Nope. We're getting close. I've been drinking a lot of caffeine recently. I promised to cut down today, so I'll probably sleep like a baby tonight."

"Sure." His boss' gaze dropped to the empty coffee cup in George's hand, then back up to his face again. He raised his brow again but didn't smile. Nothing got by that man. "You and Wood off to Strangeways today?"

"Yes, sir, as soon as she gets in."

"Good. Good. How's she doing as deputy SIO?"

George tried to hide his smile. "She's intelligent, thorough, and has a keen initiative, sir. The utmost professional. I've got no complaints."

"Good, glad to hear it. I've followed her career for a while, and I won't lie to you, I headhunted her from Wakefield. She's an outstanding officer, George, and judging by her reports, one who has excellent attention to detail. I suspect it's only a matter of time before she takes the Inspectors Exam."

George nodded but didn't reply. Wood had other qualities, qualities he couldn't share with his boss. She was easy to be with and was always one step ahead. Sharp as a tack. Her instincts were usually on the nose, and her questioning and observations were on point. He couldn't have asked for a better sergeant.

"I'll let you get back to whatever you were doing, George." He was taken aback by the politeness of the dismissal and wondered for a moment whether the strict detective superintendent was warming to him. As he walked back to his office, he wondered what it'd be like to have Jim Smith's job, what it would be like being in charge. His office was naturally the largest, and looked down at the floor below. There were blinds for privacy, but the DSU hardly ever used them. George suspected it was because Smith wanted to be involved at every level of every investigation. He wondered for a moment whether Smith was envious of the detectives who worked down on the floor. They were the ones who went to the crime scenes, the ones out on the streets interviewing witnesses. Smith's job was primarily managerial. He dealt with all the stuff George wasn't very good at, such as the politics, the taking of press calls, and the sweet-talking of those of higher rank than he.

George took a seat in his office and turned his attention back to the folder on his desk. David Clark. DCI Roberts had been right about Clark's youth, especially regarding how much of a troublemaker he was. Clark had been suspended frequently from school; once, because he'd lost his temper when a supply teacher asked him to sit in a seat he didn't want to sit in. A seat change seemed trivial to George, and as he read further, he saw David had received several warnings from the police for fighting. It was clear he had a temper. And tempers were usually involved when it came to crimes of passion, which was what DCI Roberts had mentioned.

There were no mentions of any offences in his file from 2012 onwards. It appeared that after meeting Eve Allgood, David Clark had turned over a new leaf. It seemed evident to George that David was trying to rectify those mistakes from his youth; he was working full time and then attending college in the evenings.

There was nothing from his youth to suggest he had any murderous tendencies. There was a proven link between killers and actions from their youth. Often, killers start abusing and killing animals at an early age, an age where they may have witnessed violence. His family life had been stable, and character references never made a mention of any animal abuse. He just didn't seem like a man capable of murder, but then, killers usually didn't.

He spoke to Wood about those concerns as they drove along the M62 to Strangeways. She was once again sat in the passenger seat of George's Honda, looking incredibly beautiful, absorbed in the case folder open on her lap.

"I agree with you, George," she said with a smile. "From a psychological point of view, I can see nothing to suggest why David Clark would kill. Maybe the retired DCI was correct; maybe it was a one-off?"

"Is that what you believe?"

"No. Clark had reformed. He was trying to get his life back on track. Why would Clark throw that away, suddenly rape and mutilate the woman he loved? He'd never laid a hand on her before. Looking at the police reports, Clark never laid a hand on any woman before. It makes no sense."

"If we consider our earlier theory, maybe Clark had caught her sleeping with someone else?" George thought about Mia but quashed his thoughts immediately. "He'd reformed, but it's not as if a person with a temper just stops being angry overnight. I opted for boxing. It helped me to expel any pent-up aggression I had simmering. I can't see that Clark did anything similar. Maybe he snapped? Maybe an affair sent him over the edge. The retired DCI could have been right. Maybe it was a crime of passion?"

Wood looked sceptical. "It's pointless guessing, but you make an excellent point, though you don't know it."

George turned to her and frowned. "What?"

"Think about what you just told me, but flip it. We have our killer. Maybe our killer was the one who Eve was sleeping with? But then Clark found out, and the affair ended. That sent our killer over the edge, and he killed her, framing Clark for the murder. Maybe that's why he's escalating."

George thought back to his conversation with Smith and the words he hadn't said. 'She was easy to be with and always one step ahead. Sharp as a tack. Her instincts were usually on the nose, and her questioning and observations on point.' He was right; he really couldn't have asked for a better sergeant.

"We'll just have to ask him, George, and see what he says. Although there was no mention of her cheating on him in the report."

"I agree, Wood. It's difficult to keep the truth from the courts, but I suppose it's possible her mother didn't know. That, or she didn't want to admit it."

Wood shrugged. "We can ask her when we see her."

"That we can."

Wood fell silent. George took the A56 exit to Prestwich/Whitefield. Being Sunday morning, the traffic was light, and he'd managed the hit speed limit the entire way there. According to his sat nav, they only had four miles to go.

Chapter Thirty-four

David Clark was the shadow of the man he had been before. That much was clear. George hadn't expected such a transformation, but then he had been behind bars for ten years. Clark's head, which had been full of brown hair in the picture from his folder, was now nearly bald. He was much thinner, too. Gone were the muscles, as was the tan. His skin was pale and thin, almost translucent. Clark barely glanced up as they walked in.

After introducing himself and Wood, he sat down. Wood scraped a chair over. The silence was deafening. He noticed the wooden table was bolted to the floor, as was Clark's chair. The atmosphere was intense, suffocating. George glanced at Wood, who nodded back. On their way over, they'd devised an interview strategy. George would clarify the basics; then Wood would step in and be the more emotive of the pair. Her questions were the important ones. George was just there to warm him up.

"Mr Clark—"

"David. My dad was Mr Clark." He didn't look up, and his voice wavered as he spoke.

At least he was cooperating, George thought.

"David, we're here to ask you some questions about Eve

Allgood and the night she was murdered."

He nodded slowly; his head still bowed down. "What happened? In your own words, David."

There was a visible shrug. "Who knows? I don't. Because I wasn't there when she died, I was nowhere near her."

"OK, so where were you?"

"I was at home watching the footy. I don't know where Eve was."

"Was that usual for Eve?" George asked. David Clark said nothing, so George clarified. "Did you often not know where Eve was?"

He shook his head. "She struggled. Daily. We had a great relationship, but sometimes she would disappear for a day or two and then show up with no warning, without apology. I got used to it. It was her birthday the day after she went missing. To be honest, it wasn't unusual for her to go missing during that time of the year."

"And why do you think she struggled?" asked George.

David took a long moment, his breathing harsh and ragged. He coughed repeatedly and considered asking the guard for a glass of water. They wouldn't allow it, though, so he never bothered. Eventually, he said, "She was on meds for her anxiety and depression. They did weird shit to her, you know? There was something about her birthday she never liked, too. She struggled. I left her to it."

"You didn't worry when she didn't come home that night?" Wood asked, her voice soft. David looked up at her, realising Wood was speaking for the first time.

David smiled at her. "No. As I said, it wasn't unusual. Look what is this really about? Eve's been dead for over ten years. She was the best bloody thing to ever happen to me, yet she was

CHAPTER THIRTY-FOUR

taken away, and I was locked up in here. You're just opening up fresh wounds, man."

"I understand that this may be difficult for you, David, but we need to ask you some more questions. Is that OK?" Wood asked.

He looked up at the recognition of Wood's voice. George, to his annoyance, wasn't getting much from him, but Wood was. "Fire away."

"Did Eve ever mention anyone following her or watching her in the days leading up to her murder?" Wood said, gently probing.

David's eyes widened. "In the beginning of our relationship, she had this ex-flame, some lad from Leeds, come over and visit. I can't remember his name, but he was looking at coming to work in Manchester. He'd been calling her and waiting for her outside her work, that sort of thing. I don't think he could accept the fact that she'd moved on. Her mum didn't like him much, either."

"Did she ever report him?" Wood asked gently. David shook his head, and for a moment, Wood met George's astonished gaze. It was a gaze that said they'd been right—a murder with a similar MO and a similar pattern of stalking just before.

George couldn't understand how the police had missed it, despite it not being reported. It was one of the first questions they asked.

"Why not, David? Why didn't she report it?" Wood was grinning.

"Because she told me it would cause too much trouble. She'd had a word, apparently, telling him to back off; otherwise, she'd make it difficult for him. We both thought it had worked. And it did, for a while. He moved to Greater Manchester. To

Middleton. I nearly went 'round to see him myself. I can be very persuasive when I want to be."

Wood nodded. "Did Eve ever go into specifics with you?" This could be their guy. Their theory of Eve being girl zero could be correct. Was Eve the girl who'd broken his heart and sent him over the edge? Was she the one who'd accidentally set this monster on the world?

David looked down again. "She said they'd never actually been in a relationship together. Eve had apparently made a mistake once, back in Leeds, one that she came to regret. We had a fight about it, but she convinced me it had meant nothing to her. The problem was that the guy wouldn't leave her alone. He'd wait for her to finish work and beg her to give him another chance. It was really pathetic. Before she'd warned him off, it was getting so bad that he'd call several times a day until she blocked him from her phone. The threat of the police worked, or so I assumed. I got fed up, though, and like, threatened to break it off with her if she didn't tell me who he was."

"And did she?" jumped in George. "Did she tell you who he was?"

"Yes, but not as much as I hoped. All she told me was that he was a nobody. Not even an ex. Just a one-off. He had been the reason she moved from Leeds to York."

"How long did contact stop before she died, David?"

David thought for a moment. "I don't believe the contact stopped, to be honest with you. But if I go with what Eve told me, then about a month before she died. She told me he got a job on the other side of Manchester and was starting that summer. That's why he stopped harassing her. He apparently needed a clean record for the job he had."

"Think carefully for me, David," Wood said. "Did she tell

you what job he had?"

"No. And I never asked. All I know is that the threat to take him to the police stopped the stalking."

George thought about the different jobs you'd need a clean record for but gave up when the list got into double digits. He could have worked anywhere, and without a name, they were stuck. But speaking to David had clarified George's thoughts about the Miss Murderer.

"Did you know Eve had once been a teacher?" Wood asked softly. George could see Wood had reached the same conclusion he had: David had been wrongly charged. He'd been the fall guy for Eve's murder, and the guy was still out there. The man without a name had subsequently become the notorious Miss Murderer.

"Yeah, she mentioned it."

"What did she tell you about it?"

"Not much," David said, a confused look on his face. "I wouldn't have known if it wasn't for the stalker."

"What do you mean?"

"Well, I saw the texts. He always called her Miss Allgood. Not Eve. She told me it was a pet name for her as she used to be a teacher. But that's it."

"Did you find it odd she didn't teach in Manchester?"

David hesitated. He shook his head. "No. Should I have? Look, I've got to ask. Is the case being reopened? Am I going to get out of here?" There was hope in the prisoner's voice. George looked him in the eye but said nothing. He had a forlorn look about him, and George thought he knew why. When David had been arrested, everyone had assumed he was guilty, and no one would have stopped to think that he was grieving, too.

He chose his words carefully. "I take it you're familiar with the Miss Murderer case in Leeds?"

"Yeah, we're allowed to read the paper, and the news is always on the TV."

"We're working on a new line of inquiry, and we think this guy, this old flame of Eve's, might be involved."

David perked up. "And you're here because you believe he was the one who murdered Eve?"

"We can't discuss the details." Like George, Wood was equally conscious of giving Clark false hope. "As Inspector Beaumont said, it's a line of inquiry in an ongoing investigation. But if you could give us any information so we can find him, we may be able to find out whether he was involved."

David's face fell. "I... I'm sorry. I don't know anything about him because I left Eve to it. Or should I say, she kept me out of it? I had a bad temper. It was for the best."

"Did Eve ever describe him to you?" Wood knew she was grasping at straws. "Did she say anything that will assist us in finding him? Such as his hair or eye colour? Or whether he had any piercings or tattoos? You understand?"

David opened his eyes and scratched the back of his head. "I want to say he had some kind of deformity. I'm sure I remember once after he'd called, she had been angry and called him a deformed freak." He closed his eyes again. "I don't know if that helps?"

"Of course, David." Wood assured him. "Did you question her about the deformity?"

He ignored the question. "Look, I need to know. Can I get out of this hellhole if you catch this guy?" A light behind David's eyes that hadn't been there earlier on in the conversation appeared.

George shook his head. "The DCI who ran the murder

investigation has a lot of evidence to tie you to the crime, David. So it's not that simple, I'm afraid. We'd have to link him to Eve's death, and after all this time, we'd be lucky to find any forensic evidence. If our guy is the guy who set you up, then all we can hope for is a confession. I'm sorry."

David's shoulders slumped. "So what you're saying is, even though I'm innocent, I have to rot in here while your guy gets to walk about and kill people. I didn't kill Eve. Believe me. Please..."

Wood leaned forward and for a moment, George thought she was going to grab his hand. She didn't. "It's the best you can hope for. Help us find him, David. Try to remember his name. We can do so much with a name. Think. Then, if we find him, we can concentrate on linking him to Eve's death."

David scratched his head more furiously as if he was trying to kick-start his brain. His other hand, the one near Wood's, taped an arpeggio on the wooden table. "I'm sorry. Since the trial, I've not thought about the guy. I've spent ten years in here worrying every day. This isn't a nice place. I'm stuck with criminals. I'm not a criminal, detectives. The only person who may know is her mum, actually."

George clenched his fist. Her mum. Of course. David had mentioned her dislike of the stalker earlier. "Thanks, we will speak with her."

A sullen look broke out on David's face. "I don't think you can... She used to visit me, you know, and would ask me why I killed her daughter. I never refused the visits because I wanted to convince her I was innocent. But she stopped coming one day. I found out that she has dementia. She might not be able to help you."

George frowned. "Thanks. I appreciate it."

"I'm sorry, Detective."

There was a pause in the interview's flow, so George repeated Wood's question from earlier. "Did you ever question her about the stalker's deformity?"

Clark shook his head and slammed his fist down on the table. Knowing they had nothing else to ask, George, smiled and stood up. "Please, David. Have a real think about that name and get in touch with me. I work out of Elland Road Police Station in Leeds."

He nodded. "Great stadium. Amazing atmosphere. Glad they're back in the Prem." They shook hands.

George left the room feeling deflated. David hadn't confirmed the information from the background check, and he also hadn't given them much information to go on. He glanced through the glass pane as the door shut, and David waved.

Wood waved back at the man, a man now filled with hope.

It made George want to catch the killer even more.

Chapter Thirty-five

The pair discussed Eve's phone records that Wood had requisitioned as George drove the five miles to the Middleton in Greater Manchester.

Wood explained to George that she would rule out the common numbers they knew first, such as David, Eve's mother, or work. Then any others, she would Google and see if they could get any results.

"The numbers you need should be in the original case file," George said as he kept his eyes on the road. It was a cold, overcast day, with a temperature of six degrees Celsius, below average for this time of year.

Wood retrieved the document she needed and scribbled the numbers down on a notepad before highlighting those numbers on the phone records.

George let her concentrate, knowing they had little time, about fifteen minutes, before arriving at Marie Allgood's.

When they pulled up outside Mrs Allgood's house, George glanced at the document on her lap. "Any luck?"

"Yeah, maybe. There's one number that starts calling and texting rather frequently but then suddenly stops."

"Sounds about right to me."

She fired off a text message and explained to George that it had been to DS Joshua Fry. "It'll be a burner phone, no doubt. But we might get lucky, and he may have used his own contract phone."

George thought the killer wouldn't have risked using his own phone, but then again, he may not have realised he was going to kill Eve. "Lucky. When have we ever been lucky during this investigation?" George laughed, trying to make it light-hearted, but Wood just raised her brow. She was thinking the same as him.

"David was right, though; about a month before Eve was killed, the calls and texts ceased."

"The warning?"

Wood nodded. "Probably."

"So, he gives up calling and texting and takes up stalking instead?"

Wood glanced sideways at him and ran a hand through her hair. She had eyeliner on, which made her dark eyes altogether more striking. She wasn't the type of girl to need makeup, George thought, but despite that, he was sure her lips were a shade more crimson than usual. He liked it. Mia always wore makeup, so George never really noticed when she told him she'd 'put the effort in' for him. Wood's looks had distracted him, and so he missed what she'd said, asking her to repeat it. She laughed. "I agree. But why the escalation to murder? What happened?"

"Yeah, I'd like to know the trigger," George said. He felt awkward sitting outside Mrs Allgood's house, but he was enjoying Wood's company. She was close to him, their elbows kissing. "But whatever that trigger was, Wood, once he'd killed Eve, I'm guessing he realised he could get away with it, and so he carried on doing it. Mark Finch said it could have made him feel empowered."

"I wonder, George... I wonder just how many lives that man has destroyed? How many more women's deaths has he had a hand in?" Her voice was weak. "Ten years is a long time. I'll bet there's more out there."

"We looked at as many cold cases as we could," George said. "Only one other matched his MO, and I put DC Scott on that. A young lady was killed in a place between Driffield and Market Weighton. Guess what the place is called?"

"Middleton?" she mused. George nodded his head, and she turned her head to gaze out of the window. "I didn't know there was a Middleton in East Yorkshire."

"Yeah, Middleton on the Wolds, a village of about 900 people. There's one in North Yorkshire, too, west of Pickering."

* * *

Mrs Allgood lived in a well-presented detached house in the Woodside area of Alkrington in Middleton, Greater Manchester. The street was lined with trees blossoming, and the houses on her side were all identical. All were constructed of orange-coloured brick that shone in the afternoon sun, all with double drives and garages with white doors. Those drives were filled with expensive motors, motors George could only dream of owning on his DI salary.

"This is definitely the place," Wood said. "No car, though. I guess that's understandable, considering what David told us. I hope she's well enough to give us something."

They'd called ahead after meeting with David to make sure Mrs Allgood would be in. Wood rang the buzzer. The door opened, and a blonde young woman wearing a blue carer's uniform stood smiling at them.

They showed off their warrant cards and, after introducing themselves, were allowed to enter. "How's Mrs Allgood today?" George asked as he wiped his feet on the doormat. As Mrs Allgood had been diagnosed with early onset Alzheimer's, Olive was her live-in carer.

"So far, so good. She seems to be having a good day." After taking George's jacket and Wood's coat, Olive ushered them in. "Welcome. She's just in there. That's the living room."

They followed Olive into a tidy living room, who approached the woman sitting in an armchair. "Mrs Allgood, the detectives are here. You know, the ones I mentioned?" She laid a hand gently on Mrs Allgood's shoulder, who looked up and nodded. "They have come to talk to you."

"Detectives. Why?"

"They want to talk to you about Eve, Marie." Olive spoke slowly and clearly. "I told you earlier they were coming?"

"Oh, yes." The woman gave them a smile and offered them a place to sit.

Wood and George sat down on an old, mulberry-coloured sofa and immediately met in the middle. The cushions below them had impacted, and it was impossible to sit upright. George met Wood's gaze, and they both tried not to laugh. In the end, they gave up trying to sit on their respective sides and nuzzled closely against each other. Wood had decided an unfamiliar scent was in order, George thought. Vanilla with a hint of black coffee. Perfect.

"I'm sorry, detectives. I tend to forget things. How can I help you both?" Mrs Allgood was much younger than George had expected. She was barely sixty, with a short blonde bob that was turning white, and wore a red blouse with black trousers.

He could immediately see the resemblance to Eve.

"No need to apologise," said a smiling Wood. "We appreciate you seeing us."

"I'll make us all tea," Olive said before she scurried off.

"I don't see many people these days. It's nice to have company," Mrs Allgood said.

Knowing Mrs Allgood's 'good day' may not last and not wanting to miss the opportunity that her 'good day' provided them with, George began to question her. "Mrs Allgood, I'd like to ask you some questions about Eve."

Her eyes, ones that were cornflower blue, darkened as she thought about her daughter. "Of course. I miss her. She was the perfect daughter. Beautiful, intelligent, and respectful. Yet all of that was taken away from me. From the world. By that man. She promised me he'd changed, but clearly not."

George was taken aback. He hadn't expected this from Marie, but he probably should have. The evidence that convicted David Clark had been 'irrefutable.'

"I'm sorry to bring up what must be terrible memories for you," George said.

She waved his apology away. "Every memory I have of Eve is good. And with my condition, I feel blessed to remember them," she said. "This terrible disease has only made me struggle with my short-term memory at the moment," she added.

Olive walked in carrying a tray with a pot of tea, three cups, and a plate of biscuits. She set it down on the table and said, "Unless you want me to stay, Marie, I'll leave you all to it." Marie Allgood ushered her away, and Olive disappeared back to the kitchen.

"She's good to me, is Olive. She reminds me so much of Eve."

Mrs Allgood leaned back in her chair. "So, what did you want to know about my daughter?"

George reached for the pot and poured tea into the three cups. Wood took hers black, as did he, and so it turns out, did Marie. He sat back down and balanced it on the arm of the sofa. "Do you know of a brief relationship Eve had before the two of you left Leeds? I don't know if you remember, or even know, because intelligence suggests it was a one-off, but he gave your daughter a hard time when she started dating David. He called and texted her relentlessly and wouldn't leave her alone."

Mrs Allgood stared through him for a long moment, and he thought he saw her blue darken further. He thought perhaps she hadn't understood the question and opened his mouth to repeat the question when she whispered, "That man. How could I forget?"

Wood had dunked one of the rich tea fingers in her tea and, at Marie's answer, nearly dropped the entire biscuit into her cup. "Please tell us everything you know about that man."

Marie crinkled up her forehead before closing her eyes. George found he was holding his breath. This could be the break they so desperately needed.

After an excruciating minute, she said, "That man ruined my daughter's life. That's all I can remember. It's why we moved to York. To get away from him."

Wood raised her eyebrows expectantly. "Anything else, Mrs Allgood? Do you remember his name?"

"I'm sorry, dear, I can't remember."

George only just concealed his disappointment, and Wood's face dropped. The woman had Alzheimer's, so they knew it had been a long shot. George thought it had been a miracle she'd

CHAPTER THIRTY-FIVE

remembered her own daughter, let alone the man stalking her.

"Oh, that's not a problem. Thank you. Any minute details help." George saw her shoulders drop.

"Is there anything you can tell us about him?" George asked. He was unwilling to give up just yet. As Wood said, the minor details mattered. "What did he look like, Mrs Allgood? Can you remember anything, anything at all, about him?" He was grasping at straws, but he was desperate.

"I'm sorry, dear, I'm afraid I can't remember much about him other than it being his fault we moved. That, to me, means he lived in Middleton. The one in Leeds, not Manchester. Her dad would have known, but he's no longer with us. He died a few years before Eve, back in York. It was why we moved here."

"Thank you, Mrs Allgood. I have just one more question if that's OK?"

She smiled and nodded her head. "Why was Eve barred from working with children and vulnerable adults?"

Marie Allgood's eyes clouded over, and, lost in her thoughts, she gazed out of the window. She sat like that for a few minutes, and neither detective dared to interrupt her.

Olive came into the room and broke the silence. "Is everything OK in here?" she asked.

George met Wood's gaze and got up. "Yes, thank you, Olive. I think we're done here. We've bothered Mrs Allgood enough."

Wood put her half-drunk cup of tea on the table. "Thank you, Mrs Allgood. We really appreciate you talking to us."

But Marie Allgood didn't answer her and instead continued to gaze out of the window.

Olive showed them out but stopped them at the foot of the stairs. "How did that go?"

Wood answered after George hesitated. "We got very little, but it's understandable considering her condition. We're sorry to have caused distress."

"I wouldn't say you caused any distress. She was happy for the company. And I don't know if it's of interest," she explained. "But Mrs Allgood's got all of Eve's things still up in her bedroom."

Wood glanced at George and then said, "Eve's bedroom is still intact?"

Olive nodded. "I clean it weekly. It's what I was asked to do. There are quite a lot of boxes and things. Apparently, the detectives checked her room, but from what Marie told me, they hardly looked. I also found some boxes that were in the loft from when Eve was younger."

George's heart began to beat wildly in his chest. "Would Mrs Allgood mind if we took a quick look?" he asked. "There might be something that could help us."

"To tell you the truth," Olive said. "She asked me to get rid of the boxes months ago, but I didn't quite have the heart to. She won't mind one bit."

Chapter Thirty-six

The bedroom was immaculate, just as Olive had explained. Sitting on the floor were two boxes, both covered in dust as if they hadn't been cleaned in years. "Look at all this stuff," Wood said as she opened one of the boxes. It was filled with folders and notebooks. George assumed they were most likely relics from Eve's teaching days.

Wood leafed through the contents of the first box. "Anything promising, Wood?" George asked.

She shook her head. "No. Nothing. Just teaching plans and notes made from several courses and training days. You look through these to see if I've missed anything," she said, "and I'll check the other box."

He knew he didn't need to double-check Wood's work but humoured her. "It's weird, you know?" George said.

"What is?"

"This is all that's left of somebody's life," George said as he returned the folders filled with teaching material back into the box. "It's quite... harrowing."

"It's so sad, isn't it?" Wood said. "She was reading what looked to be a diary, and he was sure a stray tear fell from her eye. He wanted to comfort her, yet he knew it wasn't right. "She was very eloquent. Descriptive. This is from when she was a teenager. I'll see if there are any diaries from when she was a teacher."

George nodded and clenched his fists. "For Eve's sake and the others, too, we have to catch this bastard. He's destroyed too many lives."

"I think you're right, Wood. This looks to be just teaching stuff. Nothing personal, just work."

Wood shared out the remaining diaries. George checked for dates, knowing she had been barred at the end of 2007 before being killed in 2014. There was nothing. Wood emptied the box and thumbed through the diaries again. "Did she stop writing? Or did the police take them as evidence. I don't remember seeing them in the file. Let me check with DCI Roberts."

As Wood took out her phone, a voice spoke through the partially closed door. "I'm sorry to eavesdrop, but I have a third explanation." It was Olive's voice.

Olive knocked and opened it. "I was just refreshing Mrs Allgood's room when I heard you, talking about the missing diaries."

"The missing diaries?" George's pulse rate rose. "Why missing?"

Olive looked anxious as she bounced from one foot to the other. She bit her lip. "I started working for Mrs Allgood about four or five years ago, and a detective came to the house asking questions about Eve."

Wood and Beaumont shared a confused look. "A detective?" George asked. "I don't remember reading anything about the Greater Manchester Police asking questions again. As far as we were aware, the case was closed. David Clark was Eve's murderer. We are the only ones to have questioned anything."

"Yeah, I know," Olive murmured. "I might have made a

terrible error that day."

Wood lifted her head to stare at Olive. "What error? What day?"

"Well," said Olive. "I remember the man knocking at the door. He wore a suit, showed me what looked like a warrant card and said he was working on behalf of David Clark. The man looked the part. He even had a briefcase. Apparently, David had tried to appeal his sentence, and they were duty bound to look into the case. I think now that I play the memory back that he was full of shit."

"Why?" George asked.

"Because he didn't want to speak with Marie. She was asleep at the time, and he was quite happy to check through Eve's bedroom."

George understood what Olive meant. Any detective would want to speak to Marie Allgood in a case like that. "Did you not report it to the police later on? You know, when you realised he was full of shit?"

Her face turned crimson. "I was afraid of losing my job. I wasn't sure the man wasn't a detective, so I didn't want to risk speaking with the police. It would have resulted in me losing my job. Nothing came of it."

"There's nothing in here that would help anyway," Wood said.

Olive nodded and closed her eyes. "I know that. So I let him up in the attic. I told him about the boxes. He didn't spend much time up there, to tell you the truth. The boxes had been disturbed, but I didn't see him with any diaries in his hands. Nor did he tell me he had taken anything."

"So why do you suspect diaries are missing, Olive?" Wood asked.

"Well, because Mrs Allgood told me Eve continued to write in her diaries until the day she died. It was how she came to terms with everything." She looked down again, her cheeks flushed, before looking at Wood and saying, "I've read the diaries myself, and they stop abruptly."

Wood nodded and smiled. "Came to terms with what, Olive?"

"Marie and Eve moved to Greater Manchester after Mr Allgood passed away. But they'd moved away from Leeds to York before then because Eve got pregnant."

"Pregnant? What happened to the baby?" George asked. There had been no mention of a child in any of the reports.

"I've no idea. That's all I know, I promise. But somebody had gotten her pregnant in Leeds. And I know something happened there that meant she had to come to terms with it. But that's it. I didn't pry. I promise."

"What did the man look like?"

"Average height with brown hair. He had a beard. It was so long ago."

"What was the detective's name?" She wanted to believe that the fake detective was the killer, a man who needed to take evidence to stop himself from being later convicted. But she also knew she couldn't afford to get her hopes up.

"Bill Harris."

* * *

They immediately spoke with Mrs Allgood, who confirmed that Eve had been pregnant, but when asked about the father or what happened to the baby, she said she couldn't remember. At the recollection of the partial memory, Mrs Allgood's eyes

CHAPTER THIRTY-SIX

began to glaze over, so Wood asked her about Bill Harris, but she said she had no recollection of that name.

It wasn't exactly what they wanted, but if Eve had given birth, then the father's name may have been put on the birth certificate. Wood also said they should check for any adoption records relating to Eve Allgood. George called DS Jenny Bird and asked her to check into it. He asked DC Scott to look into the name Bill Harris too.

They quickly left, Olive showing them out.

George drove as fast as he dared back to Strangeways. Despite being in his personal car, he put the siren on and flashed his lights repeatedly to warn motorists to get out of the way. As if like Moses with the Red Sea, the traffic parted, and they raced towards Strangeways with no issues.

Unfortunately for them, David Clark did not know who Bill Harris was, nor did he know Eve had ever been pregnant.

They were back to square one again.

* * *

By the time they got back from the prison, Wood and George had discussed every angle of Eve's pregnancy and the stealing of her diaries by Bill Harris before they settled on a plan of action.

George's phone rang as they walked into the squad room. It was DSU Smith. His boss hung up as soon as he saw them. "I'm glad you're back. How'd it go at Strangeways?"

George filled him in.

"Poor guy," said Smith. "Imagine spending ten years in that hellhole for a crime you didn't commit."

"Yeah, on top of losing the person you love." George shook

his head. "I think the worst thing of all is even if we catch this guy, we have no forensic evidence to link him to Eve Allgood's murder. It means David will still be stuck inside."

"The bastard could confess?" said Smith. "It's common for serial killers to want people to know what they did. Look at Levi Bellfield. They're looking into his confession of the hammer murders of mum and daughter Lin and Megan Russell. He confessed two years ago, yet they're still looking into it." At George's surprised look, he added, "You might know that Michael Stone was handed a life sentence and believed to be the murderer, but he, like David, has always protested his innocence. I'm told he'll be released soon."

George hadn't known about Stone's possible release, so he just nodded. "Sir, once I find more info about Bill Harris or Eve's pregnancy, I'll let you know."

Chapter Thirty-seven

"How about a drink and some food, George?" Wood asked George when he returned from Smith's office. Her eyes shone with excitement, and her cheeks were flushed. He thought she looked gorgeous. It had been a long day for them. They'd barely had anything to eat or drink; such was the frantic pace of the investigation. He wanted to say yes but felt guilty. It was Sunday, every member of his team was in, and it wouldn't do for the boss to leave early.

But George thought about Smith and his advice about delegating. Every detective under his command was busy, and all he had to do was update their events in Greater Manchester on HOLMES 2. Then he'd return to his cold, empty house. There seemed little point in going home. "Let me finish this report first, but why not? I know a great pub that's quiet and has good food."

They left the police station in separate cars and headed towards the pub just off Bradford Road in East Ardsley. It was a Sunday night and would be quiet, and he knew from experience that the food was delicious. He'd never taken Mia, nor had he been there with any of his mates, so he and Wood would be uninterrupted.

Not that he saw his mates much any more. He used to be

a season ticket holder for both Leeds United and the Leeds Rhinos, often going to both matches in the week if they didn't clash. Rugby league and football were good like that, where matches barely clashed. Now that Mia had left him, it made sense that he reconnected with his old pals. He shouldn't have dumped them in the first place, really, but his new relationship and recent promotion to Inspector had taken all his free time up.

After parking their cars, George led her to a table at the back where they'd have a degree of privacy. They passed a brick fireplace that crackled and threw a glowing sparkle of light onto the rosewood tables. There were a few television screens mounted on the walls showing a Premier League match, the half-four kick-off of City versus Wolves. George remembered that in the real world, the real world where people went about their everyday lives, the footy was still on. The season would be over by the end of next month, and he could count on one hand how many matches he'd seen.

Wood twisted her body towards him as he sat down, and as she removed her jacket and sat down herself, George caught himself staring at the gap in her blouse where three buttons had come undone. He instantly averted his eyes, but he was sure she'd noticed his gaze.

The hint of a white lace bra was all he could think about as she tried to talk to him about food. As was the fact that she'd decided to sit right beside him, rather than opposite, so they could both view the menu. He wasn't listening, which was unusual because he was suddenly very aware of her closeness.

It was one of those pubs where you ordered food and drink at the bar, and Wood decided it would be her treat. She returned with two pints which she set down between them. Her blouse had escaped from her skirt and his face flushed as he glimpsed a flash of tanned skin. "This place is really nice, George. Do you come here a lot?"

"Not a lot, no. Usually, I tend to come here alone. You know, when I get bogged down and need peace and quiet. It's been a while since I've had a drink, actually," he said, thinking about his pact with DC Oliver James. There was no wedding to lose weight, for now, so he'd asked Wood for an alcoholic drink.

George took a long sip from the pint glass and savoured the malty flavour. He'd needed this. Why the hell he'd decided not to drink beyond January was beyond him, and he was surprised he hadn't caved earlier. Such was the stress caused by the murder case. The bubbles felt great going down his throat, and he found he'd nearly drained the entirety of it.

"The fact that Eve was pregnant bugs me," she said. "I've been thinking about it. What if the pregnancy was caused by our culprit? During that one-off? Maybe he found out she aborted it? Maybe that's why our guy is going into a frenzy after killing."

George nodded and said, "The stabbing of their wombs?"

"Yes."

George thought for a moment and drained the rest of his beer. The food hadn't arrived yet, and he itched for another drink. "Whilst I don't doubt your logic, nor your expertise. I think the timings are off." He glanced up. "Bill Harris. If that's our culprit, the guy who stole the diaries from Mrs Allgood, then the timings make little sense."

Wood smiled and shook her head. "You're thinking about it wrong. Olive said Bill stole the diaries 'about four or five years ago', which suggests to me he did it after killing Liz Anderson. I'm thinking he lost control, thought she was Eve and punished her womb for not giving him a child."

George was about to speak when Wood continued. "I know what Mark Finch told you, George. I read your report, and at first, it made sense that our culprit attacked our victims' femininity." She gave a wry grin. "But what if it's more literal than that? What if she had an abortion?"

George nodded in response but said nothing. She had a point.

Wood carried on. "Finch said he was probably unpopular or bullied at school and maybe even had a deformity." She looked up at him. "David did say that Eve called her stalker a 'deformed freak', and well, all of that makes sense, given how he reacted to his fling with Eve. For him, it was a big deal, perhaps his first love. For her, it was a mistake."

Wood wrapped a manicured hand around her beer glass, and George noticed she'd yet to have a sip. "We really need to find some information about Bill Harris," George pointed out. She smiled and took a big drink, gulping down nearly half the pint. George laughed and offered her a napkin when she spluttered.

"I'm just trying to keep up with you," she said, pointing to his empty pint glass. "And anyway, I'm an all-or-nothing kind of girl. I don't do half measures." Wood winked at him.

He gazed deep into her dark eyes, hoping she was being purposely flirty. "From what I see, that extends to your work, too."

She smiled but shrugged. "Yeah, we all work long hours. I don't have a social life. At all." She gazed at her glass and drained another quarter. "For a woman my age, I find it a bit sad, really."

"I don't think it's sad. But I understand. I'm the same, Wood; I forgot how to socialise, to be honest. Sometimes I go out for work drinks with the team, or like the odd one after

CHAPTER THIRTY-SEVEN

a shift, like this."

"What about you?" She turned to him. "Does Mia know you're here? With me?"

So she knows about Mia. Shit... He knew what he should say, but the truth was, he didn't want to. Mia had made her intentions clear at the cocktail bar. He was single and, therefore, was doing nothing wrong.

He shook his head. "Mia and I are no longer together. We broke up a while ago. She moved out." He wasn't sure how to put his thoughts into words, and as the words left his mouth, they felt like a lie.

"I'm sorry to hear that, George. I had no idea." Wood smiled, and she removed a couple of clips and uncurled the messy bun atop her head. George thought she'd looked nice with the elegant updo and was surprised by how long her hair was as it fell down in a wavy brunette cascade down her back. "Do you think you'll get back together?"

"No," he said honestly. He didn't want her back. She was beautiful and intelligent but mean, disrespectful and very selfish. Wood was both beautiful and intelligent yet possessed none of the latter negative traits. He gazed at Wood as she played with her curls, took in her glossy red lips, and the soft blush on her cheeks. Did he want Mia back? No. He'd never been so sure. "Mia made it very clear the last time we saw each other that our relationship was over for good."

"Why did you break up, if you don't mind me asking?"

"Work. I work too many hours, I was told. Her dad was a detective, too. I think it was destined to fail like her parent's marriage had."

Wood nodded. "It's an occupational hazard," she said. "No one understands what it's like unless they're in the police themselves."

The truth. Plain and simple. George thought back to all the arguments and thought he must have been crazy to try to make it work with Mia. It was evident from the start that she disliked the police, that she didn't understand, nor even attempted to understand, the love he had for his job. Mia had no idea the pressure George was under, nor any clue as to the desire that drove him to put away dangerous criminals.

But Wood did. Just as he lived and breathed it every day, so did she. He'd seen that from the moment they'd started working together. A great team. An incredible partnership. He was lucky to have her.

"A good-looking man like you, though, George. You must have some admirers?" she said, draining the rest of her pint.

George was sure his face had turned beetroot and so made an excuse to leave the table. "I fancy another drink. Can I get you anything?"

Wood straightened and nodded. "A JD and coke?" she said, and he nodded in return. "Thanks, George. I hope that bloody food shows up soon. I'm proper starving."

Once George was back with the drinks, they continued. "So, we have our culprit, who we think could be called Bill Harris, and believe he's killed at least five women. They were all blonde with blue eyes. All were teachers. Other than Eileen, all were mid-to-late twenties." George frowned. "E and A initials. His victim selection is practically identical. So what makes Eileen different?"

Wood shuddered. "Talk about being obsessed with blondes. I don't understand the fascination, myself. A nice brunette can do wonders, you know?"

George grinned but said nothing else.

CHAPTER THIRTY-SEVEN

Their food arrived, and between sharing with each other more about themselves, they discussed the case.

"I keep coming back to Eileen Abbott. Please tell me I'm not the only one?" he said. Somehow, she'd moved even closer to him, and the heat from her thigh was seeping into his. Their shoulders were touching, and it made it difficult for him to reach his drink.

"You're not the only one. I can only guess that he must have known her. Maybe she was his teacher? Eileen could have been the one who rejected his feelings, so he went after Eve? We know Eileen was eight or so years older than her. If Eve and our culprit are the same age, then it makes sense?"

George nodded slowly. It made sense. "But that throws all our other ideas to the wind about her being his obsession."

"She must have known Eve," Wood said. "The background check shows they worked at Beeston Park Academy at the same time. Eileen also worked there when Eve was barred." She stopped talking, and she scrunched her nose in what George thought was a cute way. "Maybe I'm wrong, but I think Eileen was the one who told the school about Eve's affair." Wood reached for her glass and downed the rest of her JD and coke. He was getting the impression she was right when she said she was an 'all-or-nothing kind of girl.' "It could be she was the one he wanted to kill all along, and the others were collateral damage? Think about it, George. Eileen would have been mid-to-late twenties if she had taught our culprit. She was blonde with blue eyes. Miss Eileen Abbott. Miss. Initials E and A. Maybe she was his final victim; maybe our culprit's done."

Or maybe, George thought, another blonde, blue-eyed female teacher going by Miss with initials E and A is going to be next.

Chapter Thirty-eight

Drunk, the pair strolled through the pub doors outside towards their cars. "Do you live nearby, George?" Wood asked.

George hoped that despite their early start the next day, Wood didn't want to rush to get home.

"Yeah, I..." he pulled a frown, which she mirrored. "I live about 200 metres down there." He grinned. "I'm sorry I never said. What about you?" He knew she lived in Wakefield still but wasn't sure where.

"I live in Wrenthorpe," she said with a grin. "There's no way I can drive. I'm going to need a taxi."

George knew his following words could break their professional relationship, but the dulling sensation of the alcohol made him not care. "You're welcome to come to mine for a bit. We can have a drink, and I'll call you a taxi?" He smiled and made sure his car was locked.

She laughed. "Really? Are you sure you don't mind? Thanks."

"No, of course not. It's no issue at all."

They walked out of the car park and down Fall Lane past the primary school. As they got closer to his home, he became aware of the sound of her heels clicking, and the sound of her giggles as his arm brushed against hers every so often. He wanted to pull her into a kiss, right there and then.

Wood waited while George opened his door. He fumbled for the lights, and the floorboards creaked as he stepped into the dark hallway.

He'd been barely home since the murders, which was lucky, as Mia had always complained about him being messy. "How about that drink, Wood? I've got beer or wine, or I think there's a couple of alcopops left in the fridge."

He saw her hesitate before she answered. "I'll have a beer, thanks." She helped herself, grabbing a beer for George, too. "This might sound ridiculous considering we've just eaten, but do you have anything to eat? I'm starving."

George laughed and told her to help herself to anything she wanted. After finding a bottle opener, he opened both bottles of beer.

He watched in amazement as she pulled a loaf from the bread bin and the butter tub from his fridge. "I know just the best thing to eat when you're drunk," she said. Wood looked around and spied a tall kitchen cupboard. She ushered him out of her way, but he stepped to the right instead of the left, and they bumped into each other. Her palms were against each side of his collarbone as she balanced on him. She laughed again, and as her hair moved, he caught a faint smell of vanilla and coffee.

Wood was close, her arms bent at the elbows. Her gaze lifted until it met his, and slowly, without really thinking what he was doing, he drew her towards him, his arms encircling her petite waist. She didn't hesitate and slid her hands up from his clavicle to the back of his neck, running her fingers through his hair. She drew him closer, gripping at his hair, pulling his lips towards hers.

She closed her eyes, and they kissed George, holding her close against his chest, feeling her heart hammer against his, losing himself in the moment.

Chapter Thirty-nine

The following day, it took a moment for George to realise it wasn't Mia lying next to him. Instead of straight blonde hair spread across the pillow, Wood's hair was curly and chocolate coloured, and unlike Mia, who had pale skin and a toned body, Wood's skin was tanned and soft, her features more rounded and sensuous. He lay silently comparing the two ladies, knowing he shouldn't and wondering what had gotten into him to act so rashly the night before. Wood was fantastic, there was no doubt about it, and they had a connection. But because of their association, he didn't want to ruin it.

George shut his eyes as the guilt sprang upon him. He was Wood's superior, and she was part of his team. Both those facts meant they really shouldn't have done this, and he worried DSU Smith would have a fit if he ever found out.

"Regretting last night already, George?" Still naked, she rolled onto her side, a sardonic smile carved on her face. She looked even better than he remembered last night.

He grimaced. "Not one bit."

She frowned. "Tell that to your face."

"I was just worried about work finding out, that's all. Honestly, Wood, I regret nothing." She shrugged and sat up, the cover falling, exposing her breasts. He desperately wanted her again, right there, right at that moment.

"Well then, you don't have to worry. I'm not going to say anything. For the record, George, I don't regret it, either." She moved in close and snuggled George, her breasts crushed against his chest, before saying, "Do you mind if I take a quick shower?"

He shook his head and kissed her on the head. "Sure, go ahead. I'll see if I've got anything in for breakfast."

"Thanks, George, I'm starving. I never got around to making my speciality." She got out of bed, not bothering to take the duvet with her. He took in her incredibly curvaceous yet lithe body as she winked and threw him a mischievous look. He beamed. For George, last night had been excellent, an unexpected change from what he was used to. It had felt good to be wanted, to be enjoyed. The lovemaking with Mia had always been frantic, and whilst it had been a heat-of-the-moment situation with Wood, theirs had seemed more profound somehow and more significant. He found that even though they had to leave for work, he didn't want to. He simply wanted to spend the entire day with Wood.

Wood was wearing the same clothing she wore yesterday when she returned downstairs smelling of Mia's shampoo some twenty minutes later. Her hair was sleek and damp down her back, and her face was clean and make-up-free. That was something else he wasn't used to. Mia always put on make-up as soon as she got out of the shower in the morning, and she'd never leave home without it. Wood didn't seem bothered, but then she didn't need it. She looked fantastic as she was.

He made a conscious effort to reassure Wood that last night hadn't been a mistake. "I'm sorry about this morning. I was surprised by what happened last night. But I don't regret it. Not one bit. I don't want you to think that you're just a—"

She grabbed him and kissed him on the lips, long and slow with a lot of tongue. "Stop worrying, George. I understand you're worried about work. Last night was great but will have no effect on our working relationship. And I know I'm not just a fling. But you're just out of a relationship. Let's take things slow, and see where they lead. No pressure."

No pressure? Take things slowly. He wanted neither. The kiss had made him want to grab her right then and take her back upstairs to explore every inch of her body. George wanted it all; however, he decided not to argue the point. "I made cheese on toast." He pointed to the table where he'd arranged two plates, each with two slices on them. A bottle of HP Fruity and a bottle of Henderson's Relish. "The coffee's almost ready."

"Thanks." She sat down and squirted fruity sauce over her toast before she tucked in.

George sat opposite her and, by habit, kept an eye out for any signs of annoyance. There were none, just appreciative glances. Mia hated cheese on toast and was fond of showing George her annoyance at the breakfast table. "You know, you're so easy to be with," he said, squeezing relish over his toast. "I was really expecting this to be awkward."

"I'm guessing that's why you looked the way you did this morning?"

"Partly," he said between mouthfuls.

"Well, there's no need, George," she replied, her mouth full. "We're both consenting adults, and both wanted it, right?"

He nodded, not wanting to shower her with spit.

"So, then there's no problem? Not for me anyway. You're

single. I'm single. We're not hurting anybody. I don't feel used. Do you?" When he didn't answer, she laughed at his raised brow and said, "Could you pour me some of that coffee, please? I'm gasping."

"Sure." He pulled the jug out of the machine and poured them each a cup, then he sat back and observed her as she took a sip. He didn't answer because he *wanted* her to *use* him again. She didn't look as if she was lying. Maybe she was right; perhaps nothing would change moving forward. "How do you stand the awful coffee at the station when you drink this at home?" she said with a laugh.

"Usually, I need the caffeine," he said with a grin. After their antics last night, he desperately needed all the caffeine he could get. "I need to go to Beeston Park Academy today and speak with the deputy head. You want to come?"

Across the table, her dark eyes met his. "Of course. But we can't go directly from here, even though it'll be easier. It's bad enough I'm wearing the same clothes as yesterday. We have to go to the office separately, then leave from there together. Especially if you don't want people finding out what crazy shit we got up to last night," she said with a wink.

He had visions of last night when he'd hastily unbuttoned her blouse and peeled it off her and thought that despite her clothes looking very good on his bedroom floor last night, they suited her.

Knowing it would take too long for her to get to Wrenthorpe, he said, "I think Mia left some of hers when she left. You're welcome to one." He quickly regretted it, realising she probably wouldn't want to wear his ex-girlfriend's clothes.

To his surprise, she nodded and said, "Sure. If you're OK with it. We really could do with getting to the station soon."

CHAPTER THIRTY-NINE

"The clothes she left are in the wardrobe to the left," he said, directing Wood upstairs.

In less than five minutes, Wood was back downstairs, tucking a yellow blouse of Mia's into her black skirt. With her dark, curly hair, which fell down her face in wispy strands, it looked great.

"It's probably best if we don't turn up at the station together, too," Wood said when they'd got to the cars they'd left outside the pub.

He nodded, and for a brief moment, the atmosphere was awkward. He wanted to kiss her or embrace her, but she took the option away from him.

"I'll see you at the station," she said, smiling and meeting his eye. But, without waiting for a reply, Wood, wearing Mia's blouse, her brunette hair flowing out behind her, got in her car and sped off.

* * *

After spending the entire morning, and most of the afternoon going through the information they had on the Miss Murderer, George finally admitted to Wood that he was stuck. The killer wasn't Preston Blake because he had been at the station whilst Eileen Abbott was killed. They'd eliminated all current partners and family members from their investigation. "That just leaves old connections, current colleagues, or, I hate to say this, Wood, strangers."

Having a man on the streets who killed three women unknown to him was dangerous, and it could only be a matter of time before he killed again.

"I don't think it's a stranger. I think it's Bill Harris, whoever he is. It has to be. He's not a detective," she said, and George, about to speak, paused as Wood continued. "I checked for detectives named Bill Harris on our database. No detectives by that name were employed in the last ten years by any police force. None in the last twenty, to be exact. The man definitely lied to Olive. Has DC James got the information back from the Royal Courts of Justice?"

George thought back to his earlier conversation with DC Oliver James. Then a sharp knock on his office door interrupted his thoughts. "Sir," DS Yolanda Williams said. "We've got information about the killer's van."

"Get everybody in the Incident Room, Yolanda," George said. But when she didn't move, he added, "Now, Yolanda. Please!"

"Right then, what have we got?" demanded George as they marched into the Incident Room. It was late afternoon, and the room felt hot and stuffy after spending hours in his air-conditioned office.

"We put a camera in the blind spot between the two CCTV cameras situated on Town Street, between St. Phillips Avenue and Moor Flatts Road. On Saturday, after Eileen Abbott was killed, the camera picked up footage of a man wearing a black hoodie entering this van and driving away, but the number plates weren't clear," Yolanda said. "We followed the white Ford Transit Connect using CCTV footage, but it went missing somewhere in Belle Isle. We thought we'd lost it, but this morning, Jay canvassed the houses where the van was last seen."

"Why wasn't this done sooner? It could have been done Saturday night. Why wasn't I informed? The killer could have left the county, or even the bloody country, by now!" George was furious. He'd heard nothing yesterday about any CCTV.

CHAPTER THIRTY-NINE

"We weren't even sure where the killer escaped to," Smith said, his booming voice coming from the back of the room. He'd just entered. "The chief superintendent held off until we had more information. I trusted his judgement, George, and so should you. It gave time for us to check for more footage whilst you were in Manchester yesterday."

"And what did you find?" Because George was angry, he quickly added a sir to the end of his question. This was his case. Why wasn't he informed? Surely they weren't still suspicious of him? They had footage of him entering the house after the killer had.

"Tell them what you found, DC Scott," DSU Smith said.

"We found private footage from a couple of back gardens which showed the killer running away from Miss Abbott's house. We needed concrete evidence that the hooded man was the killer. And we got it last night. As DS Yolanda said, sir, I spent all morning canvassing houses. One person I spoke with told me about a van that had been parked up outside the back of their house over the past three weeks, which kept coming and going. It was a white Ford Transit Connect. It was gone when I checked myself. They've been burgled quite a lot in the past three or four years and put up two cameras in the back garden, one on the house facing the shed and one on the gate facing the back. They were tiny cameras. I'll be honest; I didn't see them until they were pointed out to me. We took the footage, and DS Williams and I have been going through it for the last two hours."

"And?" George asked impatiently.

"The owner deletes the footage weekly, so nothing on the night of Erika's death, but we have clear footage of the Ford Transit Connect and its driver both leaving and arriving at specific times. And these times correlate with the murders of Emma Atkinson and Eileen Abbott."

"Right, that's great, but without a number plate and an ID, it's circumstantial at best."

"I agree, sir," DC Scott said. "So we did some more digging. The council provided all CCTV footage in the area, and we checked through it for white Ford Transit Connects. We found only one, and we managed to follow it back to an address in Middleton using the CCTV footage. Before getting you, we checked the PNC, and we matched the address to, yeah, you guessed it, a white Ford Transit Connect 2016 and found details of the registered keeper," DC Scott said.

"Go on, Jay, tell me."

A grin broke out on Jay Scott's face. "It's registered to a person named Adam William Harris."

"William Harris? Not Bill?" Smith asked.

"Bill is short for William, sir."

"We've got him, we've fucking got him." George looked at Wood and grinned. Wood filled them in on Eve's stolen diaries whilst DC Jay Scott wrote Adam's address up on the whiteboard, pinning up a map of the local area.

"So, who is he?" Wood asked, circling Adam's house. "Please tell me someone's running a background check?"

George and Wood hovered while the team checked the various police databases. They knew for a fact Adam hadn't committed a crime before because he didn't show up on any of them. The blood their culprit was trying to clean up had been sent to the lab for extraction, and a mixed profile had been identified whilst they had been in Manchester. Later that night, the scientists isolated their culprit's profile by subtracting Eileen Abbott's DNA profile. It matched the DNA found in

CHAPTER THIRTY-NINE

Cleethorpes and the DNA harvested from the cellular material the killer had left on both Erika's and Emma's bodies. George was always amazed by forensic science. Now they just needed to find Adam and take DNA from him to match him to his crimes.

An hour later, Smith came out of his office. "The chief super is asking for an update on who Adam Harris is?" he asked.

"We're waiting on the background check but have requested information from the DVLA to see if we can get the photograph from his driving licence," Wood told him. "That's if he even has one."

George thought he would. The van was insured, and it would have made little sense to drive without a licence. "I've got some of the team searching for references online and on social media," George said.

Smith nodded briefly. "Let me know when you have something, Inspector Beaumont."

An air of expectancy hung over the room, and George continued to pace up and down while DS Fry and DC Scott went to get them coffee. He watched his team whilst they clacked away at their computers.

"Did you have any luck tracing Adam William Harris on Facebook?" Wood asked DS Williams.

"Nothing, Wood," she said without looking up.

She sighed in frustration and said, "Thanks, Yolanda; good work, as always."

The clock in the Incident Room showed them it was just after four. Another day would soon be over, yet they weren't any closer to finding Adam.

The DVLA records should be with them soon. He'd have liked a background check, but they were taking their sweet time.

Then suddenly, Wood asked for silence and said, "The DVLA has just sent through Adam's information."

His team paused whilst the printer whirred and spat out a sheet of paper. Wood snatched it up. George stood by Wood's side as she held up the driving licence photograph. George gazed at it, then blinked. He shook his head, snatched the photo from her, and then looked at it again.

"I know this guy," he said.

Chapter Forty

"What? What do you mean, you know him?" Wood said as she turned to face him.

The colour drained from his face as he said, "He's Mia's colleague. He was with Mia at the cocktail bar the other night. The night Eileen was killed. He was wearing gloves. I thought it was weird."

"Are you sure it's him?" she asked. "Take another look. It could be a different guy?"

George didn't need to study the picture again. It was obviously him. William. A chill went through him.

"It's definitely him. He works at Hunslet Park Academy with Mia but goes by the name William. I don't know why he's using his middle name if he's called Adam."

"But how can you be so sure?" Wood said, her dark eyes creased with concern.

"The facial scar. Mia had a right go at me for staring at it. Maybe it's why our killer's been wearing a mask?" Wood nodded weakly.

"Oh, shit! Eve had called him a 'deformed freak', if you remember?" He looked around at his team in horror. "That fucker! He's going after her."

"Who? Mia?" Wood grabbed him by the arm as DSU Smith

walked in. "How do you know Mia's next?"

"George, what's going on?" Smith's booming voice said.

"Don't you get it?" He used a shaky hand to pick the sleep from his eyes. "That fucking journalist was right. The initials, E. A. Eve Allgood. Elizabeth Anderson. Erika Allen. Emma Atkinson. Eileen Abbott. Emilia Alexander..."

"Emilia?" Wood stared at him. "Oh shit! I had no idea her name was shortened. She's blonde, too."

"And a teacher. Somebody call the school."

Smith, when nobody moved, shouted, "Now! And somebody send uniformed officers down there to pick her and Adam William Harris up!"

Wood nodded and called the control centre. A moment later, George's mobile rang. He hoped it was Mia and went to answer, but his shaking hands meant he dropped the phone to the floor.

By the time he picked it up, he'd missed the call.

Smith put a large hand on his shoulder and said, "She'll be OK, George. It's only just gone five. It's getting lighter by the day, and that bastard won't risk anything in broad daylight."

George didn't correct him, knowing that their culprit had killed Eileen in 'broad daylight.' "Mia's not answering her phone. I need to get down to the school."

Smith nodded.

"Wood, stay here and keep in contact with the uniformed officers picking her up. I want to know when she's safe and when Adam's in custody. That's a priority."

"Will do, George."

As George fled from the Incident Room, he stopped by his office and put on his soft vest and duty belt. He didn't know why, but he felt as if he needed to, especially with how close he'd come to their killer before. All he knew was he needed to

CHAPTER FORTY

get to Mia before that bastard did.

George sprinted down the steps and didn't bother to sign out as he burst out of the door and into the car park. He thought about Mia. About what she'd told him about Bill. The bastard had wanted her to remain teaching. Why? So he could kill her, or so he could continue fucking her? Probably both.

This was all his fault. He should have known last night; he should have put two and two together. His infatuation with Wood had blurred his thoughts. No wonder Mia had wanted to know everything. He'd probably asked her daily for updates on the case, acting concerned for his colleagues when he'd been the guy killing them.

As he drove towards the school like a man possessed, his phone rang. He answered it, pressing the button on his steering wheel. "Mia?"

"Hello, Detective Inspector Beaumont, I'm not Mia. I don't know if you remember me, but my name's Janice Mitchell, Edith Jackson's daughter."

"Oh yes, I remember. I'm sorry, Ms Mitchell, but now isn't a great time." He swerved around a car and up a junction, his tyres squealing.

"You said I could call you. I've been digging and have some news. That teacher I told you about? Her name was Miss Allgood. A friend of mine told me last night. Eve Allgood was the one shagging that kid from my class. His name was Adam William Harris, but he preferred to be called Bill. Do you remember I said he had some kind of face deformity? Well, it was a nasty scar from his cleft lip surgery. A massive scar. Wondered if you fancied coming 'round mine? I have a yearbook photo of him. Annie Scanlon was who told me, Jimmy's older sister. Year older than us at school. She'd left before us, obviously, but had gone to work in the school office. It was definitely Adam that Eve had been caught sleeping with. Eileen Abbott was the one who grassed them in."

"Thanks, Janice. I need you to get to Elland Road Police Station right now. Take the yearbook. Take Annie with you. It's important, Janice. Ask for DS Wood. I'll call her now and let her know you're on your way. It's important. Thanks for calling." He hung up via the button on his steering wheel and put his foot down, the lights flashing and siren blaring.

Everything made sense now. He called Wood and explained. Now the motive for both Eve's and Eileen's deaths was clear. Adam was the one who Eve had had an affair with. The father of her child.

Five minutes later, he pulled up in front of the school, abandoned his car and with the door open, rushed inside, flashing his warrant card to a member of staff staffing the reception desk. "I need to find Mia Alexander. Where is she?"

Three uniformed officers, two males and a female, pushed through a door to his right, accompanying the deputy head, Charlotte Gleeson. George knew Charlotte from social events. He ran up to her and said, "Charlotte, where's Mia?"

A mixture of both sadness and confusion spread across her face. "As I was just telling these officers, Mia didn't come back from break. It was a long staff meeting, so I gave them a fifteen-minute break. I was just about to ring her when the officers arrived. It worried me, George because it's not like her to be late."

He turned to the uniformed officers. "Have you got Adam Harris into custody yet?"

Charlotte answered for them, a concerned look on her face. "William? He went with Mia." She checked the computerised log, her fingers clacking away at the keyboard. "Yeah, they left the premises together. He didn't come back, either."

George clawed at his face and roared in irritation. Adam had her; he just knew it. He turned back to Charlotte. "We need Adam's number." She didn't move. "Now, Charlotte! Please. We need to find them."

George ran outside to check for Mia's car. The flame red coloured Clio was parked up.

"What type of car does Adam drive, Charlotte?" he snapped.

"I... I don't know. I'm sorry, George. Look, what's this all about?"

"Wood, did you manage to find any other vehicle details for Adam?" he rasped down the phone, chest heaving. He'd run back outside again for a signal.

"Yeah, a diamond black-coloured Renault Megane." Wood told him the reg number, and George committed it to memory.

As the panic set in, he said, "We're too late, Wood. Fucker's got her. What do I do?" pacing up and down.

"George, calm down. Think." Despite the urgency in her tone, Wood's voice was steady. He liked that about her. "Is her phone on?"

He thought for a moment. "Yes. I tried it earlier, and it was on. She didn't pick up, though."

"What about Adam's? Do you have his?" He provided the number Charlotte gave him and heard her writing it down. "We're going to do a trace on both numbers." *Oh, thank God for Wood,* he thought. Because of the shock, his brain wasn't functioning correctly. "I'll let you know when we get something, George. Stay on the line. Tell the school not to contact either of them, or it'll raise suspicion."

"Will do, Wood. Thanks." The notion of Mia being in the

clutches of that monster made George sick to his stomach. "We need to find him, Wood. I know we're not together, but I couldn't bear it if anything happened to—"

"Nothing's going to happen," she interjected. "We will find her, George. Don't fall apart on me now. I need you on top form."

She was right but was far too kind about it. He had to get a grip. He needed to calm down and start thinking straight if he was going to find this bastard. Replacing the shock he felt earlier, adrenaline coursed through his veins.

"What's taking so long, Wood?" he grumbled. "Come on; I need to know where to go."

"DS Fry's working on Mia's number now," she replied. "He's on the phone with another tech guy who's tracing Adam for you."

"Thanks," George told her. He was still pacing. Charlotte and the three officers had followed him outside. He tried to think about where Adam would take Mia. It was getting dark, but it would still have to be somewhere deserted, somewhere they wouldn't be interrupted, somewhere close by. George was also unsure how he'd lured Mia away. Then he thought about their affair. She had been fucking a murderer behind his back. Was she in on it? An accomplice? Maybe he hadn't kidnapped her after all. "Hurry, Wood. I'm losing my mind."

"We're on it, George," barked Wood. He heard her issuing orders to someone in the room about ANPR—the registration. Of course. "Bad news. Adam's phone is off. I'm just waiting on Mia's—" George heard a voice interrupt her. "Mia's pinged a cell phone tower just five minutes ago. It's the one at the park gates on Town Street."

"Middleton Park again?" George asked. It was where Erika

CHAPTER FORTY

Allen was killed. The area was heavily wooded, with lots of places to hide. Wood confirmed. "Right, Wood, I'm on my way."

"I'll meet you in the car park with the dog squad, George," she said before she hung up.

He raced back to his car, leaving the uniformed officers and deputy head in his wake. His phone rang almost immediately, and he put it on speaker. It was Wood. They didn't bother with any pleasantries.

"George, Adam's Megane was clocked by the ANPR camera on the Newhall Road junction turning right onto Town Street. I've put out an APB in case he hasn't driven down into the park.."

"He's definitely heading towards the park, Wood."

"The canine unit and Uniform are on their way, George," said Wood. "I'll meet you there."

George swallowed. "I just hope I'm not too late, Wood." He knew a lot could have happened in the time wasted at the school.

Chapter Forty-one

Adam William Harris, or Bill, as he was sometimes known, glanced over to where Miss Emilia Alexander was slumped unconscious in the passenger seat of his Renault Megane. The Rohypnol he'd put into her coffee during their break had taken effect. It had been so simple with Emilia. The flirting had turned to kissing, and then that had turned to sex. She'd leapt at the opportunity to skive the rest of the meeting with him.

At the very least, he could finally stop pretending to be William, the caring teacher who wanted to love her in ways her fiancé couldn't. He'd had enough of her problems, enough talk about her fiancé's demanding job and the fact that he was never home. He understood how she felt neglected but so fucking what? She should try getting teased at school every day for being the freak with the lip, try having the opposite sex laughing in her face and whispering denigrating remarks behind her back. How would she react then?

Probably terribly. Despite losing her parents, Emilia had a spoiled existence. She was gorgeous, adored, and had a figure that most men would kill for. As did Eve—the forbidden fruit. He'd tasted that forbidden fruit before her mother had moved her away. As a teenager, he had no means to track her, to keep

CHAPTER FORTY-ONE

her nearby. But that all changed as an adult. Like Emilia, Eve had used her body to entice men. Their fiancés were a prime example of this. Emilia didn't love that dickhead detective, just like Eve hadn't loved that wanker mechanic, but at first, both women enjoyed how the men made them feel. Both women were wanted, appreciated, and loved. All the emotions he'd never felt before, not even from his parents, who had died in a car crash just weeks after he was born, and especially not from Eve or Emilia. They both used him to get back at their partners. He laughed bitterly. His experiences shaped him into the man he was today. And because of that, Emilia was going to pay.

His anger towards Eve was still there, and after meeting Emilia, an untamed beast had awoken within. He'd had a slip with Elizabeth, but she hadn't been enough. *Clearly.*

He knew he would never see Eve again—and yet Emilia had come to him one day out of the blue. Practically a clone. A Belle Isle born secondary school teacher with blonde hair and cornflower blue eyes. Emilia Alexander had been easier to seduce than Eve, much easier, but every time he thought about her, he thought of Eve. Every time he saw her, he thought of Eve. When he grabbed her tits and tight ass, he thought of Eve. When he entered her, he thought of Eve. They were painful memories, memories where Eve taunted him, and they lingered in his mind. She humiliated him, rejected him, and even terminated what was his. And so he'd decided to end her, to end them all, every single one of them. That was the only way to end the memories. He'd already decided to move on and find a new Eve in a different part of the country.

A car horn cut through his thoughts, and he had to swerve to avoid a collision. There was no use in being caught now, especially now he had his Eve back.

The sun was low in the sky, and he thought about his nickname. The Miss Murderer. He still felt shivers when he remembered the name they'd given him. It had a terrifying ring to it. Along with Stephen Griffiths and Peter Sutcliffe, he would go down in history as one of the county's, if not the country's, most infamous serial killers. Yet he knew he was only getting started. There would be more Eves working around the country, and when he was finished with them, he'd travel abroad and continue his work.

As Adam slowly drove down the slope towards the car park for the woods, he thought about the intrepid investigator George Beaumont and how he'd nearly caught him at Miss Abbott's house. The descent was agonising; the speed bumps were like small mountains on the road. He'd always hated parking here, preferring to walk in by the side of St Mary's church. The gruelling pace didn't bother him, though. He didn't believe anybody could find him. His phone was turned off. No one knew his identity, and the foolish detective did not know who he was, despite staring straight at him the night he killed Miss Abbott. He was just William, Miss Alexander's work colleague. The look on his face the night at the cocktail bar had been priceless. The Inspector had been there, with the killer in the flesh. He had questioned him on his gloves, the idiot. He laughed hollowly.

Despite the chill, he spotted several dog walkers as he pulled into the car park at the end of the long slope. He knew it was risky to leave the car here, but he hoped that by hiding it in plain sight, it wouldn't bring suspicion. Adam looked around at the woods that surrounded him, knowing he needed to get her into the woods on the opposite side of where he'd killed Miss Allen.

CHAPTER FORTY-ONE

He murmured the song that had been on the radio to himself as he unbuckled Emilia's seat belt and attempted to rouse her awake sufficiently for her to walk. Carrying her would draw too much attention to herself. He smacked her across the face when she didn't answer. She sighed, and her eyelids opened for a split second before closing again. He hadn't even given her that much, just enough to make her drowsy. Nevertheless, the idiot bitch had passed out. He smacked her once more.

"What—?" This time, she turned her unfocused gaze to him, and he grinned as he noticed the confusion in her eyes. "How did I fall asleep—?"

"Come on. I want to go and fuck in the woods. Sound fun?" He stepped out of the car, opened the door for her, and assisted her. She leaned heavily on him, wobbling dangerously, but he closed the door and supported her as they moved to the right, into the vast wooded area that led into the dark bank of trees that would surround them. Emilia tried to speak but couldn't get the words out. Anyone observing would think he was bringing his drunken girlfriend for a much-needed walk to clear her mind.

Despite her pixie-like frame, Adam had worked up quite a sweat by the time they arrived at a secluded spot in the woods. It was a perfect place, perfect for her to receive what she deserved.

First, he'd have a taste, and then he'd destroy her.

Her phone rang.

He couldn't believe he'd been so idiotic as to forget about her phone. He located it, removed the SIM card and bent the card in two. Adam then pocketed the handset. He knew her detective ex-fiancé would attempt to ping it as soon as he found out she was missing, but because she wasn't living with him at the time—she'd explained to him in excruciating detail how she'd moved out to be with him—that wasn't likely to happen just yet.

But it wouldn't matter. By the time the police attempted to find them, he'd be long gone, and Miss Emilia Alexander would be dead.

* * *

George raced through the park gates and sped down the path to the car park, his Honda Civic practically flying over the mountain-like speed bumps, the car's suspension crunching on its way down. The tyres grumbled on the gravel behind him, kicking up stones and dust. When he reached the car park at the bottom, he slammed on the brakes, bringing the Honda to a screeching halt.

Despite it being late, unkempt hyper schoolchildren and their irritated parents were still hanging around. He kept his eyes alert, roaming up and down the aisles in search of the black Renault Megane.

There!

It was parked in the final berth of the last aisle at the far end of the car park. There were no other vehicles in the vicinity. Adam had obviously not wanted anyone to see him with Mia.

They couldn't possibly have gone very far. Mia would have been screaming or struggling, most likely both. He grimaced. Adam couldn't afford for her to make a disturbance or draw attention to them, so he would have to restrain her in some way. He shoved the image of Mia lying on the ground with duct tape over her mouth out of his thoughts. No, not yet. He didn't want to go there just yet. There was still plenty of time to find her.

George rested his hand on the bonnet of the Megane. It was hot, but the engine had begun to cool. He could smell fuel and hear a faint ticking. It had been here ten to fifteen minutes at most.

That was too long.

George had a look around. Off to his left was the pond, with fishermen milling around, no doubt chatting about what they had caught during the day. He knew from his teenage years how popular fishing was in the park, having been fishing himself repeatedly. He missed it and made a mental note to come down after he caught this fucker.

Before him was the Middleton Park Visitor Centre that housed a café that he and Mia had regularly spent time in, but it had shut for the day, and there were now only a sprinkling of people sitting at the wooden tables outside, resting before they headed home. Since there was a barrier and around fifty metres of wooded area between where he stood and the centre, none of them would have seen anything.

To his right was a vast wooded area criss-crossed with walking routes that led into the dark bank of trees that surrounded him. George raised his eyes to the darkening sky. Night would fall soon, and he estimated he had only twenty minutes of light remaining, bringing with it acts of terror he didn't want to think about. The car park had streetlights, but the wooded area before him was covered in shadows, and it was already dark beneath the canopy of trees ahead.

He'd spent a lot of his childhood here and was familiar with the park's general layout. Adam wouldn't have risked walking past the centre, and he would have avoided the children's playground next to the pond. It left only the woods to his right.

He slid through the gap in the barrier, turned to his right, and started walking along the path that led straight to the cluster of trees ahead. A mud trail ran down to the wooded area, and it was the only place Adam could have headed without attracting attention.

When he arrived in the woods, the temperature dropped, and the noises of children's laughter and dogs barking were replaced by sounds that terrified him, those of scuttling creatures, trilling insects, and groaning branches. The wind had picked up, blowing leaves at a rate of knots between the carpet of rotting leaves below and the canopy above.

"Mia!" he screamed, hoping she'd still be able to scream or shout or in some way give him a clue as to where she was. His only response was a scampering squirrel darting across the path in front of him. Or at least, that's what he believed it was. It was almost impossible to see in the dim light.

Whilst he knew it was a risk, he pulled out his mobile and turned on the light. He followed the route, his senses heightened, listening for anything out of the ordinary—the sound of a footstep, a groan, or a cry—but there was none. The path curved to the left, becoming slick and irregular, the decaying leaves mixed with the morning's rain hampering his trek. Instead, he walked to the side, where the tufts of grass around the edge provided some traction.

"Mia!"

Still, George heard nothing. He spun around slowly, focussing on his breathing, making sure his ears and eyes were open.

Nothing.

Where the hell were they? What the hell had happened to them?

CHAPTER FORTY-ONE

George knew they had to be there somewhere. From the car park, this was the only area of the woods that made any sense; it was the most secluded. George knew Adam would have been spotted if he had gone anywhere else.

He abandoned the trail, knowing that it led to the Manor Farm estate, and considered his options. There were only two. He gazed into the gloom that reached out for him, attempting to imagine himself in the killer's shoes. With a hostage, there was only one place to go, and that was north, deeper into the woods.

Taking the high ground on the left, George walked through the heavy foliage, stepping through vegetation and avoiding the broken branches and fallen tree trunks.

"Mia!" he tried again. George believed he heard something this time, a rustle that cut off abruptly. He turned off the light on his phone and crept closer, keeping his hands out in front of him to hold the low branches hidden by the blackness at bay. "Is that you, Mia?"

The response was urgent yet suddenly hushed. A groan followed. Then he heard the sound of skin on skin—a slapping noise punctuated with cries.

"I'm coming, Mia," he whispered as he dashed through the woods like a maniac, following the sounds he had heard.

George cleared the foliage and saw that Mia was on her knees on the cold, wet ground. Her ankles were taped together, and her hands were bound behind her back.

Adam was above her, unzipping his trousers.

"Adam Harris, this is the police! Stop what you are doing and raise your hands."

He raised his eyebrow at George and turned to face him.

"Adam Harris, I am arresting you for the murders of Erika

Allen, Emma Atkinson, and Eileen Abbott. You do not have to say anything, but it may harm your defence if you do not mention when questioned something which you later rely on in court. Anything you do say may be given in evidence."

Adam smiled a cocky smile and shook his head. "Put your hands behind your head. Now, Adam!" Adam shook his head again and charged at him.

As Adam charged, George was distracted by a rustling sound coming from the tall trees to his left. The second that he was distracted cost him because Adam sprinted, wielding a thick, wooden branch. He hit George at the side of the head, just below the temple, and knocked George off his feet. George's jaw throbbed, and he spat blood as he scrambled to his knees, hissing.

"Get the fuck away from her, you monster!" George screamed.

But as the thick piece of wood came down again, an immense pain erupted from his skull, and George passed out.

Chapter Forty-two

George awoke to the sound of billowing leaves above him. An overwhelming feeling of nausea rose from his stomach into his throat. The light was intense, and he blinked, rubbing his head until his eyes adjusted.

He winced in anguish as pain erupted from atop his head down through his jaw.

Through blurred vision, he could see Mia's powerless prone figure a few metres away.

When he tried to roll over, he discovered he couldn't move his arms. As his jumbled mind struggled to understand the situation, he realised he was taped to a tree, his arms above his head. Mia, who was now wholly subdued by Adam, looked as if she wasn't moving.

George blinked his vision clear, strained against the intense light, and looked at her chest to see if she was breathing. It was hard to tell because of the low position she had been forced into, but he was sure he had detected a slight rise and fall of her exposed breasts. The gap in the canopy above helped, but it made him aware that the rapist had sliced off her dress and was in the process of cutting off her panties, the fixed blade hunting knife glinting in the fading light.

Desperately attempting to get free, George struggled against the tape that bound him.

The rapist shifted his gaze from Mia. "Hello, Detective Beaumont, you've woken up just in time for the show."

George twisted his wrists and pulled his arms. He felt it begin to slip, the tape giving way. With a little more twisting and pulling, George knew he could get free. There was a hole in the tape, and George ripped his right hand away. He turned and, using his teeth, tore the tape binding his left wrist. After that, George stood up. He still had his vest on, but his duty belt and baton were nowhere to be seen.

Adam hadn't expected George to get free as easily as he had done and was used to overpowering the vulnerable women he preyed on. George sprinted and threw himself at the stalker with a frantic howl, the knife flying from Adam's hand into the undergrowth near Mia.

Adam landed on his back next to Mia, with George on top. George jabbed him in the face twice before he head-butted him and heard a satisfying crack as his nose or cheekbone shattered. Adam had been flailing, so he couldn't tell which, not that George cared. The murderer pushed George away and rolled away from Mia, into the undergrowth, inside the shadows. George swatted the ground but stood up and cricked his neck. He took a deep breath. He was a boxer, not a wrestler.

By the time George had taken his breath, Adam had jumped to his feet and charged. He slammed into George, sending both of them flying into the undergrowth. His attacker landed on top of him, and George felt something sharp impale his back. George jabbed him with a quick right and rolled away before he scrambled to his feet. Adam was breathing heavily now with blood running down his nose, knife in hand.

George had both the height and the reach, but Adam was

CHAPTER FORTY-TWO

broader, a man who trained in the gym with thick, muscled arms and strong fingers. He also had a weapon.

Despite this, George knew he could beat him in a fair fight, not that he expected Adam to fight fair. His vision was still partially blurred from the smack to the head, and he was sure his jaw was broken. The pain in his back was intense. George's feet swayed, but he clenched his fists, waiting. He was ready.

Adam, sensing his advantage, closed the distance and, instead of attacking with his knife, fired off a nasty left hook. George stepped into it and ducked under him. He buried his own left hook into Adam's ribs. He staggered, dropped the knife, but remained upright. With a roar, Adam looked around for it, confused. He picked up a large rock with two hands and threw it at George. It rocketed towards him.

George ducked to the side as he saw it coming, the sharp edge cutting his right arm. He felt no pain, but a rush of adrenaline was released. It elevated his heart rate. This guy was dangerous, and there was no way he was going to allow Adam to escape.

George charged forward, and they exchanged blow after blow, both men suffering from exhaustion, but both men continuing to fight. "You should never have gotten involved with her, Adam," George shouted. "It'll be something you regret for the rest of your pitiful life."

"She needed to pay, Inspector. I'm surprised you care after what she did to you."

George clenched his fist, a red mist descending over him and sprinted towards Adam whilst shouting, "Why Mia? Of all the blonde teachers with initials E and A, why her?" He slipped. The murderer stepped back towards Mia and collected his other weapon, the thick branch that he had used to knock

George unconscious.

"She was the most like Eve, Inspector. I thought that fucking her would give me what I'd always wanted. She was going to leave you, you know? Until you proposed. We were going to be together." He spat at the floor. "She betrayed me just like Eve did. So, I tried very hard to project my feelings elsewhere, which was why I killed Erika and Emma. They rejected me too. If only Miss Alexander had stayed with me. Nobody would have died." Adam stepped forward, a toothless grin warped by the scar from his cleft lip and the smattering of blood in his beard. "I'm going to kill you now, Detective Beaumont. Then I'm going to enjoy my time with Emilia like I did the others." He ran, the wood high in his hands, ready to bring it down crushingly on George's head.

But George had expected the attack and stepped diagonally to the side, the weight of the missed blow throwing Adam off balance.

George delivered a devastating blow to the side of Adam's head. It was a short, hard blow, and the killer collapsed to his knees. He let the wood go, and it hit the ground with a muffled wooden clonk. Adam followed it flat to the floor.

George picked up the piece of wood and examined it in his hands. It felt hard and heavy. He liked Adam had fallen that way, low and powerless like his victims, and had wanted to show him the same respect he had shown him when he was down. He stood over Adam, the wood high in his hands, ready to bring it down crushingly on Adam's head.

He hesitated and asked, "Tell me why you did it, you bastard! These women were innocent. You had Mia; she was yours. She chose you, you fucking idiot! Or was it just a game to you? Was it all planned?" The killer ignored him. "I'll fucking do it,

Adam. Give me a reason not to. I'm already losing my fragile grip on sanity, Adam. Confess!" He grasped the wood tighter as his woods were ignored.

But in the end, George couldn't do it. He didn't have it in him. His deep breathing was already calming him down, and he began to shake.

Satisfied Adam was down, he dropped the wood and walked towards Mia to check that she was OK. But, in a last-gasp attempt, Adam gripped George by the ankle.

"Get the fuck off me, Adam," he said. But the man's strength was phenomenal. He pulled his foot away from Adam, his standing foot slipping on the wet leaves. A smear of blood painted the leaves as he fell on his back, and Adam pulled him closer. George kicked out at Adam's wrist, releasing himself. "Just stay there, Adam. Stay still."

A low groan erupted from his throat as if Adam were trying to tell him something. "What?"

Another low groan.

"Tell me, Adam." George stood up and edged closer, bent down low, but then became aware of a rustling in the trees behind him.

He turned to look, and Adam seized his chance. The knife Adam had lost earlier was in his hand, and he attempted to stab George with it again.

But the attempt was feeble, and George's fingers found the large rock Adam had attacked him with earlier to knock the knife from Adam's lethargic fingers. With both hands, he brought the rock down against Adam's head, and with a sickening thud, it crashed into his brow.

He hit the killer with the rock again, and again, and again until his face was nothing but a bloody mess. He only stopped when he heard someone shouting behind him. That and the sounds of dogs barking.

Chapter Forty-three

"Stop! George! Stop!" DS Wood's voice pierced through the red mist that had swallowed him whole. "Please, George. Drop the rock."

George did as she asked and sat back, panting. She threw her arms around him, and he nestled his head between her neck and shoulder. She smelled of vanilla and coffee.

"You got him, George," she said. She was out of breath, her chest heaving. "You got the bastard. Mia's safe."

"Mia!" George turned to see a crowd of paramedics leaning over her body. "Is she OK?"

"Yeah, she's OK, George," DS Wood said, still gripping him tightly. "You got there just in time. He didn't rape her."

"Thank God." He tried to get up, but his legs buckled. He shivered, and his vision spun.

"It's OK, George," DS Wood said. "Everybody's safe, and I've got you. Don't try to move." She turned to someone perched behind her. "He's shivering. Is there anything you can do?"

A medic appeared with a blanket and draped it over the pair of them. George didn't know how long they stayed that way, but when the shivering abated, the pain subsided, and his vision stabilised long enough for him to see properly, he stared at what he assumed was the head of Adam Harris. A team of SOCOs, led by Stuart Kent, lit up the area all around them.

"Oh shit, I did that, didn't I?"

DS Wood hesitated, her smile not reaching her eyes. "Yeah… Do you think you can get up yet?"

He nodded, feeling a pain deep within his back he hadn't noticed before. Every movement made him feel sick. "I think I was stabbed. Is there a wound on my back?"

DS Wood turned him around and looked at his back. She nodded, a serious look on her face. "I think you need to get looked at by a paramedic. You've got a nasty bump on the back of your head, too."

"Shit. Isn't the vest supposed to protect me? As for my head, the bastard hit me with that." George pointed at the long chunk of wood. "It knocked me out."

She nodded. "A soft vest only slows a blade. It could have been a lot worse," she said with a thin smile. "OK, let's go get your back looked at." With her arm gripping his upper back, they walked together up a path towards where an ambulance was parked. They were closer to the car park than he realised. He'd wasted time running around the woods searching for them. The thought made him dizzy, and his legs buckled once again. "It's OK, George," DS Wood said, "I've got you."

"Let's get you sat down," a paramedic with a kind voice said. With DS Wood's help, George delicately sat on the ledge at the back of the ambulance. The paramedic immediately inspected the wound on his head. "That's a rather nasty bump you have there."

"It's nothing compared to the pain in my back."

The paramedic also had kind eyes and winked at him. She looked at his back and nodded. "Does this hurt?"

CHAPTER FORTY-THREE

George nodded, then immediately wished he hadn't and closed his eyes against the pain. "Knife wound?" George tried to smile his agreement, not wanting to nod. "It didn't hit any vital spots, though. You were lucky. You'll be healed in no time, but I think you should go to the hospital now."

"Thanks, Wood. Thanks for coming after me," he said, ignoring the paramedic's advice. She was standing in front of him, looking down at him, and he thought that, for once, she looked dishevelled. Yet it only made her more beautiful.

"Mia's phone had pinged, and we managed to map it, with a rather large radius, to this area. But it was the sniffer dogs. I had them sniff the blouse." Her face turned maroon. "They went mental and ran off, clearly having got yours and Mia's scents. We wouldn't have found you otherwise. But George, how on earth did you manage to find them?"

"I know these woods pretty well, and when I found his car in the car park, I put myself in his shoes and took the most direct route into the woods. I think I got lucky because I heard them before I saw them."

"Yes, George, you were fortunate," she hissed. "Mia too. I saw the knife he used. He could have killed you. And Mia. If you'd have been any later, she may have—"

He closed his eyes. "I know, Wood, I know."

"Sir, I need you to look at the light," a male paramedic said five minutes later as he shone a torch into George's eyes. DS Wood hadn't left him. They'd spent the minutes in silence. George blinked and tried to concentrate, but all he could think about was the pain in his back.

"Sir, you have a concussion," the paramedic said. "We also need to do something about your back. I'm going to have to take you to the hospital for treatment."

"What about Adam?" George glanced into DS Wood's eyes. He thought he already knew.

"I didn't want to be the one to tell you, George," she said, a thin line for a smile. "You hit him with that rock more than once. He deserved everything he got, mind you, and he's going to the hospital, too. But he won't be on a ward, George; he'll be in the morgue. DSU Smith has already said there will have to be an investigation."

George gave a terse nod and closed his eyes. He had murdered their suspect.

"The guy had a knife, George, and given your injuries, it's obvious you acted in self-defence." George began to cough. "I don't think it'll be the end of your career, though, because we have a witness—a dog walker. And for God's sake, you caught the Miss Murderer. That has to be worth something."

George frowned. "Yeah, I caught him. Then I murdered him."

"You didn't, though, George. You defended both yourself and Mia. We can get his DNA and match it against the database. I know we'll be able to match his fingerprints to the duct tape partials. I've spoken to a fingerprint expert, and there's ridge detail on tape. All we have to do is get her to match it. It probably doesn't feel like a win for you right now, but it is. We can show he was responsible for the murders of Erika, Emma, and Eileen."

"The technicality matters to me, Wood," he mumbled. The three women and their families deserved justice. They were innocent victims, and George had denied them that. "I am sorry. If I'd kept my temper in check, he might have confessed to killing the others, too. Poor David is locked up for Eve's murder, yet he didn't even do it. How am I supposed to tell him I killed his only shot of getting out of prison?"

Eve Allgood, Elizabeth Anderson, Erika Allen, Emma Atkinson, Eileen Abbott. He'd failed every single one of them. But it wasn't just that; it was their families and friends, too.

A ping interrupted the silence.

"Look, George, I know it's hard right now, but it's not all bad." DS Wood had a smug grin on her face.

"What exactly do you mean?" he asked. "Have you discovered something?"

She showed him her phone. "Just after you left, I sent a team led by DC Jason Scott to Adam's house. The address from earlier. They discovered a box filled with trophies under a loose floorboard at the back of a wardrobe."

"Trophies?"

She nodded. "Trophies. The women's phones, too. Five of them. We'll have to send them to the lab, of course, but I know, I just know, there's something of Eve's in that box."

"Oh, I hope so," George said. "I need there to be something in there. David Clark doesn't deserve to be behind bars."

"I promise you, George, that once the items come back from the lab, if there's anything in there of Eve's, then I'll petition for an overturn of his conviction. We can't let this miscarriage of justice go."

"Thank you, Wood. You're incredible, you know?" He reached out and squeezed her hand.

"Any time." She smiled, but their moment was ruined by the paramedic. He got George to agree to lie down on his side on the gurney and take some painkillers. DS Wood lingered nearby and kept a close eye on him.

From his viewpoint, George saw a group of paramedics emerge from the woods carrying a stretcher. Mia was on it. He knew she was alive, but she wasn't moving, and that panicked him.

Despite what Mia had done to him, he still loved her. He still wanted to protect her, to care for her. But she had been right before. Their relationship had been over for a while. In fact, it had probably been over before he'd even proposed.

"She'll be fine," DS Wood assured him. She lowered her voice to speak, but George spoke first.

"About last night—"

She locked her gaze on him; her smile was high and wide. "We can talk about that when you're better."

He nodded and retook her hand. He saw Mia as she was wheeled into an ambulance. She looked pale; her eyes were closed.

George got up from the gurney and hobbled over to her, despite the paramedic warning him not to. "How are you, Mia?"

She didn't open her eyes, and she only managed a whisper when she said, "I'm OK. Thanks to you. I'm sorry, George. Really sorry. Listen, come and see me at the hospital. I need to tell you—I'm pregnant." Her voice was cut off as the ambulance doors slammed shut. Then, with its sirens blaring, the vehicle shot off.

George stood there, stunned. Pregnant? Was it even his?

It felt like hours to George as he ambled back over towards his own ambulance, lost in his thoughts. He sat back down, not wanting to lie on his side. "Are you OK, George? You look as if you've just seen a ghost. Is Mia OK?"

"Yeah, Wood. She's fine." He gripped her hand and smiled. The smile hurt. He felt numb yet in pain. It was a strange feeling.

CHAPTER FORTY-THREE

Smith's car stopped behind the ambulance. He exited his vehicle, and they stopped holding hands as he walked up to them. "Beaumont, how are you?" He was smiling, but George expected what he said next. "I need to see the crime scene, but I'll be back to talk to you soon."

The crime scene George had created. "I'm so sorry, sir. Please accept my apologies, I..."

"It's all right, George. I know it was self-defence. I heard you took quite a thrashing. That he had a knife and stabbed you with it? Are you sure you're alright?"

George sighed with relief. "I am, sir. Thank you."

"Get yourself to the hospital, son. I mean it."

"Yeah," he said, his words still a little wobbly.

She encircled him with her arms and held him close. He could smell Mia's shampoo in her hair. "Listen. We did what we did, and I don't regret it. I know I shot off after Mia, but trust me when I say it's over between us and has been for a while. I really like you."

Epilogue

Two weeks later

George was struggling over Adam's death and didn't expect the guilt ever to fade. He was struggling with how he had killed Adam and what Adam had done to Mia. It didn't matter how many times George was told it wasn't his fault, that he acted in self-defence, that he'd saved Mia's life, the fact that he'd pushed Mia into Adam's dirty arms hurt him.

That he had killed Adam wasn't what bothered him the most. It was the fact that he'd let it reach that stage in the first place. Three women had lost their lives, five if you included Eve and Elizabeth. George felt as much to blame as Adam, despite others telling him otherwise.

It was the weekend. It wasn't even dinnertime, and he had already started drinking. Despite his Dry January challenge, he'd never been much of a drinker in the past, yet as he poured another shot, the irony wasn't lost on him that he seemed to be making up for lost time. George had visited Mia that morning, her last day in the hospital, before being discharged. Their relationship was still over. She had been a victim, yet she felt guilty. Guilty that she had survived when others hadn't; guilty that she'd been having an affair with the killer. She had PTSD and was in a bad way. They'd had a fight over the pregnancy, George accusing her of it being Adam's. A colleague from work had come to collect the rest of her belongings.

The families of the victims had said nothing, and he wouldn't imagine they ever would, but he was sure they blamed him for killing Adam. They knew who the killer was, but they didn't understand why he'd committed those heinous acts, nor did they get justice. They would deny it, might not even know for sure they felt that way, but George didn't have any doubts. It was the way he felt, so why shouldn't they?

DS Wood had come to visit bearing good news. George handed her a coffee, and they stood together by the glass door in the living room that led to his small garden. She didn't judge him for his drinking, but she had mentioned it. He would stop soon. He only drank to help numb the pain. The doctors had kept him in the hospital for three days, making sure that the knife wound wasn't infected. They'd used surgical glue to close his head and back wound that third day and given him painkillers before discharging him.

He was currently on enforced leave and wouldn't return for another fortnight. DS Wood had taken over as interim inspector in his absence. Smith had said it was to give him time to come to terms with what he had done to Adam, but George suspected otherwise. Despite the dog walker's statement that George had acted in self-defence, he was still waiting to be summoned before Professional Standards, and his future was unclear.

With DS Wood in charge, his team had managed to tie Adam Harris to some of his past victims, meaning the families finally had closure on who killed their loved ones. It also meant that David Clark would be released from prison. Using DNA profiling, they proved the items found in the hidden box in Adam's house belonged to his victims.

Wood had also contacted DCI Brown from Cleethorpes and

confirmed with him the DNA found under Elizabeth Anderson's fingernails matched that of Adam's. After a bit of digging, and information received by DC Oliver James from the Royal Courts of Justice, the pair proved Adam Harris hadn't changed his name. Data from their smartphones confirmed the woman he killed in Cleethorpes, and the three women he'd murdered in Leeds, knew him by the name William 'Bill' Harris. He had been Elizabeth Anderson's colleague. He'd worked at two different schools after killing Elizabeth, so Wood had put DC Jason Scott on cold cases in those areas.

The partial ridge details found on the tape binding Emma Atkinson matched Adam's prints, too. Wood also explained they used his mobile phone data to trace his movements on the days the three victims were murdered, his mobile putting him in the right areas at the right times. The Ford Transit Connect was found and contained bags of blood-stained clothing. Two sets of DNA were found on each and were a match to Adam and each of his Middleton victims.

But that wasn't all. DC Scott had found two separate boxes. One contained Eve's diaries, whilst the other was filled with Adam's diaries. He stole Eve's diaries so they couldn't be used against him, knowing after killing Elizabeth, he would kill again. Adam wanted every woman who reminded him of Eve dead, which was why he explained in his diaries that he killed Elizabeth, Erika and Emma.

She had been pregnant when the school found out about the affair and wrote in her diary she'd had an abortion in York. According to his own diaries, Adam knew which was why he killed her. As they thought, the diaries also explained the knife blows to the women's wombs. DS Wood had tried to confirm the abortion, but there was no record, so they only had the diaries to go on. Despite the loose ends being tied up nicely and with everything Wood told him, he still couldn't find a way to be happy about it. He'd killed a man. Yes, it was in self-defence, and yes, he protected a victim, but it still felt wrong. DSU Smith hadn't berated him. In fact, he'd even privately congratulated him, yet George still wasn't happy. Through his actions, he'd removed a killer from the streets and caught the Miss Murderer, but it was how he'd removed the killer that bothered him. George had lost control. And he was disappointed in himself.

He'd never forget Erika Allen, Emma Atkinson, or Eileen Abbott. He'd never forget about their families and the way their cries sounded whilst they shed their tears for their loved ones. George swore never to forget that he was responsible for their lack of justice. He wouldn't forget Elizabeth Anderson, or Eve Allgood, either.

And, as Isabella Wood walked barefoot across the wooden floor and smiled that beautiful smile of hers, and even though George knew he would carry those names with him forever, for the first time in a while, he felt optimistic about the future.

Afterword

Thank you, reader, for reading my debut novel. I was born and raised in South Leeds, and have spent my life working and living in West Yorkshire. It has been such a pleasure to write about the places I know and love.

All the locations within the book are based on real settings, though some details may have been fabricated, such as the changing of school names. Middleton Park is somewhere I often visit, a beautiful, ancient woodland with a small lake and recreational areas. I've fished the lakes myself as both a teen and an adult, and it's a lovely place to feed the ducks and swans. Thankfully, I have never found any bodies there, and I hope I never will.

I'm excited to take you to more amazing places in Leeds as you follow George and his team, and I hope you enjoy the adventures. If you enjoyed this book, I'd really appreciate it if you could leave a positive review and comment on Amazon. I promise you George Beaumont will return soon.

Take care,
Lee

About the Author

Lee is an author who lives in Middleton, Leeds, West Yorkshire, England with his wife and three children. He spends most of his days writing about the places he loves, watching sports, or reading. He has a soft spot for Japanese manga and anime, comic books, and video games.

You can connect with me on:

- https://www.leebrookauthor.com
- https://www.facebook.com/LBrookAuthor

Subscribe to my newsletter:

- https://leebrookauthor.aweb.page/p/cfff8220-7312-4e37-b61a-b1c6c2d15fc2

Also by Lee Brook

The Detective George Beaumont West Yorkshire Crime Thriller series in order:

The Miss Murderer

The Bone Saw Ripper

The Blonde Delilah

The Cross Flatts Snatcher

The Middleton Woods Stalker

The Naughty List

More titles coming soon.

Printed in Great Britain
by Amazon